THE CAPITAL CONSPIRACY

JEFF NESBIT

OLIVER NELSON

THOMAS NELSON PUBLISHERS
Nashville • Atlanta • London • Vancouver

Copyright © 1996 by Jeff Nesbit

Published in Nashville, Tennessee, by Thomas Nelson, Inc., Publishers, and distributed in Canada by Word Communications, Ltd., Richmond, British Columbia.

Library of Congress Cataloging-in-Publication Data
Nesbit, Jeffrey Asher.
    The capital conspiracy / Jeff Nesbit.
       p. cm.
    ISBN 0-7852-7812-5 (pbk.)
      1. United States. Congress. Senate.—Officials and employees—Fiction. 2. Nuclear weapons—Developing countries—Fiction. 3. Conspiracies—Fiction. I. Title.
PS3564.E73C37 1996
813'.54—dc20   95–20502
                                         CIP

Printed in the United States of America.

1 2 3 4 5 6 — 01 00 99 98 97 96

Prologue

A trained observer would have noticed something out of the ordinary at the dull gray building a few blocks from the White House. But no trained observers were anywhere near the place. That had been taken care of, as had many, many other details.

The drivers of the dozen or so dark blue Town Cars let their solo passengers off at the front entrance to the building, which conveniently had more than one tenant. None of the passengers signed in at the front desk; they did not have to follow the guidelines set for visitors to nearly every building in Washington.

There was no record of such a meeting on the voluminous daybooks that swirled around official Washington. The secretaries to the men—there were no women in this group—did not know where their bosses were, except at a meeting in Washington, D.C.

None of the staff to these men knew who would attend their meeting or what they were meeting about. The staff had prepared briefing papers, as they did for countless other meetings, but they were on such broad issues as water resource management, currency evaluation, agricultural stabilization policies, power resource development, legal challenges to the international General Agreement on Tariffs and Trade, and biodiversity of species.

These men all carried a single file with them, known only to those involved as the Wormwood Project. Only these men looked at and added documents to the file.

They were all dedicated to a single human resource management issue, one that had been under development for quite some time. It was the single solution to a thousand problems. The time was right. The principles needed for the solution were established.

The world had seen many revolutions and dozens of wars since Adolf Hitler had nearly won the Second World War, but it had still managed to learn its lesson from that war. Every policy up to and through the cold war had been held up to a single standard—how to make sure there was never a third world war. Every international trade agreement, global nuclear disarmament treaty, nuclear test ban accord, multinational environmental pact such as the vaunted Biodiversity Treaty, Group of Seven accord, or European Community financial stabilization package had this common goal—to avoid a single conflagration that could lead to a world war among major, well-armed nations.

Still, there had been scares. A terrible peso devaluation in Mexico had nearly sent the global currency market into collapse. Pakistan had come close to launching nuclear weapons at India. Both Iran and Libya had almost triggered a massive Middle East war. Two devastating earthquakes had leveled Tokyo and

Los Angeles. And two severe droughts had killed millions in desolate parts of Africa.

These scares were the true genesis of the Wormwood Project. The people of the world were nervous, not quite sure what might happen next. They wanted help, though they knew not what form it should take, and leaders and others were out there willing to deliver such help in small and large quantities.

The meeting took place late in the morning, after the breakfast meetings had broken up but well before the power lunch period when so much business was conducted up and down the K Street corridor in downtown Washington.

While most of the Town Car drivers went elsewhere to wait for the meeting to finish, one driver did not speed away. After letting his passenger out, he parked a half block down the street where he could watch the entrance.

A second car, with several black antennas on the back, followed closely behind. Two men in tight-fitting suits got out. One entered the building. The second positioned himself as unobtrusively as possible just a few feet from the entrance. Both had a receiver in one ear, and one of them lifted the cuff of his shirt to his mouth every few minutes.

By Washington's standards, it was a relatively standard security detail. Only the president traveled with a much larger detail team. This particular detail could be protecting almost anyone in the three branches of the U.S. government—the secretary of state, the secretary of defense, the vice president, the Speaker of the House of Representatives, a Supreme Court justice, or the Senate majority leader.

Washington was quite used to seeing such security details in and around the many public, private, and quasi-governmental agencies near the White House or Capitol Hill. It was not unusual to walk up and down K Street or Pennsylvania Avenue and see as many as three such details cooling their heels outside building entrances.

All anyone knew was that someone of importance was inside, discussing something of some consequence in some nice conference room. Beyond that, no one knew or even cared really. That was the way Washington did business.

This particular meeting lasted an hour or so, long enough to confirm last-minute details that could be decided only by this group in person. The project was not discussed by phone or fax, the usual way in which business was conducted in Washington.

The plan had been set in motion. One of their very well-paid employees at an international firm would deliver necessary and timely information to one of their usual conduits. That contact, they hoped, would inevitably lead to the usual high-level meetings at the White House, with the president involved. Decisions would be made, they hoped moving in the right direction—their direction.

But to assure success, they had carefully nurtured a project, through a trusted subsidiary, that guaranteed a direct link to the president's national security apparatus and personnel. It would be the final piece to fall in a quite elaborate puzzle.

The group had worked this particular line for several years, and their efforts were about to pay very big dividends, setting in motion a series of very carefully planned and timed events.

There were still risks. Large ones. But the quite realistic and possible gains—both financial and diplomatic—were now within their reach. Every participant in the room could sense that it was within their grasp.

After the meeting, they left as unobtrusively as they entered. Their drivers came and went, with the experienced ease of professionals who had done this for years and knew how to slip in and out of Washington's lousy traffic with a minimum of fuss.

There would be no story in the *Washington Post* recording the gist or direction of the meeting. It was not an official meeting. There was no public docket, no chance for the public to comment or even ask about it. There was no regulatory agency or congressional committee with oversight responsibility. There were no shareholders who could question the motives of the group.

There was no necessity to file a report with anyone because the group had no formal affiliation. It was not incorporated. It did not have a name beyond a nondescript definition as a working task force of the organization where the members met every so often.

The goals of the group were clear, precise, defined, and well organized—better than any plan of even the best-run multinational corporations, federal agencies, or international bodies.

They were not subject to any form of outside scrutiny. There was no need, in their view, and no legal requirement in either U.S. or international law requiring such scrutiny.

Their word was their bond. There was no need for anything else. They had set in motion a plan that was finally coming to fruition. Others would judge the results after the fact.

Chapter One

FRIDAY, JUNE 12, 1998

It always made him pause. But this particular document made him pause a little longer than usual. It was stamped EYES ONLY. It meant that you absolutely, categorically, emphatically could not make a copy of any portion of the document. You had to have code word clearance to look at the document.

Which Daniel Trabue had. He'd seen scores of top secret documents on all sorts of subjects. But he still had to pause, for just a moment, when he saw it stamped on the outer covering to the document that was hand delivered to him in his office deep within the confines of the Senate's Russell Building.

Daniel stared hard at the subject heading for the document, which he'd just received from the NSA courier. Employees of the National Security Agency rarely stopped off at Capitol Hill. They hated giving information out to members of Congress and their staff. Especially the anonymous, ever-present staff.

But Daniel had specifically asked for a briefing on this subject. He'd gotten a tip from perhaps his best source in Washington, a lawyer at one of the big bipartisan international law firms in D.C. that did code word work for the CIA, the NSA, the Pentagon, DARPA (Defense Advance Research Projects Agency), and other assorted programs that operated under black programs.

Daniel hated black programs, and he was always searching for ways to find out what actually went on in them. Black programs were very top secret programs that Congress threw money at, without knowing how or where or why the money was spent. The various agencies asked for billions of dollars each year to run such programs, and Congress always granted money for them without asking any questions.

Only if someone like Daniel's boss, the chairman of the Senate Intelligence Committee, asked about a specific program would the "community" come up to the Hill and brief them alone on the subject. But that rarely happened.

Still, Daniel always searched because every so often something would turn up, and he'd pass the information on to his boss, who would make a request and then get briefed. Sometimes, and sometimes not, Daniel's boss would tell him the results.

But this particular lawyer had always been dead on the mark. Absolutely, positively right in the center of the bull's-eye. It was uncanny. He always came to Daniel with exact information, which always led to something quite interesting.

At times, Daniel wondered who was using whom. Clearly, the lawyer was giving the information to Daniel for his own purposes, in his own time, under his own agenda. But it didn't really matter to Daniel why the lawyer gave him the information. Daniel weighed each "leak" on its merits and acted accordingly.

In this case, the information tracked exactly with a theory he'd been following diligently and painstakingly for two years, a theory involving a rather bizarre chain of events in places like Iran, Algeria, Russia, China, and even the United States.

His theory had its roots in an international banking scandal of the late 1980s—the infamous BCCI network of illegal arms sales, currency transfers, and loans to clandestine terrorist networks in more than a dozen countries around the world—that had never really been run to ground.

Daniel was convinced, based on repeated clues from his sources like the lawyer, that the octopus-like network had simply changed leaders and venues and was now operating in different places and different networks—but with its hidden goals and objectives still intact.

This particular piece of the puzzle was especially intriguing, and Daniel was anxious to confirm the tip. It involved oil cargo shipments and a clandestine operation in a remote location of northern Africa.

So he'd taken a risk and asked the NSA for its latest satellite photos over a particular region of the world, a place where the "community" had earlier been shocked to find some startling evidence of a new nation joining the exclusive nuclear club.

As always, Daniel had made the request on behalf of the chairman of the committee, not on his own merits.

He had the authority to make such requests for his boss because they'd worked so closely for so many years. Because he'd asked under the auspices of his boss's authority and power, Daniel knew there would be no hesitation about honoring the request for information. The document he now held in his hands was the result of that request.

He unsealed the document carefully, pulled it free, and began to thumb through the pages gingerly. It was almost as if the document itself was dangerous, like the subject matter it covered.

It took him a while to discover it. But it was there, on page 17 of the written briefing. Daniel smiled and looked up at the ceiling briefly. The NSA. They never gave it to you straight. They gave you everything but the kitchen sink first, and then buried the essential information well within a thick document.

The NSA claimed it was because they gave out information, not analysis. They always said it wasn't *their* job to figure out what the stuff really meant. But Daniel was never quite so sure of that explanation.

He looked at the few key paragraphs for almost a full five minutes. This kind of information would certainly set them buzzing at the White House. But should he raise it?

The White House always treated news like this as if someone had set the place on fire. He knew the drill by heart. First, they'd send out a call for background information to half the intelligence world. Then they'd gather again for a second meeting, task a whole new set of questions and briefings, and then re-form a third time to set policy. By then, events would be off in a new direction, and they'd go through a whole new fire drill.

Daniel grimaced at the thought. The worst part was that he *knew* the information he'd just asked the NSA to deliver to him would come back to him in another form at some future date. He'd give the information to the White House; they'd ask the CIA for an update; the CIA would snoop around and get back to the National Security Council.

Then the White House would send a few people over to Congress for a closed briefing to select members of the Senate Intelligence Committee. And then, sure as day follows night, the White House would give the senators the information as if they'd dredged it up themselves and were only sharing it benevolently because the law required them to.

Fortunately, Daniel's boss didn't care much for those games. Oh, he never called their bluff. But whenever they started to deliver old information as new, the senator would glance over at Daniel, who would be sitting in a hard chair up against the wall of the soundproof briefing room. That was all it took. Just a glance. But Daniel would know.

He pulled a yellow pad over and jotted a few notes to himself. He didn't quote from the document. You couldn't do that. But he'd have to brief his boss before he went to the White House with the information, and he didn't want to waste the senator's time.

He was also curious how his boss would deliver the unwelcome news at the White House over the weekend. The senator's political instincts were second to none, and Daniel trusted them without question.

He glanced at the few select paragraphs certain to set off a chain of events that, he knew, no one would be able to predict accurately. He made a note to himself to make sure the senator himself made the request for the lone NSA photo that the raw information was based on.

Thanks to the lawyer's tip—which he'd given from his usual pay phone somewhere in Washington—Daniel had been able to make an educated guess about the time and place of an NSA satellite run in a region of the world most people paid very little attention to.

In some ways, it had been a lucky guess on his part. Or unlucky guess in a way. No one wanted to hear about something like this, especially not this White House, which dreaded foreign policy crises.

But he had no choice. Not now. He had to start delivering the news, step by careful step.

And then? Well, it was above his pay grade, as the omnipresent staff always said. Others in positions of power and influence would have to decide how to proceed then. Or at least, so he hoped.

Chapter Two

It wasn't that Loren Anders was afraid. She wasn't. Not really. But she couldn't shake the feeling. As many times as she'd joined her boss on his regular routine, there was still that little spine-chilling moment as she crossed through the doorway to the office.

The Oval Office wasn't all that different from other offices. Generals at the Pentagon had bigger, nicer offices. Bigger desks. More secretaries. More aides scurrying around with important messages for very important people. She'd been to see ordinary assistant secretaries of state at Foggy Bottom who had better, more awe-inspiring views.

After all, the Oval Office wasn't exactly shaped so that the furniture could fit. The president's desk kind of jutted out into the oval-shaped room a little. The couches and tables for visitors and working groups were the same way.

Oh, he had a nice view of an immaculate lawn and gardens—especially the roses right now in early summer—but it was still no nicer than the view at a country club. There were plenty of pretty roses in the world.

But it was the Office. The Place. Where Reagan, Kennedy, Roosevelt, and Lincoln had run the nation. Where big decisions were made about whether to send troops into places like Bosnia, Iraq, or Nicaragua. Where colossal, world-shaking events sometimes had their origins.

Loren knew her boss, Dr. John Sullivan, felt much the same way. He tried not to show it. After all, he'd been to the Oval Office to brief the president dozens of times. But she could always tell. The way he fidgeted with the wire frames of his glasses as he waited in the lobby for the secretaries to tell him he could enter to see the president each morning. Or the way he twirled the wedding band on his left hand. He felt it.

Dr. Sullivan, the president's national security advisor, had that same feeling in the pit of his stomach as he entered. It was something that never really went away, even after you'd been sitting there for a while going over things, just talking about world events.

Watching John sweat over his daily security briefings always made Loren feel slightly more at ease. John had a Ph.D. in international relations and conflict resolution from Johns Hopkins University. He'd been an ambassador to two large nations, France and Brazil. He'd been an undersecretary of state in charge of every major diplomatic initiative for several years.

And he was still nervous. He felt that little emptiness as he entered. Like you were at the center of the world, and a whole lot of people were marking every step and every phrase.

Loren was no slouch, either, though she couldn't match Sullivan's credentials just yet. She had a master's from Stanford, also in conflict resolution. She had worked for a large defense firm for three years, then left for a detail at the CIA where she'd gotten to work directly for the deputy director of intelligence. And then this job with Dr. Sullivan.

Loren glanced around at the various people gathered for the briefing today. More often than not, it was just Dr. Sullivan and her. The CIA director, Kenneth Branigan, showed up about twice a week. The president's chief of staff, Will Samuels, sat through one or two a week. Sometimes the secretary of state or the defense secretary would come over as well. That was usually the size of the briefing contingent. Small, efficient, routine. They'd go over the summaries from the State and Defense Departments and the CIA, and then the president would ask a few questions.

But not today. For some reason, there was a full house. Besides Loren and Dr. Sullivan, Samuels was there. So were the secretaries of state and defense. The only significant presence missing from the room was the vice president, Lucius Wright, who had flown up to New York for an 8:00 A.M. United Nations meeting and wouldn't be back in the city until midmorning. But no one ever missed Wright really because he gave his advice to the president privately, and he always seemed to be operating his own network in and around the system.

Even the NSA chief, General Jake Allen, was there.

He was off to one side talking quietly to Branigan. That was strange. Loren couldn't remember seeing Allen at a briefing. The guy was an inveterate networker, but it required a special invitation to get into the president's morning security briefing. The CIA must have gotten him in, Loren figured. His office hadn't placed a request to attend Friday afternoon, so Branigan had to vouch for him this morning.

Loren wondered when Allen had called Branigan to get in. She glanced at her watch. It was 6:50 A.M. The briefings usually started at 6:45. To get in, Allen had probably placed a call to the CIA at 5:00 A.M. Loren shook her head. Sometimes the people in this town were mad beyond belief. Who in his right mind plotted to get into a meeting at that time of the morning?

Allen must have something, Loren thought. *That's why he's here. He's planning to drop some kind of a bombshell on the group.*

The word must have gotten around as well. It was like that in Washington. When there's a really hot piece of information, it doesn't take long to get out onto the street—the street being a little like Main Street in a small town without all the buildings. People bumped into each other at lunch or in the hallways of the Capitol, and they passed on information.

Loren thought about it for a moment. *For all these people to be here, they'd all heard something after Allen had called Branigan to get into the meeting. Which meant there had been a whole flurry of calls between five and six o'clock. This morning. Just an hour ago. While everyone else was sleeping, aides to all these pow-*

erful people had been deciphering some bit of information.

The president's longtime personal secretary, a middle-aged woman with steel gray hair and a demeanor to match, emerged from the Oval Office, walked past the guard stationed just outside, and took the few steps to the lobby. "The president will see you now," she said to the assembled group.

"Watch yourself," Dr. Sullivan whispered to Loren as they stood to file into the Oval Office.

"Do you know what's going on?" Loren dared to whisper back as they began to walk slowly in the direction of the office.

"Yes, a little. Keep your attention on Branigan and Allen. They've got a hot one."

"From where?"

Dr. Sullivan let an involuntary snort of mild disgust escape. "The Hill, of all places."

"The Hill?" Loren was incredulous. No significant piece of information ever actually originated from that swamp. It was where rumor and gossip galloped wildly, not where important national security information was discovered. No original idea or thought ever came off Capitol Hill. It just wasn't possible.

"Yeah, if you can believe it," Dr. Sullivan continued, "the Senate Intelligence Committee chairman sent something over to Branigan Sunday evening. Something from an NSA photo file."

"And we didn't have it first?"

"Apparently not."

Loren glanced down at her folder. She always read her briefing materials closely. There hadn't been anything all that unusual from the satellite reconnaissance data this morning. The usual troop movements in places where there were regional conflicts—and there were too many these days—as well as a couple of training exercises by Russian and Chinese forces. Nothing out of the ordinary.

Once upon a time, when the cold war was still on, the NSA had been front and center. The agency tracked the Soviet threat all around the globe. But not anymore. There was no need to worry so much. Everything these days was small potatoes compared to the former Soviet threat. There was only one superpower these days, not two. No need to worry anymore about who was doing what.

Loren watched as General Allen took a seat outside the "rim of power," as she liked to think of it. The president was already seated at the corner of one of the long couches, his customary cup of coffee cradled in both hands. It usually took him the entire briefing to finish his first cup of coffee. Immediately in front of the couch were four chairs facing it. Just four, and no more. Other chairs were arrayed a row behind, against the slightly curved walls.

When it was just Loren and Dr. Sullivan at these briefings, with either Branigan or Samuels, Loren could take a seat at the rim, facing the president directly. But when other, bigger guns were present, there was a silent, but established, pecking order to where people sat. Cabinet members first, senior White House staff next, and people like her—a mere special assistant to the national security advisor—last. At least General Allen was stuck in the cheap seats with her, Loren mused ruefully.

The secretary of state, Elizabeth Barton, took the seat closest to the president. Liz Barton had risen through the ranks of the world health and nongovernmental organizations (NGOs) in meteoric fashion, going back and forth between the NGOs and the government like a Ping-Pong ball. She'd started with World Aid, then gone to a desk at the State Department, back to another NGO, America Cares, then on to head up the U.S. Agency for International Development where she funneled billions of dollars to developing countries, then back to World Aid, and finally to her job as the first female secretary of state in U.S. history.

The defense secretary, "Big Bill" O'Donnell, sat down next. O'Donnell had come into the Department of Defense (DOD) from one of the megaconsolidated defense firms that depended so heavily on the Pentagon for its survival. His route to power had been far more ordinary than Barton's. He had been an engineer who had become CEO and then raised nearly a million dollars from his "friends" for a senator from his home state who happened to be running for president. That senator won, became president, and appointed O'Donnell to the job.

Samuels took a seat beside O'Donnell, and Branigan quickly settled into the last remaining seat before the president.

Loren glanced over at Dr. Sullivan. By rights, he should have been in one of those four seats. He was on the Cabinet. He clearly was a peer to both Samuels and Branigan. Actually, in the invisible, unspoken chain of command, he was a little higher than Branigan because he was closer to the president, their boss.

Loren knew her boss wasn't too happy, but he didn't let it show. He shook his head once to her—signaling to Loren to let the little indiscretion go—and then took a seat immediately behind Barton. He'd been around long enough to know when not to rock the boat over protocol.

Samuels took over the meeting immediately. That was his style. He was ruthless in managing the president's affairs, and he wasn't about to let an opportunity such as this spin out of his control if he could help it.

"Mr. President," he said before everyone was even seated, "you're probably wondering why so many of us have gathered for your morning briefing."

The president didn't smile. Smiles were for the public when the cameras and lights were on. "The thought did cross my mind," Franklin Shreve said evenly.

Shreve, who was in his first term of the presidency, hated surprises. He hated them more than anything he could possibly imagine. Just to make sure that he was always fully briefed on everything under the sun, and that nothing slipped through the cracks, he had people on his staff assigned to information patrol.

These people did nothing but cross-reference information gleaned from newspapers and magazines across the globe, from cyber-info networks like Internet, or from dozens of other linked computer databases.

President Shreve received summary briefings virtually every hour during each day. He had mastered the information highway and, as a result, had mastered at least some corner of the world. Very little slipped through his net or his radar screen.

Shreve had leaped onto the national stage in very short order, largely because he always seemed to know how to be in the right place at the right time.

His first elective office had been a statewide race. When no gubernatorial candidate emerged for the Republican Party in Virginia, he left a high-paying job with the World Bank and ran uncontested in the primary. He raised plenty of money from his friends in the international banking community and won easily, surprising the self-styled pundits.

Four years later, he raised $30 million for a run at the presidency, took the party by storm, and won the primaries with hardly a fight. His Democratic Party opponent self-destructed in the last weeks of the campaign, and Shreve took nearly four hundred votes from the electoral college.

He'd come into the White House at the age of forty-eight, relatively young by presidential standards. The presidency had already taken a toll on him. His temples were now gray, and his otherwise black hair was showing flecks of gray.

But he still ran five miles every morning without fail, and he could play three solid sets of tennis in the afternoon. One cup of coffee was all he needed after lunch to get him through the afternoon meetings at the White House and into the evening hours.

Getting up before dawn for his daily run and then meetings such as this one wore him down. But that was the burden of the office—too many requests for his attention and time, not enough hours in the day for all of them.

Will Samuels met the gaze of his boss without flinching. Liz Barton shifted in her seat, as did Branigan. The others waited.

"Sir, we may have something. A problem perhaps," Samuels said finally.

"A problem?" the president asked.

Samuels glanced over at General Allen, who nodded once. Samuels returned the gesture and turned back to the president. "It's something we picked up—NSA picked up—from a satellite pass over northern Africa."

"Northern Africa?" the president asked, more than just a little surprised. Nothing ever happened in northern Africa. At least, nothing of a strategic nature. Famine and drought, yes. But nothing strategic.

Two "problems" had cropped up in recent years in Algeria and Sudan—thanks to Iran's constant efforts to foment a fundamentalist Islamic uprising in both those Arab nations—but they were seemingly well under control, everyone assumed.

Samuels waited a few moments for it to sink in with his boss. "Something is there, sir," he said finally. "Something that doesn't make sense."

"What?"

"Well, there are . . . there appear to be hardened underground bunkers in the mountains south of Algiers," Samuels said. "At least, we think there are. We have only one picture."

There was a deep stillness in the room. Every one of them knew this information made no sense. Not now. In a few years, yes, perhaps, but not now. Not this soon.

A few years ago, another NSA photo surveillance pass over northern Africa had discovered a shocking truth, one that had rocked the intelligence community and the world at the time.

When Algeria had signed a contract in the late 1980s to have China build a small nuclear reactor, the CIA and other U.S. intelligence analysts had told everyone quietly not to be concerned. They said, at the time, that it was nothing more than a research facility.

But in 1991, NSA satellites spotted what were almost certainly antiaircraft defenses that had been set up—rather illogically—in the middle of the Algerian desert near the mountains.

NSA and other agencies ordered a closer look, which then turned up signs of construction of a nearly complete nuclear reactor. There was vegetation planted around it in patterns similar to the way the Chinese planted such vegetation. So it was obvious the Chinese were building the nuclear "research" facility for Algeria. And from the size of the cooling towers, the reactor was roughly four times the size of the original estimate. It was, without a doubt, much larger than a research facility.

No, the experts concluded, a reactor that size had only one purpose—to produce plutonium for nuclear bomb fuel. Further strengthening that argument was the simple fact that there were no power lines or electrical generating equipment anywhere near the site.

Even now, no one knew the true size of the reactor, how far along it was, or whether it was capable of producing fuel. The experts did know, though, that Algeria was making every effort to build a bomb and was helping others to do so as well.

But no one expected deployment. That seemed impossible. Even a country like North Korea, with its full-blown nuclear program, was thought to be years away from actual deployment. It seemed impossible that Algeria had leapfrogged the rest of the developing world and had actually deployed.

In addition, while it was one of the wealthiest of the African nations, it was still poor by world standards. It couldn't *afford* to deploy nuclear weapons. Not yet, at least. Or so it had always seemed to the intelligence community.

There had been rumors for years, of course, that Algeria was obtaining hard-to-get nuclear technology from somewhere in the world, perhaps from Iraqi nuclear scientists, perhaps from Iran, or perhaps even from Libya to the east.

But Libya was the nation everyone had feared. It had the resources, and the will, to deploy. Not Algeria really, despite the intense efforts of the Islamic Salvation Front to push the country into Iran's orbit.

Libya's Mu'ammar Gadhafi had tried for years to use the wealth of his nation to purchase strategic weapons systems of one kind or another on the black market. But not the Algerians, other than the one reactor the Chinese were building for them in the desert.

Branigan cleared his throat to speak. The others instinctively turned to hear him. If there was something in Algeria beyond the reactor site—and the CIA had missed it all these years—it would likely mean his job. Branigan knew it. Everyone in the room knew it.

"Mr. President, we don't know conclusively that there's something in Algeria," Branigan said somberly. "As Will said, we have one picture, taken at night through cloud cover. It does appear that there is an opening of some sort—an unnatural opening—within one of the mountain ranges south of Algiers. But we really can't be sure."

Branigan reached down and unclasped the briefcase at his side. He fished for a file, extracted a glossy black-and-white photo, and handed it across the table to the president.

The picture was clearly taken with the longest lens NSA had from one of its low-orbit satellites. It looked straight down onto the tops of several mountains, through a heavy cloud cover. Because it was night, the picture was shot with infrared.

And there *was* an opening—a black maw at the center of one of the mountains, perhaps one hundred feet across, illuminated faintly from within. It was clearly unnatural and almost certainly constructed by humans.

"It could be a man-made cavity," General Allen finally spoke up. "It's not unlike the ones we've seen in eastern Russia where they once buried some of their intermediate-range missiles and then hardened them to attack."

"Those intermediate-range missiles are all gone now. The INF Treaty finished them off. We watched them be destroyed," Loren said tentatively. No one paid any attention to what she said.

"We've never turned up anything even remotely like this in Algeria before," Branigan said quickly. "The reactor in the desert, yes. But since we discovered that, Algiers has been mostly political. Not strategic.

"The Algerian military has had its hands full with the Islamic Salvation Front since the fundamentalists won the national elections and then the military threw out the results and took over. I checked with our station chief just this morning, in fact, before this meeting."

The president looked up sharply. "Pictures don't lie, do they? Do they?"

Branigan tried to meet the president's gaze. He didn't do very well. "Well, no, sir, but . . ."

The president turned to General Allen. "How long have you had this picture?"

General Allen shifted uncomfortably in his chair. "Two weeks."

"And how did it surface?" asked the president.

"The . . . uh . . . the Senate Intelligence Committee asked to see the picture file reports for Africa. From the past month. It was like they knew what they were looking for. We delivered it late Friday."

The president leaned forward on the couch. His eyes didn't blink. "Congress asked for these?"

"Yes, sir," General Allen said. "We'd included a mention of the photo in our usual reports. Somebody on the committee staff must have stumbled across it and asked for the files."

Loren held her breath. If Congress knew, it was only a matter of time, perhaps days, before the word would spread like wildfire across the town. Nothing remained secret on Capitol Hill for very long. They all knew that. Gossip spread faster there than it did in every Mayberry township in America.

She glanced over at her boss. Dr. Sullivan was ashen-faced. Loren knew it had all come as a complete shock to him. And she also knew that it would absolutely consume the White House and his time in the coming weeks. There was no way around it.

Samuels stepped back into the conversation. "Mr. President, I think we need to call the security council together immediately. Perhaps we can . . ."

The president shook his head quickly, cutting him off. "No, we don't. We won't. Not yet. We don't have any kind of information yet. If we call a full council, we might as well just leak it to the *Washington Post* and declare war on Algeria. And I don't think anyone in this room is ready for that. Are they?"

No one spoke up, so the president continued. "I didn't think so. No, what we need is information. We need to send a team over there. Immediately." He looked at Dr. Sullivan. "You'll arrange for one?" Dr. Sullivan nodded.

The president turned to Branigan next. "And you'll tell your station chief to cooperate with the inquiry? To *facilitate*? Discreetly, of course?"

Branigan frowned. "Well, yes, of course, but our people can handle any kind of a . . ."

"They will cooperate, Mr. Branigan, won't they?" the president asked sharply. Branigan nodded glumly. He could only hope that this didn't amount to anything, that the CIA hadn't missed it. Time would tell.

The president turned at last to Samuels. "And Will, you'll take care of Congress? You'll try to keep a lid on this?"

"I'll try, sir. But you know what it's like there. And with it coming off the Hill to start with . . ."

"Do more than try, Will," the president said. "At least until we have some harder answers to this. We don't want this public until we have answers."

Chapter Three

9:00 A.M., MONDAY, JUNE 15

"FORE!" the congressman bellowed loudly. The golf ball, hooking sharply to the left of the immaculate fairway at the Congressional Country Club in the suburbs of Washington, hit a tree hard with a loud "thwack!" and then bounced once into the golf cart of a twosome playing on a parallel fairway.

"Too much right hand," the congressman muttered to one of his playing partners, a senior vice president at the World Bank.

"Take a mulligan," his partner said sympathetically, glossing over the fact that it would be his fourth mulligan on this nine alone.

The congressman, the chairman of the House Ways and Means Committee, yanked another ball from his pocket, set it on the tee, and hit quickly. It, too, hooked sharply to the left and disappeared into the trees along the left side of the fairway.

Amy Estrada winced. She hated this kind of detail.

Hated it with a passion. But there wasn't much she could do about it. Her Secret Service team leader had specifically asked her to serve out a tour of duty on the vice president's detail.

Amy had wanted to be a Secret Service agent for as long as she could remember. She'd stood in awe once as the president of the United States came through her hometown of Dublin, Ohio, during a presidential campaign.

For some reason, she'd admired the stoic agents who were omnipresent in and around the crowd, protecting the president. She decided, at that moment, that she would be an agent someday.

Little did she know just how difficult that would be. Oh, the job itself wasn't so hard. It was getting to the job, and then doing it among so many men that was hard. That, and putting up with the sideways glances at her because she was a minority woman in a job traditionally done by white men.

Early on, Amy had grown a thick hide. She was proud of the job she did. She knew her career didn't depend on the fact that she filled some kind of a minority quota because she was Hispanic. She was a Secret Service agent. Period.

Still, every so often, a snide comment would rub her the wrong way, and a little kernel of doubt would creep in. But only for a moment. Then her mind and her heart would be back on the job.

The way Amy viewed life was very straightforward and simple. She served God first, the president and the country second, and herself last. One day, when she was married and had kids, she'd probably move family up the list.

But at least for now, she was devoted to her local Catholic parish—she volunteered in the church's free medical clinic every chance she was on the ground at home—and to her job protecting the leaders of the U.S. government. She was devoutly religious, and that helped carry her through the hard parts of her job.

And she'd needed a lot of that strength of conviction for her latest detail. From what she could tell, the vice president she was now covering, Lucius Wright, really had no job at all. Thus, Amy had no real job.

Vice President Wright traveled from country to country, meeting with officials, with no apparent purpose other than to serve in the president's stead at some function or attend some international meeting the president was too busy to attend. The vice president seemed to have a fondness for meeting with international banking, trade, or financial world types. Perhaps that was because he was plotting his own campaign for the presidency down the road, and he knew he would need a great deal of money for such a race.

It made no difference to Amy. She just knew that she hated the detail because she was forced to protect someone who was such a nonplayer in the arena of national politics. She wanted to be where the action was, and covering this guy wasn't it.

But her team leader had insisted. He'd promised her that if she did this assignment well, she'd get a crack at one of two jobs she'd always coveted—leading a detail covering the president, or taking control of a special projects assignment in Treasury securities fraud.

So she was willing to bide her time and forgo any serious entanglements in her personal life because she did so much traveling with the vice president aboard *Air Force Two* and *Marine Two*.

Wright, who was remarkably fit for a man in his late forties, stepped up to the tee box. He meticulously placed the white ball on the tee, took his customary waggle as he addressed the ball, and then crushed a long drive down the center of the fairway.

Wright was a very good golfer, his handicap easily in the single digits. He got out to play a lot because no one paid even the slightest bit of attention to his comings and goings. His favorite course was at Andrews Air Force Base, a secure course where he could play day or night with generals.

In fact, Amy often surmised, Wright could probably play golf five times a week, and no one would know. Or care. The White House press corps slobbered after the comings and goings of the president. They didn't care a whit about what the vice president did.

The final member of their foursome stepped up to address the ball. It was someone Amy knew only by reputation, the director of the FBI, John Wilkinson. Wilkinson had been in the job for years. But he rarely hobnobbed with the political types. This was, apparently, a special occasion.

Wilkinson was a lousy golfer. Amy instinctively shied away as he began his swing, even though her cart was a good fifty feet or so behind the tee box, off to the side.

True to form, Wilkinson topped the ball. It dribbled down the fairway, just seventy-five yards or so from where they all stood.

"Hey, good news, John," the vice president said in a loud, boisterous voice. "You're in the fairway."

"Great," Wilkinson muttered ruefully. "Eight more shots and I'll be there."

"Could be worse," Wright added. "You could be out in the boonies with the chairman."

"I'll find my ball," the congressman growled. "You'll see."

"Under a tree stump most likely," the vice president laughed.

Amy started her cart and drifted up as close as she dared to the cart the vice president and the FBI director were riding in. She was close enough to hear their conversation, but far enough away from the two of them to be discreet.

For the first few holes, neither Wright nor Wilkinson said much. Wright was deadly earnest about his golf. He concentrated intently before every shot.

But now that they were well into the course—and Wright was seemingly playing well within his game— the vice president started to loosen up.

"So you got any hot ones these days?" Wright asked his playing partner as they drove up to his ball, making sure that they approached it by driving at a ninety-degree angle to the ball. Amy waited off to the side.

"This and that," Wilkinson said with a shrug.

"So the FBI's bored these days?" Wright asked.

"No, not bored. Just nothin' all that unusual really." Wilkinson slid out of his cart and ambled over to his ball. He pulled out a fairway wood.

"You sure you wanna use that thing?" the vice president called over to him. "Wouldn't an iron work better?"

Wilkinson said nothing and just gripped the club

harder. He set his sights on the green some three hundred yards away and took a mighty swing at the ball. Chunks of grass went flying in all directions. The ball dribbled another fifty yards down the fairway.

Amy did her best not to laugh. But it was hard not to. The FBI director really was a pathetic golfer.

Wilkinson stomped up to his ball. The vice president eased the cart down the fairway, keeping his distance from the fuming FBI chief.

Wilkinson took another mighty swing at the ball. This time, he hit it fairly solidly, and the ball leaped into the air and rolled nearly to the green. Wilkinson nodded once, hard, and then dropped his club into the bag with a satisfied "thunk."

"Hey, what did you make of that report on those members of the Islamic Salvation Front who just arrived in the United States?" the vice president asked him as Wilkinson climbed back into the cart.

Amy sat forward in her cart a little. This was news to her. What was the Islamic Salvation Front?

Wilkinson gave the vice president a curious glance. "What's that? I haven't seen a report on that."

"I guess it's new," Wright said. He pulled up to his own ball and selected the club he'd use. He didn't hesitate over the club selection. He knew precisely where he was on the course at all times and what he wanted to do.

"And where did you see it?" Wilkinson pressed.

"Oh, some report, from somewhere. Probably some CIA briefing or something I had to sit through," Wright said, not looking back as he sized up his shot. "I don't remember exactly. I could be wrong."

"But you think it was the Islamic Salvation Front? Some of them had entered the U.S.?" Wilkinson said anxiously. "Like from Iran?"

"Someplace like that. But not Iran. Algeria maybe," the vice president said as he focused intently on the ball. He had about 125 yards to the green, which was an easy nine iron. He took a deliberate backswing and then lofted the ball quite high into the air and dropped it right in the center of the green.

The other two playing partners applauded the shot. Wilkinson continued to glare at the vice president.

"You're sure it was the Islamic Salvation Front?" the FBI director asked him.

"Pretty sure," Wright shrugged. "I could be wrong. But you might want to check it out. Just to be sure."

"I will." Wilkinson nodded. "Don't worry, Mr. Vice President. I will, just as soon as I get back to the office."

It was all Amy Estrada could do to sit still in her seat. She wished she could radio this in, but that wouldn't be prudent. No, she, too, would have to wait until the round was over and then begin to check into the report.

If it was true, then it had the potential for something huge. There hadn't been an international or domestic terrorist scare in the U.S. since the bombings of a federal building in Oklahoma City in 1995 and the World Trade Center two years before that.

She wished the information had more of a direct impact on her job. But no terrorist would target the vice president. One or two of the Cabinet secretaries, but not the person she was supposed to protect.

Still, it wouldn't stop her from investigating and discussing it with others in the Service. There was no chance of that. Every instinct told her she was on to something, and she wouldn't give it up easily.

Chapter Four

9:00 A.M., MONDAY, JUNE 15

The meeting was to take place in the less-than-ornate small conference room of the Senate Intelligence Committee in the oldest building of the Senate, the Russell Building.

It was a secure room, one of the few such rooms on Capitol Hill. There were very few truly private places on the grounds of the Capitol, and this was one of them.

The most interesting "private" Senate facility was the indoor tennis court on the fifth floor of the Dirksen Building that few people—not even most of the Senate staff— knew about. A handful of senators played there with trusted aides or confidants. The blinds were drawn so no one could see them play. Senators had their aides carry their bags up to the court so no one would catch on.

There were also a few hideaway offices for senators that were off-limits to all staff. These offices were generally small and spartan, but several—like those of certain senators in their fourth terms in Congress—were known to be *slightly* more than spartan.

There were also the secure briefing rooms in the Capitol that the Pentagon's generals came to when they met with various members of Congress. The generals liked to meet in these rooms, even when national security wasn't involved. The rooms spoke of power, and generals liked the power. So did the Senate and House members, for that matter.

But the conference room of the Senate Intelligence Committee was where Daniel Trabue liked to meet. There were no trappings of power in the room—just a small conference table, soundproof walls, a back entrance for staff, and one telephone tucked into a corner of the room. You could not hide in the room, which was just the way Daniel liked it.

It was also the way his boss, Senator Cedric Jackson, liked it. Senator Jackson was a direct descendant of Stonewall Jackson, though he never said much about that. He never said much about himself. He left that up to others. But Senator Jackson liked the room for many of the same reasons Daniel did. You could not duck or bob and weave in the room. You put what you had on the table, and you hashed it out.

Senator Jackson had not been completely startled by the news Daniel gave him. Nothing surprised him anymore, not in today's world. Russia sold arms and babies to almost anyone who asked these days. Brazil was on the cusp of becoming a greater superpower than Russia. Israel had given away half of its country in a futile hope for peace.

North Korea had nearly built a nuclear weapon. Both Iraq and Iran had scoured the world for years in search of parts and fissionable material for some sort of a nuclear device. Pakistan almost certainly had at least short-range ballistic missile capability, as did several other lesser nations.

So it took a lot to truly surprise him these days. But the Algerian situation had given him pause. It was clearly out of the ordinary path of things. Algeria wasn't a country that had ever been known as a place willing to risk the wrath of the international community for the sake of some insane quest. Libya, yes. Algeria, no.

In fact, Algeria had carried on its own socialist revolution somewhat out of the global picture, other than the extraordinary assassination of its president several years ago and the startling national elections that had brought the Islamic Salvation Front to power—until the military had staged a bloodless coup d'etat and taken back the reins of the country.

Algeria's socialist monarch—which is the way the senator thought of presidents for life of countries like Algeria—had actually instituted a few democratic reforms. Not many, but more than other countries of similar stature and socialist history.

Algeria spent nearly all of its collective and national efforts on securing export markets for its national treasure, oil. It lived and breathed oil. Its import market was directly linked to its success at finding and exporting oil. Nothing else seemed to matter, nor should it. Until Algeria established itself in stable oil export markets, it was pointless to attempt anything else. The nuclear reactor being built by the Chinese, for instance, was almost certainly paid for by other forces around the globe—not Algeria.

So the photo Daniel had dug out really made no sense. Senator Jackson half suspected that there wasn't much to it, that, in fact, the photo was an aberration. Still, he'd go through with the briefing and see what would come of all of it. He'd seen more than one wild goose chase amount to nothing. More than likely, this would come to that as well.

Daniel had known that his boss would be skeptical even as he'd briefed him. Senator Jackson was a hard man to convince, and it would take more than one NSA photo to convince him of the merit of the case Daniel had been working on for some time.

The NSA photo was the first real hard piece of information to surface. But Daniel felt certain it would not be the last piece in a trail of puzzles.

Daniel was convinced that parts of the former Soviet Union were beginning to vanish to different parts of the world, and he'd been trying to track them for months. It was a daunting task. The warring states of the former Soviet empire were like the Wild West of the early days of the United States. There was very little authority, and almost no record of transactions.

It was funny. At odd moments, now and then, Daniel felt like he'd caught a vision of the future—a future where no one really ruled and where the boundaries were no longer clear. In that future, information was shared freely, and those who controlled that flow controlled the world. Or manipulated it to their advantage.

One example of that uncertain future was an international movement called Unity, which had captured followers and leaders in nearly every developed country of the globe. Unity had begun as a private nongovernmental organization, but had quickly evolved into a virtual offshoot of the United Nations Office of Humanitarian Affairs, the World Bank, the International Monetary Fund (IMF), and a host of other global bodies.

Unity was comprised of the leaders of all the major religious denominations around the world. It was the first group to include senior leaders from the Protestant, Catholic, Islamic, Buddhist, and Jewish faiths in its upper management ranks.

Unity thrived on information. Because it had been set up as a humanitarian outreach program, it was nearly always first on the scene of every major disaster. But it also used its vast information network and resources to work its way into major development schemes in many nations as well. It just seemed to be in dozens of places all at once, working side by side with the ruling governments.

Daniel had researched Unity only a little, enough to know that it received grant money from the U.S. Agency for International Development (AID) for development projects in a handful of countries around the world. It also represented the United Nations in many places and worked closely with both the UN and the State Department in reconciliation efforts in countries decimated by civil wars.

In short, Unity was the model of the new international organization that now flourished in the world where rapid access to information and the ability to move money and resources quickly were the keys to success. Unity could get jobs done that no one else could get done. So the organization was always in demand, and it always received funding and support from governments that needed its help.

But Daniel saw only fleeting glimpses of that future, where groups like Unity flourished and former superpowers like the Soviet Union collapsed. Events crashing down around him usually kept him focused on tasks at hand. Like the one today.

Daniel arrived at the secure briefing room a full half hour before the meeting. As usual, his worn leather briefcase was nearly overflowing with documents that were still unread. He pulled out his Algeria file and reread all the documents.

There was an unusually terse communiqué to Senator Jackson from Ken Branigan, the CIA director. It basically conveyed only that the CIA was fully exploring the situation and would facilitate any efforts by Congress to raise questions.

Which meant to Daniel that the photo had caught the CIA completely by surprise. Branigan was probably turning the world upside down now trying to get to the bottom of what was in the picture.

There was also a fairly detailed memo from Will Samuels, the president's chief of staff, to his boss. Daniel laughed out loud again as he read it for the second time. He could spot the sections of it that would almost certainly be used as direct quotes in the *Washington Post* should it ever need to be leaked.

Daniel actually admired the work and effort Samuels put into the memo. It was masterfully done. The memo never once mentioned how the information about the Algerian situation had come to the White House, only what the White House's national security team was doing with the information it had. An uninvolved observer would naturally assume that the information had been gathered by the administration's vast network of intelligence agencies. But at the same time, Samuels was already distancing the president from any responsibility for what had happened in Algeria—*if* anything had happened—just in case the whole thing should happen to blow up in the White House's face.

Samuels wrote that the president stood ready to take all means necessary—including some form of military force, should it be warranted—to "secure" the Algerian situation. But he emphasized that any such action was premature in light of the scarce amount of information as yet provided by the intelligence community serving U.S. interests.

Daniel almost felt sorry for the CIA station chief in Algiers. His career, most likely, was finished. His only hope was that there was nothing to find in that mountaintop. He would try vainly to funnel information back as rapidly as possible. But it would not matter. He would be held accountable.

Daniel was so absorbed in his Algeria file that he didn't hear the door to the briefing room open. He looked up and was startled to see his boss standing over him, gazing over Daniel's shoulder with a bemused smile.

The two of them were an odd couple. Senator Jackson, true to his heritage, had a face that almost looked as if it had been chiseled from stone. With a square, broad chin, a high forehead with three deep lines running across it, a nose that still bore the scars from when it had been broken by the butt of a rifle in military training school, and steel gray hair that was cut to the point of almost vanishing, Senator Jackson was quite easy to spot in every crowd.

Daniel, on the other hand, looked like he was still a senior in college, with light blue eyes that never seemed to blink, wavy brown hair that sometimes fell across his eyes, and a wiry frame that never seemed to gain any weight. Daniel blended into crowds easily. He faded into backgrounds.

"Figure it out yet?" the senator asked him.

"Almost," Daniel mumbled, embarrassed that he had not been aware of the senator's entrance.

"You saw the Samuels memo?"

That made Daniel smile. "A piece of work, wasn't it?"

"One of his best efforts, I think," Senator Jackson said, laughing. "I was actually surprised he didn't just claim credit for finding the information in case he should need documentation."

"I think he left it out, just in case."

The senator raised his eyebrows. "So you actually think there's something to this?"

Daniel looked intently at his boss. He'd never really discussed his pet theory with the senator, not in any specific terms. Oh, they'd both had long discussions about the fall of the Soviet empire. But Daniel had never let on that he'd been attempting to track certain developments. And now wasn't the time to begin that dialogue.

"Yes, I think there might be something to it," Daniel said evenly. "Perhaps not what we think right now. But something, yes."

The senator nodded. If Daniel took it seriously, then

that was enough for him. He would pay close attention when the White House contingent arrived in a few minutes.

Neither of them was entirely sure who would show up. It could be the full armada—one or two generals from the Joint Chiefs of Staff, Branigan, the secretary of state, the secretary of defense, Dr. Sullivan, and various assorted others—or it could be a small, stealthy team sent to determine just what Senator Jackson and his staff knew.

Daniel was betting on the latter. He was sure they didn't know enough to send in all the troops. They'd send in the reconnaissance team first, and then blister the Hill with briefings later when they knew what they were dealing with.

Senator Jackson took his place at the head of the table, and Daniel moved his papers back into their file and then the jammed briefcase. Then he took his customary seat in the corner of the room, away from the table. He was an observer, not a principal, and he knew his place.

When the White House group arrived moments later, though, Daniel was surprised. The team consisted of three people, two of whom he'd never seen in this briefing room before—Will Samuels, who *never* came to Capitol Hill unless the president ordered him to; Dr. Sullivan, the national security advisor who probably had no choice in the matter; and a woman Daniel had never seen before.

The woman was striking, even to Daniel, who was usually oblivious to such things. She wasn't dressed in the usual attire of the professional woman in Washington, with the power suit, pearl necklace, and sharp heels. She was dressed much more casually, with a soft gray skirt that matched her full black hair and pale features and almost no makeup or jewelry. She had the look of someone who felt at home wherever she went. Even here.

From the way she shadowed Dr. Sullivan as he entered the room, Daniel immediately guessed that she was one of his aides. Dr. Sullivan almost always came to the Hill without an entourage, and Daniel rarely telephoned the White House for information because the president was a Republican and his boss was a Democrat. So their paths would likely not have crossed, except by accident.

He knew the names of Dr. Sullivan's senior aides, though, and there were only two women at a level high enough to come to a meeting such as this. One of them was an expert in Japanese affairs, so he ruled her out instantly. Which meant that the woman had to be Loren Anders, a special assistant who was fairly new to the White House compound but who had already earned a reputation for her hard work and quiet resolve.

As Dr. Sullivan and Will Samuels moved around the table to greet Senator Jackson, Daniel hurried across the room to intercept her.

"Ms. Anders, how nice to see you. Thank you for making the trip here," Daniel said somewhat awkwardly. It took a little effort to keep his gaze from wavering.

The surprise registered on her face. "Have we . . . have we met?"

"No, we haven't, I don't believe," he answered quickly. "But you're Loren Anders, right?"

"Well, yes, I am, but how in the world . . . ?"

Daniel glanced over at the other group in the room. "I saw that you came in with Dr. Sullivan. I just assumed you were with him."

Loren bristled. The thought unnerved her slightly that she could be so easily pegged. "I might have been anyone at all," she said, unable to keep the ediginess from her voice.

"Yes, but you aren't, though," Daniel said softly. "My assumption was correct, wasn't it?"

"You shouldn't assume so quickly. It'll get you in trouble someday," Loren said curtly, her eyes now riveted on Daniel's. She was clearly angry, though Daniel felt sure she didn't really know why.

They stood there like that for several long moments— worlds apart even though they were just a few feet from each other. They instinctively mistrusted each other, though she knew nothing about him other than that he was some anonymous aide to a senator from the other party, and he knew nothing of her, other than that she was a political lackey of a president he had only the faintest regard for.

But just as Daniel was about to write her off as yet another self-important White House aide who meant to take the world by storm, Loren suddenly smiled and held out her hand. The distance between the two wavered momentarily. Daniel took her slender hand and squeezed it gently but professionally.

"Congratulations," Loren said, still smiling as she withdrew her hand.

"For what?"

"For the photo, of course. It was you, wasn't it?"

Daniel grinned. "You're not supposed to admit that."

"I didn't. To admit to something means you're guilty. And we're not guilty of anything as far as I know. But it was you, right?"

Daniel hesitated, and then nodded. But before he could say anything else, Senator Jackson took his seat at the table, along with Dr. Sullivan and Will Samuels. Loren and Daniel quickly took their seats behind their bosses, on opposite sides of the table.

"All right, let's get this over with," the senator said briskly. "There aren't enough of us in the room to make this complicated, so let's get right down to it. I'm assuming you all knew nothing about what was in the photo, or you'd have been up here before?"

"Senator, we've had intelligence in Algeria about shipments of imports," Samuels answered. "Remember, NSA discovered the nuclear reactor in the desert. We've monitored the progress of that reactor for several years, and there had never been any indication that they'd moved beyond the research phase."

"No indication?" the senator asked incredulously. "If I remember correctly—and I'm certain I do—none of us in this room had an inkling that Algeria had such a large reactor under construction until the blasted thing was almost complete. Right?"

"Well . . . um . . . yes, Mr. Chairman, that is correct, but . . . ," Samuels said hesitantly.

"Will," the senator interrupted him quietly, "there are no cameras here. This stays in the room. We both know the Algerian reactor took us by surprise. This thing could be like that as well, couldn't it?"

Will paused. "Yes, it could, I suppose. But our CIA chief there says that . . ."

Senator Jackson held up a hand this time, cutting him off. "Yes, I know you've got the poor man pulling every scrap of paper he's sent you in the past year, trying to sort through it. You can let that carry on as long as you like, I don't care. I just want to know—just for me, not for anyone else—that this represents new information. Right?"

Will Samuels nodded slowly. "Yes, it is new information." How he spun the story outside this room was one thing. In here, it was easier to tell the truth to Senator Jackson.

"Good," Senator Jackson said. "And I assume you want to get to the bottom of it as rapidly as you possibly can. Correct?"

"It is," Samuels acknowledged.

"Then I have a proposal," the senator said. He glanced over at Daniel, and then back to the table. "I'd like the White House to send a team there."

"On the ground in Algiers?" Samuels asked.

"There, and wherever you think they need to be or go," the senator responded promptly. "It's your call."

"And you'll support us?" Dr. Sullivan offered, chiming in for the first time.

"As long as you shoot straight with me, of course," the senator said sternly. "That's all I ask."

Samuels pursed his lips. "Well, we could send General Sanderson from the air force and perhaps the undersecretary of state, along with Dr. Sullivan here. And there's also . . ."

Senator Jackson held up a hand, cutting him off. "No, a small staff, a small mission. We don't want this thing noticed, do we? Not yet, at least, until we know what we're dealing with."

"I suppose you're right," Samuels agreed.

"So I'd propose Daniel Trabue of my staff," the senator said, gesturing toward his aide, "and someone from the White House staff who isn't easily recognized."

Dr. Sullivan and Will Samuels both glanced over at Loren, who did her best not to show just how panicked she suddenly felt.

"Loren?" Dr. Sullivan asked.

"I'd be happy to go along on a fact-finding mission," Loren said, her voice surprisingly calm.

"I'd like to send a military aide," Will Samuels said.

The senator knew the military aide would, in fact, be CIA. Samuels had long had a direct line to the CIA. But he didn't care, not as long as Daniel was along for the trip. He stood up and held out his hand. The meeting was over. "You've got a deal," he growled. "Don't make me regret it later."

Will Samuels shook the senator's hand, relieved that it had gone as well as it had. There would be no leaks to the press, at least not yet. The president would be pleased.

Loren's eyes met Daniel's only once more, as they exited the room. She tried not to let her fear show. She wasn't sure how well she'd succeeded.

Their fate was now intertwined, for better or worse. Neither knew whether that was good or bad, only that their futures were virtually the same for a time.

Chapter Five

MONDAY, JUNE 15

Colonel David Asher was trooping up the side of a mountain in the middle of the night with a dozen soldiers beside him in full gear. They'd been at it for several hours already, and the end wasn't in sight yet. The problem was that the trail switched back and forth like a very long dragon's tail. It would take them three days to reach the summit. And they still had no idea where to search once they hit the summit.

It had been a mistake to cede this territory back to Lebanon. Peace was nice, but giving up a strategic mountaintop that overlooked the northern plains of Israel was foolish at best and quite dangerous at worst.

Their mission right now was clear proof of that, as if any were needed. If any of his men were caught on this mountain, they could be shot by Lebanese patrols. They weren't on Israeli soil. They were technically in Lebanon.

But it was a mission they had to undertake, as quietly as possible. They'd had a fluke report of a mobile short-range missile position being set up here, overlooking the countryside. An Israeli jet, shooting infrared pictures for a topography project that wasn't even secret, had picked up something. Army had decided to check it out, as a precaution.

So the army had sent Colonel Asher, a repatriated American Jew. He had officially been an Israeli citizen for close to twenty years. He loved Israel—more than life itself almost.

He was a Talmud scholar and a devoted, traditional Jew who believed in God's presence and protection of the Holy Land. He would serve that land with his blood if necessary.

His Hebrew was flawless now, though he could still speak English almost as well as he had when he first visited Israel in the 1970s and stayed. It was easy actually. So much English was spoken across the countryside, keeping it up wasn't difficult.

He was a full-bird colonel in the Israeli army, and one of the best they had. He was an expert at covert missions such as this one, and he'd been on more than his share of raids in remote or forbidden places. He knew how to be careful.

He had, for instance, been in and out of Gaza and the West Bank so many times he'd forgotten the number of missions he'd undertaken there. He'd been in and out of Syria, Lebanon, and even Egypt on a handful of occasions as well.

But tonight it was Lebanon. The mission this time was different from the others. He'd never hunted hardware before. Before, it had always been soldiers or arms caches. Not actual weapons positions.

There really wasn't any way to take a helicopter—even under radar—north into Lebanon and drop in without alerting half of the monitoring posts that something was happening. The generals had felt an on-site look was needed. And that meant literally walking up the side of the tallest mountain overlooking the plains of Israel.

At some point in time, Colonel Asher knew instinctively, Israel had given over too much land in its hard-won efforts to win peace with its neighbors on every border. Israel had given back so much land to Lebanon and Syria that those two countries felt as if they'd actually won a war with Israel.

Giving away that much in the quest for peace signals weakness. At least, that's what Asher had always believed. Better to have held what they'd fought so hard for, and given other things—like information or technology. Just not land.

But land was the quid pro quo for peace in this part of the world. It was what the nation's rulers bargained with.

Israel's neighbors had gotten most of what they'd always sought. Land north, northwest, and west of Israel now belonged to those neighboring countries again. Once, the mountain they were on had belonged to Israel. A satellite surveillance station had operated on top of it. Several missions into southern Lebanon had been launched from it.

That was, of course, why Lebanon's leaders had insisted on its return to Lebanon. They were as sick of the successful Israeli raids into Lebanon's interior as they could be. The only way to stop it, they felt, was to take the mountain back. And what they could not achieve militarily, they had achieved through diplomacy.

The report of a short-range missile position on top of the mountain was a recent development that the Israeli army had not expected. Such missiles were expensive, and Lebanon had not had that kind of wealth for quite some time.

Which meant that, if they were here, they most likely belonged to someone else. Syria perhaps or Iraq. But what were they doing in Lebanese territory? It made no sense.

All Asher knew was that if he found them, he was going to take them out. He didn't much care who they belonged to. A well-installed missile, with the proper circuitry and guidance in the nose, could reach Jerusalem.

Once, that hadn't been the case. Syria and Iraq, for instance, had tried for years to get their hands on sophisticated weapons that actually worked. But the best they'd ever been able to find were the Scud missiles that couldn't hit the broad side of a barn.

No longer. These days, expensive, intelligent weapons were leaking out of the former Soviet Union at an alarming rate. Russia, the Ukraine, and other nations that had once made up that military power were selling major weapons systems for hard cash on the black market.

So-called experts always said they weren't, but they were. And everyone who knew anything about weapons systems knew it as well.

So it was entirely possible that Asher would find Russian missiles at the top of this mountain. Entirely possible. And those missiles might just have the range to get to Israel's major population centers.

What he wouldn't know until he got there was who they belonged to. If missiles were up there, who was operating them?

Chapter Six

Daniel looked down at the three matching immaculate suitcases Loren Anders had brought with her. He glanced at his own somewhat battered duffel bag, which had a rip in one corner, a zipper that was half off, and at least three coffee stains in the canvas.

He thought—just for a brief moment—about dashing over to one of the all-purpose stores in the lobby of Dulles International Airport and buying a new piece of luggage. Maybe Loren wouldn't notice. Somehow, though, he doubted that would be the case, so he resisted the thought and plunked his bag next to Loren's belongings.

Anyway, he *liked* his duffel bag. It had been with him since his days at Yale University. It had been through both lean years and years of plenty. Once, it had carried all his worldly possessions from job to job. He hated the thought of parting with it. But, man, it sure was ugly and disgusting, especially compared to Loren's things.

It wasn't that Daniel was a slob. He wasn't really. All right, so he left his dishes in the sink for a day or two. Or three. And he never actually put his dirty clothes in a basket so he could wash them. He piled them all in the closet until he couldn't close the door, and then wore the clothes for a second (and sometimes a third) round.

And, okay, so he sometimes had a hard time finding his other shoe in the morning, and sometimes his keys were in a weird place like the soap dish in the shower. And every once in a while he went to his cubbyhole office in the Russell Building with one black sock and one blue one.

You weren't a slob just because you wore striped pants and checkered shirts at the same time. You were just fashion dead. You weren't a slob because you had to search for a piece of paper under mounds of old newspapers and files that never got smaller, only bigger. You were just disorganized.

About every six months, Daniel went ballistic. He'd spend an entire Saturday throwing everything in sight away or into drawers. He'd clean out every cobweb in his apartment and rearrange everything, then vow it would never get that way again. He wasn't a slob. He was just really busy, and he never got around to keeping things together.

Slobs left half-eaten pieces of pizza under couch cushions. Daniel carefully closed the box lid on his pizza boxes and kept them stored in proper places—like the top of the TV console or on top of the kitchen cabinets where the mice (supposedly) couldn't get to them.

Slobs left clothes and towels and coats and other assorted objects lying around on the floor. Daniel was careful to drape his towels on the arms of chairs or on the door handle in the bathroom. Never mind that you couldn't find a free doorknob or unencumbered chair anywhere in the apartment. At least everything was in its proper place.

Daniel actually watered his plants, and some of them stayed alive for long periods of time. He swept the floors at least once a month, and he'd even bought Lysol for the bathroom. He hadn't really *used* the Lysol, but it was there. Slobs never even thought to buy that kind of stuff, Daniel reasoned.

Daniel frowned nevertheless as he looked over at Loren. She was wearing a nicely tailored suit, the kind that you had to spend a little time to find. There was no way she'd just plucked it from a rack somewhere, the way Daniel bought his clothes.

It was funny. Loren didn't dress flashy. She didn't wear a lot of colorful makeup or paint her fingernails bright red. She didn't have that walk some women have that almost orders members of the opposite sex to take notice. And yet every man glanced at her when he went by. There was something so striking about Loren that every man saw it and stared for all he was worth.

Daniel was annoyed that men did that. He had the same urges sometimes, but he tried his level best not to look women up and down. It wasn't that he was trying to be moralistically superior to other men. He just thought it was incredibly rude and obnoxious the way men sized women up constantly.

In fact, Daniel had never really had time to think about ethical or moral things. In college, he'd been a political science major, with his eyes firmly on good grades so he could get into one of the top law schools in the country. He'd succeeded at getting into the best law schools—just as he'd succeeded at everything he'd ever done. He chose Harvard and blazed through, finishing third in his class.

After law school, he'd clerked for a federal appellate court judge for two years. It was a tremendous experience, but one that hadn't given him much of a life beyond work. From there, he went to work first as a legislative aide and then as chief committee counsel to his current boss, Senator Jackson.

In the process of establishing his career, Daniel had never taken time to think too long and hard about anything beyond work. There had been no need to think beyond school or work. That had been more than enough to consume every waking moment of his life.

But when he looked at someone like Loren, he wondered if he hadn't missed something. He wasn't exactly sure how to approach her. Not like he had a choice anyway. She was the enemy, and he'd have to go after her, hound her intellectually, like he did any adversary.

"You ready?" he asked her.

Loren glanced at the slim watch on her arm. Daniel instinctively glanced at his watch as well. Their plane would leave in about thirty minutes. The third member of their party, the military attaché who would accompany them on their trip, had not shown up yet. They'd decided to wait in the lobby area just outside the entrance to the airport hangars where their plane would leave from.

"I guess so," Loren sighed. "But I don't know what we do if he doesn't show."

"He'll show. Maybe he's already over at the terminal, waiting for us."

Loren got up slowly and stretched. Two men walking by at that moment watched every movement she made, and they even craned their necks as they walked off into the distance. Daniel felt a wildly irrational surge of adrenaline and almost took off after both of them. He wasn't exactly sure what he'd do if he caught them. Maybe just ring their necks.

"Whatcha starin' at?" Loren asked him, a funny look on her face.

Daniel felt his face grow flush. "Oh, nothin'," he mumbled. "I was just lookin' out for our guy."

"You looked like you wanted to punch somebody."

"No, no, I was just . . ." Daniel looked away. This was embarrassing. He decided to change the subject. "Hey. By the way, did you get a chance to look over the State Department briefing on Algeria?"

Loren nodded. "Yeah, I looked at it. Not much there. I didn't learn anything I didn't already know from the news clips my staff pulled for me."

"But what did you think of those export numbers on oil?"

Loren thought about that for a moment. "Well, that's right. Those numbers haven't been in any news stories."

"Don't you think they mean something?" Daniel pressed, anxious to turn the conversation away from his previous thoughts as quickly as possible.

"Maybe," answered Loren. "It's interesting, I guess,

that their oil production has all but collapsed in the last three years."

Daniel nodded eagerly. "While—at least for now—the price of oil has fallen right through the floor OPEC tried to set because Iran was so desperate to find cash to pay for the four nuclear reactors it's buying from Russia."

Algeria's economy was almost wholly dependent on exports of oil. When oil prices were high and the wells were flowing, the socialist government had more than enough money to dole out to its citizens.

But as Loren had noted, both the production and the price the Algerians could get for their barrels of oil had fallen dramatically in the past three years.

The drop in oil prices recently was due almost solely to Iran's efforts to sell crude oil on the world market for any price anyone would pay. The Iranians had to have the hard currency. They'd recently signed an agreement with Russia to purchase technology to build four light water nuclear reactors near Bushehr.

The total cost of the reactors was about $8 billion, and Iran didn't have it. So the Iranians were willing to violate OPEC's price setting to get the currency. It had driven all oil prices down in the process.

The United States had done everything in its power to block the Russia-Iran nuclear power deal. Because it was clear what Iran wanted. The Iranians planned to take the spent fuel rods and extract the plutonium from them.

Daniel had done enough research to know that the Iranians were well on the way to acquiring reprocessing technology sufficient to allow them to take what they extracted from the spent fuel rods and turn it into weapons-grade plutonium. They had to be at least five years away from such a capability, but it was still absurd for Russia to sign such an agreement, no matter how badly Russia needed the currency.

The Russia-Iran deal was the best example Daniel could think of to illustrate just how insane the world had become after the cold war had ended. Everyone thought the collapse of the Soviet Union had ushered in an era of global peace.

Far from it. There had been nearly one hundred wars around the world in the past five years alone. It seemed that everyone was fighting everyone else. And Russia seemed willing to arm anyone who wanted what it had to sell. Even Iraq, which had been condemned by every civilized nation during the Persian Gulf War.

Algeria was typical of what was happening to a lot of countries these days. The Algerians were right on the edge of financial collapse. They were so dependent on oil production and exports of oil that their current predicament may have driven their government's leaders to desperate measures.

There were signs to watch for when countries got in trouble like that. If they tried to take out IMF loans, or tried to arrange deals for new industries with other countries, that was a sure sign that they were in big trouble and heading in the wrong direction.

Loren and Daniel both knew from their oral briefings by the CIA that Algeria's leaders had been to the World Bank and the IMF on several occasions—as well as to several bankers in Geneva—to discuss bridge loans for new industrial development.

Algeria was clearly in trouble, and there seemed to be

no immediate solution to the problems. The Algerians had to hope that their national oil company would discover some new, productive wells, or that the price of crude oil would start to go up sharply again as it had, once, in previous decades.

Loren and Daniel didn't want to leap to any conclusions until they'd had a chance to look at the place for themselves, but both had independently begun to form a theory about what the NSA photo had revealed. It was entirely possible that some third party—Russia, China, or even a second-tier country like India—had promised Algeria cash for the right to test or site nuclear weapons on their sovereign territory. Both of them were thinking that, though neither would speak of it to the other.

Most of the nations of the world had signed both the nuclear nonproliferation and the test ban treaties that had been around for years. Most nations adhered to the treaties.

But countries like Russia and China were almost certainly looking for ways to escape the scrutiny of inspectors who could go in and look at facilities and plants. One sure way to continue testing or actual deployment of intermediate-range or intercontinental ballistic missiles was to cut a deal with a friendly country and then give it so much money that it would do as you asked.

Perhaps Algeria, in its desperation, had done just that. It was possible. Not likely, but at least possible. Government leaders did foolish or reckless things when their political lives were in very serious jeopardy—and Algeria's socialist leaders were certainly up against the wall.

There was a great deal of civil unrest in their society

as workers got laid off or saw their wages severely cur-
tailed. There had been a few riots in the streets of Algiers in the past year alone, and there had been reports of a
rebellious opposition party being formed in shadow village
councils around the country.

"What I'd like to know is just how desperate the Algerians are now," Loren mused.

"Me, too. If they're really desperate, then that could
mean something."

Loren looked straight at Daniel, which unnerved him
a bit. "Do you think we'll get a chance to visit the
mountain site? Are you prepared to force the issue?"

Daniel took a deep breath. He'd thought about it, of
course. But he hadn't reached any firm conclusions.
"The problem, you know, is that we don't have the
same status or rights that the nuclear inspectors have.
There's no way we can demand to see their facilities."

"They're not going to even admit to any facilities,
Daniel. You know that," Loren said somberly.

"I know. You're right."

"So can we demand to see a mountain?" Loren asked.
"I mean, that'll sound crazy."

"I don't know," Daniel joked. "Maybe we can just
rent a car and drive there."

Loren smiled. Daniel couldn't help noticing that her
teeth were all straight and even, with no gaps or blem-
ishes. She must have worn braces as a child, unlike
him. His teeth were crooked, and he had a severe over-
bite. "Better yet," she said, "maybe they'll just let us
hire out a helicopter pilot and fly over the place."

"We can dream, can't we?"

They looked at each other, the same thought occurring to both at the same moment. Yeah, right. Fat chance. They were never going to get near that mountain. Not in a million years.

Loren glanced down at her watch. They had twenty-five minutes until their plane left for London, and then Algiers. They had to board. "Look, maybe he'll catch up with us," she offered.

"Sure, maybe. And, anyway, we can always hook up with someone from the embassy on the ground there."

Daniel picked up two of Loren's suitcases before she could grab them. He slung his own bag over his shoulder and then took off for the terminal. They piled their luggage onto the conveyor belt, walked through the metal detector, and headed quickly to the terminal area from where their plane was to depart. People were already starting to board.

Their attaché was nowhere in sight. They were on their own. Daniel looked over at Loren and broke into a wide smile. "Well, guess it's just you and me, kid."

"That's a scary thought," Loren said, frowning. "I presume I can trust you to behave yourself?"

"I was an Eagle Scout," Daniel said, still smiling. "You can trust me with your life."

"Not my life," Loren said, half seriously. "Just be a gentleman. Okay?"

"Always and forever. You have my word," Daniel said, actually vowing at that moment to be faithful to the pledge. It felt funny, too, because he'd never even thought about such a concept before. He kind of liked it.

Twenty minutes later, as the plane began to taxi away from the port, Daniel looked over and saw a *very* angry man shouting at the airline representatives inside the lobby. He could see the man, who was in uniform, gesturing wildly, flashing a badge, and pointing at their airplane. He kept gesturing and shouting, sometimes at the same time.

Daniel started to laugh. Loren looked at him like he'd lost his mind. "What is it?" she asked.

Daniel pointed over to the plate glass window. "Our escort, I do believe, has arrived."

Loren started laughing, too. "Slightly late, I'd say. He's in a heap o' trouble now."

"Yep. I pity the poor guy when he gets back to the office. Wouldn't want to be him."

They kept expecting the plane to turn around, to go back and get the military aide. But—though he was undoubtedly invoking every name up to and including the president, he did not have the authority to make a plane turn back once it had begun its route. They were on their own.

Daniel noticed that Loren closed her eyes and clasped her hands silently just as the plane was revving up for takeoff. She remained that way for a while.

As the plane lifted off the ground, Daniel was certain he saw her say "Amen" quietly and then open her eyes. She'd been praying. He was certain of it. He wondered, just a little, what her prayer had been about.

Chapter Seven

Sarah Jons stared at her computer screen for a long time. A very long time. Phones rang incessantly all around her, demanding her time and attention and those of everyone else in the room. But Sarah didn't hear them. She didn't hear anything.

It isn't possible, she thought. *It can't be true.* But she knew it was. Every instinct she'd honed over the past five years screamed out to her that it was true. The one thing she didn't understand—the common thread, so to speak—was an organization she'd never heard of before.

Sarah had the knack, the one that every really successful trader had. She knew when things were going to go up—and when they were going to go down.

She was the only major currency trader who'd guessed right about the Christmas 1994 crash of the Mexican peso. The only one. Every other major currency trading firm—and the institutions that took currency positions

---

61

through them—had taken a huge, huge hit in the peso crash.

It had happened so fast. In a matter of days, a third of the peso's value had dropped off the table. Vanished, gone, devalued beyond belief. Whole fortunes were lost because the Mexican government had botched its calculated effort to devalue the peso and pay off a few debts.

The peso had gone into free fall overnight, and no one could catch the currency before it had plummeted out of control.

But Sarah had known. She'd guessed right, as she had on so many other occasions. She'd quietly moved her positions and investors out of the peso into dollars just two days before the crash. She'd seen something and guessed right.

The way she did it was simple. She'd learned how in her early twenties as a trader in a crummy brokerage house that traded dollar stocks on third-tier exchanges.

Sarah had grown very, very adept at surfing the World Wide Web on the Internet, the on-line services like America Online and CompuServe, various financial bulletin boards that had sprung up all over the computer world like weeds, and even the government's own on-line computer offerings.

Sarah got special enjoyment reading the State Department's unclassified descriptions of comings and goings between various countries. That's where she'd gotten her lead on the Mexican peso.

Sarah also enjoyed using her ability to gather information to the advantage of her clients, many of whom had never seen her in person. They knew her as a voice over the phone.

That was nice because Sarah had been forced to fight every stereotype imaginable in the trading world. She was very pretty, with naturally blonde hair and a fair complexion. People took one look at her and figured she was somebody's secretary.

She wasn't. She was maybe one of the toughest traders around, who could move aggressively when the position warranted it or patiently wait out storms when that was called for.

Another aspect set her apart from her colleagues on Wall Street. Largely because of her deep Christian faith, she had no ambitions to become wealthy. Greed did not drive her. Success and hard work did.

Her competitors and coworkers now recognized her abilities. Some of them were even a little afraid of her ability to get in and out of positions before anyone else knew what was going on. She never let on how she came up with her "guesses."

For Sarah, ripping through all the computer networks had been a cheap, easy way to gather thousands, even millions, of scraps of information. And information *was* power, as trite as that saying was. Information meant access to the right decision, and the right decisions led to money. Big money.

In the early days, Sarah had spent a great deal of time gathering information without using much of it. Every so often, something would pop, and she'd find her surfing useful. But as she got better at trading stocks, and then eventually currency, she began to learn the delicate and global relationship of the financial markets.

Everything seemed to be interconnected. There was

no getting around it. If Japan did something that affected the balance of trade with the United States, then the dollar was affected. That was simple. But it went much deeper than that.

Taiwan, for instance, invites a U.S. assistant secretary of commerce over for a conference. Several American corporate CEOs come along for the ride. During that conference, the trade press in Taiwan reports on progress toward a new bilateral trade agreement between the two countries.

Meanwhile, two of the corporations involved in the conference have initiated talks with mainland China over a block of exports. China, hearing of the conference, threatens to sever the talks with the two corporations.

The corporations quickly look to a third country, Venezuela, to sell their export. And in a day or so, an event in Taiwan has potentially had a major impact on the balance of trade with Venezuela, even though the two things don't seem to be connected at all.

Sarah was especially adept at following these trails, especially the ones that wandered through several countries. She loved following the invisible thread that ran from one seemingly unconnected event to another.

But never had she seen so many tangled threads, all leading in one ominous direction. At the heart of each—and perhaps the only thing standing in the way of a global financial collapse—was a private global organization called Unity.

Whoever was masterminding the events—if there *was* a mastermind—had covered his or her tracks pretty neatly. Other than the Unity connection, there was very little to latch onto, should anyone actually look. All she could tell was that Unity was waiting in the wings with offers to help.

Sarah thought she had tripped across a series of crippling actions in several countries, all of which would follow one after another, circling the globe. By the time one part of the world reached its particular day two, several financial disasters in other parts of the world through the night would likely throw the entire currency system into near collapse.

None of the countries seemed to know or care what was going on in the other parts of the world. None of the events seemed to be related. But they were. Sarah *knew* they were.

And all that would keep disaster from spreading from continent to continent like an unwanted cancer was this vast well-financed, wonderfully philanthropic and humanitarian organization, unlike any the world had ever seen.

But who could she tell? Her boss? That was pointless. Her boss was responsible for just one thing—the $3 billion in currency they traded. He'd ask Sarah to protect their investment. The problem was, there wasn't a place to run and hide.

So should she tell her congressman? Her fellow traders? Perhaps the *Wall Street Journal*? Sarah didn't know where to turn.

So she decided to do what she'd always done before—rely on the network. She'd log onto the Web of the Internet later in the week, put out a request for information and help in several different directions at once, and then wait to see what came back to her.

Chapter Eight

Loren hadn't said much on the flight from Dulles to London. She'd slept for a good part of it and awoke only to eat a snack. In London, they'd grabbed a quick bite and then boarded the flight to Algiers. She'd explained to Daniel that she was catching up on sleep before the time difference took effect.

It hadn't been much different on the second leg of the flight, though. Loren had brought a book with her, and she'd buried her nose in it almost from the moment the plane lifted off from Heathrow.

Daniel wanted to talk to her, to work this whole thing through. He felt out of place for some reason. He was much more comfortable behind a desk, working the phone. He was out of his element like this, in the field.

Daniel kept glancing over at the book Loren was engrossed with. He didn't recognize the author or the subject matter, either. Something about the role of women in a secular society. Not exactly his kind of book.

Daniel couldn't remember the last novel he'd read or even a decent movie he'd seen in a theater. It had been years. He'd been pushing hard to succeed almost from the moment he entered Yale University. He hadn't let up through Harvard Law School or his first job clerking for the appellate court judge.

Working on the Hill, of course, chewed up his time. It wasn't unusual for him to stay in his office until ten or eleven at night. Every so often he'd go curl up in the sofa chair in the corner of his office and start all over first thing the next morning.

He didn't regret his decisions. He was happy and successful. He knew his way around the labyrinthine mazes of Congress and the committee rooms. He knew virtually everyone connected to the foreign-policy-making apparatus in Congress. He could call on anyone at any time. Everyone returned his phone calls.

Still, at times like this, he was like a fish out of water. He was profoundly uncomfortable around this woman, and he didn't know why. It wasn't that he was intimidated by her. No one intimidated him. Not anymore.

No, there was something else, something intangible, undefinable. She had a center to her, a firmness, that scared Daniel a little. She seemed so sure of what she was doing, why she was doing it. Daniel always acted out of fear that perhaps someone knew something he didn't know. This woman, Loren, didn't seem made that way.

Daniel had to admit he didn't know what drove her. And he hated that. He always knew what drove people.

Loren put her book down when they finally served breakfast, about halfway through the trip. She rubbed her eyes, slid her book under the seat, and made room for the breakfast.

"Must be a good book," Daniel said.

Loren looked over at him. He felt as if she looked right *through* him, not at him. It unnerved Daniel.

"Yes, it is," she said firmly. "It is quite good."

"What's it about if I might ask?"

"Oh, nothing really," Loren said, clearly distracted. Something was on her mind, and it wasn't the book. "Look, can I tell you something? It may be involved in all of this."

"Sure. Shoot."

Loren took a deep breath. She was uncertain. She wasn't sure she could trust this guy. But she almost felt like she had no control. Everything seemed to be spinning in the same direction.

"It's about my brother."

"Your brother?"

"Yes, I have an older brother, Michael, who lives in Washington, like I do. He used to work at the Pentagon. Now, he's retired, and he has a new business."

"What kind of business?"

"An export-import company of some kind. He had a business on the side for years while he was at the Pentagon."

That wasn't new. Daniel knew of plenty of people who did that sort of thing. He wasn't into it, but he wasn't about to condemn others for the practice.

"But pretty recently," Loren continued, "Michael got into something else. He won't talk about it much. We only spoke by phone a couple of minutes the other day. But I think he's trading information to other countries."

"What kind of information?"

"High-tech stuff. Things that used to be controlled by the Commerce Department, but that have loosened up."

"Like computer or defense technology? Things like that?"

Loren nodded. "Yes, like that."

Again, that wasn't all that unusual. American defense companies, trying to keep from going under in the new budget-cutting era, were selling very sophisticated weapons systems to places like China these days—sales that would have been unheard of just a few years ago.

A couple of years earlier, one of the large jet propulsion contractors in the U.S. had sold manufacturing technology used to build gas turbine engines to China. With that kind of technology, China could build engines designed for aircraft—but also engines for cruise missiles, enough to allow them to fly one thousand miles or more.

No one had blinked or batted an eye. The sale went through, and for all anyone knew, China was busily building—or perhaps had already completed—cruise missiles to be targeted at Japan, South Korea, or even India.

The world had become a funny place since the end of the cold war, Daniel often thought. A very funny place. More dangerous in many ways than during the cold war.

"So?" Daniel offered. "That's not a big deal."

Loren looked down at the floor of the aircraft. "He mentioned Algeria once, Daniel. He told me his company—his new partners—had sold technology to Algeria."

Daniel looked at Loren. She seemed so vulnerable right now. He wanted to reach out and hold her. "Look. It's probably nothing. Really. But I'm glad you told me. Sometimes it helps just to tell someone a thing like this. Lifts the burden."

Loren closed her eyes. She *was* glad to give this burden to someone else. She wasn't sure if she could trust this guy, but it made no difference. The die had been cast. She'd have to trust him now.

"Thank you," she said quietly. "You're right. I needed to tell someone. You got elected."

Very few people had ever trusted Daniel before. Used him, cajoled him, persuaded him, lobbied him, yes. But trusted him? No, that was something new, something quite unexpected for Daniel. He wasn't sure what to make of it.

He glanced down at her book again. He was even unfamiliar with the publisher. "So, what's your book about anyway?" he asked gently.

Loren blinked a couple of times and then turned in her seat to look at him directly. She didn't flinch. "It's about the proper role of a Christian woman in marriage today, how she should relate to her husband in such a marriage."

Daniel felt like he'd been shot. It wasn't the answer he'd been expecting, not by any means. Daniel had long ago given up on religion. There was no room for it in his life. He'd never had any desire to see or experience God.

His parents had quit going to church when he was eleven. He'd never been back, had no need to go back. It wasn't that he despised God or those who chose to believe in Him. It was simply that God seemed irrelevant to him, to his life.

He had no idea who any of the people of the Bible were, who Jesus had been, who Moses or Abraham or Joseph or John the Baptist or any of them had been. They were in the same category to Daniel as the Abominable Snowman, the Easter Bunny, and Santa Claus. He had no use for any of that.

His religion, the one he adhered to faithfully, was the religion of the mind. Whatever you could learn, what you could grasp with your mind, that was his religion. He had no need for anything beyond that. Or so he had believed for years.

Daniel had a great deal of faith in his ability to master almost anything and any situation. Even now, with a woman such as Loren.

"Yeah? Really?" he answered.

"I doubt it's something you'd be interested in," she said, "but you asked."

"Yeah, I asked. You're right about that." Daniel nodded. "But you're wrong if you don't think I'm interested."

"You're not religious, though, are you?" Again, that look. Like she saw right through him.

"Well, no, I guess not. But," he added hastily, "it's not like I have anything against people who do. Who are, I mean. You know, religious and all."

Loren smiled. It was a radiant smile, the kind that lights up rooms and makes people happy to be alive. "I'm sure you don't. You probably don't have time."

Daniel shrugged. "I'm pretty busy. You know the Hill."

"Yes, I think I can imagine. The White House is no piece of cake, either."

"I'll bet," Daniel replied. "It's probably a zoo, like the Hill."

Loren leaned forward in her seat, close enough so Daniel could smell her perfume. "I've found, though, that there's always time to have a life. Even in what we do, you and I. You just have to work at it, like everything else."

"I guess so."

Loren looked out the window. It was almost as if she was waiting for some signal, a sign of what to say next. Perhaps she got it because there was a sense of urgency, of resolve, when she turned back to Daniel.

"What we're doing, where we're going," she said, her eyes almost glowing with intensity, "I know in my heart that it's important. This isn't some mind game. This is the real thing. What we do will have a profound effect on *something*. I don't know what that is yet. But I know it's important. Don't you?"

Daniel tried to meet her gaze. "I've . . . well, yes, I guess I know it, too."

"There are only two paths in life, Daniel," Loren said. It was almost as if someone else were speaking to him, speaking to him through Loren's voice. "Either there is meaning in the world, or there isn't. Either God exists, or He doesn't. There is no middle ground. There is nothing in between those choices.

"For those who do not believe in God, their world—their existence—rests on a simple principle. How much power, fame, glory, money, or things they can achieve or accumulate. There is nothing else for them. But for those who believe in God, there is a deeper meaning to what we do. A much deeper meaning."

"And what is that?" Daniel asked hoarsely.

"You will see," Loren promised. "In time, you will see. Perhaps we will get a glimpse or two where we are going."

Loren said nothing for the rest of the trip. Eventually, Daniel forgot her words, said with such force and earnestness. But he knew the words would come back again at odd times during the next few weeks. That was the way his mind worked.

Either the world has meaning, or it doesn't. Either God exists, or He doesn't. There is nothing in between those two choices.

And where did Daniel believe? Where was he? Was he, in fact, in between those two choices? He didn't know. He just didn't know.

Chapter Nine

11:30 A.M., TUESDAY, JUNE 16

Michael Anders eased his red Ferrari past the gate that led into the underground parking garage of his office building. He was meticulously careful to keep at least a foot between his car, which was less than a year old, and the retracting arm at the entrance to the garage.

The underground garage of his office building at 1801 K Street NW—a prime corner location in the heart of the capital's power corridor, nestled in among big law offices, huge public relations and lobbying firms, and megacorporate offices—was nearly full this late in the morning.

Michael knew he would have to go clear to the bottom of the garage to find the right kind of parking space for his new car, but he didn't mind. Not at all.

In fact, Michael didn't mind much of anything these days. For a change, everything was going right. Or at least, it was much, much better than it had been during his days as a sludge bureaucrat in the bowels of the Pentagon.

Michael was, or had been, the typical bureaucrat—by the rest of America's standards, at least. He had lost his hair by his late thirties and had gained a paunch at roughly the same time. It had become quite a substantial paunch, which he did his best to obscure with loose-fitting shirts and oversized suit coats.

His wife and he had never been able to have children. It had devastated his wife, Charlene, but Michael had always secretly thought he'd been blessed.

With no kids to pay for and no college education to plan for, Michael had been free to indulge each and every one of his hobbies. His salary at the Pentagon, combined with his wife's earnings as a staff assistant to the executive director of a large Washington trade group, had guaranteed that they had plenty of extra money each month.

During his long career—first at the CIA as an analyst and later at the Pentagon—Michael had also been free to do what so many bureaucrats did "on the side." It wasn't illegal, though it wasn't exactly encouraged by the senior executives at the agencies and departments, either.

Michael had started a second career—a business, to be more precise—when he was in his late twenties and had continued the business to the present day. He had always been amazed that you could do such a thing while you worked for the U.S. government. But you could, and he did, just like thousands of others.

The business had begun as a tiny export-import company. Michael and a partner, who was not in the government, basically tried to arrange for the purchase of fruits or vegetables in places like Brazil or Chile, and then sell them to large restaurant chains or food co-ops in the United States. They also traded other commodities as well, over time.

On the export side, Michael's company would find products like blue jeans in warehouses and then sell them at marked-up prices in Russia or the Middle East. People loved American blue jeans, and they were easy to unload.

Michael was not supposed to use the phone or his office to conduct any business beyond the Pentagon's business, but he had saved on phone bills and other overhead costs by making all his calls overseas from the Pentagon.

It had been easy to mask what he was doing because so many overseas calls went out from the Pentagon daily. Ten or fifteen calls more—in the middle of tens of thousands of such calls—were never noticed.

Michael felt like he wasn't *really* breaking the law, just bending the rules a tiny, little bit. There was no harm, no foul, he felt. Anyway, he always rationalized, he was working for the taxpayers for less money than he might get in the private sector, so no one would mind if he did a little business on the side at their expense. It all evened out, he figured.

Over the years, the business had begun to make more money, occasionally coming close to matching his Pentagon salary. He wasn't going to get rich, though, not by his standards.

When Michael thought of rich, he thought of the CEOs of companies like Lockheed or Martin Marietta or

Boeing who came in to see his superiors at the Pentagon. Those guys made millions each year and lived the life of kings. They were rich. They were where Michael wanted to be someday.

Michael had planned for his retirement a full five years before he walked out the door. He'd been able to do so because he'd long ago mastered his job as an analyst within the Pentagon's nonproliferation office, the place where they tracked nuclear developments in far-flung places like North Korea or Pakistan, and he was able to devote much of his time to pursuing other things.

He'd seen his chance to move the timetable up during the Clinton administration, when the "reinventing government" guys were handing out a $25,000 check to anyone who retired early. Michael pulled a few strings he'd latched onto during his years there, got someone to "abolish" his job, and took an early out—complete with the $25,000 check and full retirement benefits.

He was just fifty-one when he walked out the door six months ago, plenty of time to start a second career building on his already established export-import company. He took some of the more interesting files he'd developed over the years with him, some of them still classified but none of them central to the security of the U.S., he figured. Just in case he might need them.

It was a nice deal. In "retirement," Michael got 50 percent of the salary he'd earned during the last three years of service in the Pentagon. He would get that for the rest of his life.

He and his partner had opened a little office in Rosslyn, Virginia, and had begun to expand the business in other commodities. Life was good. Michael's house was paid off, so when they sold it for a handsome profit and moved to a smaller, custom-built home in McLean, he still had plenty of money left over. His health was fine, and he had no other outstanding debts of any kind.

And then, out of nowhere, life had gotten even better. A much bigger, more successful export-import company, Peramco Ltd., had approached his partner one day about acquiring their little company and some of the interesting projects and files Michael had spirited away from the Pentagon.

Three weeks later, after several dinners and lunches in quite nice restaurants and two conferences in the law offices of Smith, Exner, and Milhouse, they had become a subsidiary of Peramco Ltd.

In return for giving up control of his company and some information from a couple of his files—for which he'd felt a little nervous, but not enough to squelch the deal—Michael received an immediate check of $500,000 for the purchase of his company, as did his partner, with a guaranteed annual salary of $175,000 plus bonuses. Michael simply had to promise to make an effort to move into some of the same kind of export and import business Peramco was good at to earn those bonuses.

The Peramco deal had proved to be mindlessly easy. Peramco was a broker of information more than goods, it turned out, and one of its specialties was information—nearly all of it unclassified or newly declassified—from the Pentagon to places overseas.

Michael found that he could go back into the Pentagon with a special projects, top secret clearance pass and literally walk the corridors of his old building, pick up information that others would find hard to track down but that was ridiculously easy for him to locate, and then turn it over to Peramco officials by courier to their offices in New York.

It was really that simple. So simple, in fact, that he and his partner had almost dropped their earlier business relationships altogether. Why bother tracking down fruits and vegetables from Brazil when it was much more lucrative to peddle easily obtained information to their new business partners and make so much more money at it? It was a no-brainer, they always laughed.

In the past few months, things had gotten a little more complicated. The requests for information from Peramco officials had been in different export areas, more in line with the kind of work Michael had once done at the Pentagon.

Some of it came awfully close to the line on the type of information that could be shipped overseas, even with all the easing of restrictions on the sale of high technology to places like Poland. Michael felt twinges of anxiety when he asked old friends for some of the information.

And in several instances, Michael wondered about the unusual requests he was getting. Especially the latest two requests for access to some data in a file on a nuclear breeder reactor that had gone belly-up in South Carolina nearly a decade ago and some of the international inspection reports on the destruction of the INF missiles in Russia and the Ukraine.

Michael would likely have to work much harder to get his hands on the materials to meet these requests, but the Peramco officials said there was a large sum of money waiting on the other side of the deal—should he be able to locate the data—and he would receive an extraordinarily large bonus for success. They had even hinted at something in the neighborhood of $1 million as an end-of-the-year bonus, which was plenty of incentive for Michael.

He finally found a spot at the bottom of the garage. He pulled the Ferrari into an empty space that had no other cars near it for at least three spaces on either side, switched the car alarm on, and walked over to the elevators that would carry him up to his corner office overlooking K Street on the seventh floor.

When he arrived at the office, his secretary—newly hired by Peramco just for him—handed him a pile of phone slips, but pulled one from the top and made him look at it.

"Peramco wants a conference call with you on this in an hour," she told him. "They said that it was important, and that you need to drop everything else to take part."

Michael glanced at the slip and shrugged. The note on the bottom said it was on the INF project. No sweat. He'd made a great deal of progress on that front, and he would be in a position to deliver within days, he figured.

"Fine," he told his secretary. "I'll take it on the speaker when they call, in the small conference room."

He walked into his office. His computer was already on, thanks to his secretary. She'd set up the America Online cue for him so he could check the latest quotes of his stock and mutual fund portfolio. He'd have enough time to tinker with his portfolio, maybe even place an order or two if he found something he liked, before the conference call.

When the call came an hour later, Michael had, in fact, placed a "buy" order for a new company that had reportedly figured out a way to make a small receiver that would be used by the fledgling Personal Communications Services companies that had so recently won licenses from the Federal Communications Commission. Michael definitely wanted in on the ground floor of a company like that. Like him, it was clearly going places.

During the call, the Peramco officials asked Michael if he could move up the timetable on the INF project, perhaps by the close of business the next day. Michael sweated that request a little, but he promised to do his best.

They politely, but firmly, asked him to do more than his best. Michael agreed to deliver. He knew he'd have to call in a few chits with a couple of acquaintances, but he could get it done. He knew the route to take, and he would deliver.

He placed the first of what would be a half dozen calls to the Pentagon the moment he got off the phone with Peramco. By the end of the day, he had his files. All he needed to do was pick them up the next morning.

Chapter Ten

1:00 P.M., TUESDAY, JUNE 16

On the way to the embassy, Daniel grilled the attaché who'd picked them up at the Algiers airport. He seemed to be clueless about what was going on.

"Can we get a helicopter?" Daniel asked him.

The attaché shook his head. "The only helicopters here are military, and they aren't used by anyone outside the major general's staff."

"Well, a fast truck then? Can we get a truck, at least?"

The attaché gave Daniel a strange look. "Well, I suppose. But we have a state dinner this evening with the prime minister and his family."

"Tonight?" Daniel asked, trying not to let his anger show. "But we have things to do, places to go . . ."

The attaché seemed quite troubled by this answer. "But you cannot. You *must* go to the dinner. If you do not, you will be denied permission to go anywhere for the remainder of your stay here."

82

"What do you mean, denied permission?" Daniel asked.

"Remember, Mr. Trabue, the military *is* the government here. The military's word is the law. Everyone knows that."

"So we have to do as the leaders say?"

"Within reason. There are some liberties we can take as American citizens. But we must be careful, especially now. We will be watched everywhere we go."

The attaché glanced out the rear window. Daniel and Loren did, too. Sure enough, a black sedan trailed behind them. There was no American flag flying from the front of the hood.

"Will we get permission to travel outside Algiers?" Loren asked quietly.

"Perhaps," the attaché mumbled. "We will work on it."

"Work hard, all right," Daniel said, gritting his teeth. "Work very hard at it."

Several hours later, after a hot shower, Loren felt absolutely ridiculous, wearing the same clothes she'd worn on the flight over. Who in her right mind would go to a formal state dinner—her first ever—in anything other than an evening gown? But it wasn't like she had a choice.

"You're fine," Daniel whispered in her ear as they slid from their seats in the back of the American embassy's dark blue Town Car. "You look marvelous."

Loren didn't *feel* marvelous. It all reminded her of the way she'd felt back in the fifth grade when she'd grown a foot taller in about three months and towered over every boy in her class. She felt exposed then, just as she did now.

The dinner was held at the president's mansion in a quite large formal dining room that easily accommodated nearly five hundred people.

Loren glanced around the room as they entered, barely noticing when Daniel took her arm and ushered her over to their table.

The embassy attaché had said that the dinner this evening had been planned for some time, and that their arrival merely coincided with it. Poor timing and bad luck, Daniel had said ruefully.

Loren was surprised to see so many military officers and their wives. There were dozens of officers, all in the military dress of Algeria, milling around in different directions. They were all waiting for something.

An instant later, Loren saw what they were waiting for. Every officer in the room snapped to attention as an officer, flanked on either side by yet more officers, strode purposefully into the room.

"That must be the prime minister," Loren said to their embassy chaperon, an assistant ambassador who'd been in the country only a few months.

"No, it's the defense minister, Major General Ahmed Khali," the assistant ambassador answered.

Loren blinked. "The defense minister? But everyone in the room . . ."

"He runs the country, Ms. Anders," the assistant ambassador said quickly. "Everyone here knows that. The prime minister is run by the military. And Major General Khali runs the military."

Loren looked back at the defense minister as he continued to walk around the room. He shook hands with every single officer he came across. Every single one. He did not miss a hand.

Occasionally, he stopped to chat with other guests. But never at the expense of a chance to speak to one of the many officers in attendance.

Khali was a striking figure. His black hair was short and combed straight back. There didn't seem to be an ounce of fat on him. He walked like a man used to plenty of exercise. People in his wake continued to stare at him long after he'd passed by.

He seemed to be working his way around the room deliberately. Loren wasn't certain, but she believed that he glanced over at them on at least two occasions.

He's keeping track of us, Loren thought, trying not to panic at the thought. *But that is to be expected. Certainly, it is to be expected.*

At one point in his tour, Khali stopped and spoke with a great deal of animation and emotion to a dark-haired, dark-complexioned man in a blue-and-white uniform distinctly different from that of the Algerians. Khali and the man spoke for nearly ten minutes, with both sides gesturing emphatically and nodding vigorously.

"Who's that?" Loren asked the assistant ambassador.

"His name is Joseph Marx," the embassy official said. "He's a Unity captain, runs the Unity forces here."

"Unity forces? Like the military?" asked Loren.

"No, not exactly. They act like it sometimes, but Unity's been in here the last few years with all sorts of reconciliation and development work. They've even brought in engineers and scientists to help the Algerian government overhaul the petroleum industry, bring it into the twenty-first century."

Loren had no idea that groups such as Unity did that sort of thing. She knew they and others—symbiotically linked to the United Nations and its offshoots—were involved in development. But working hand in hand with government? The world had changed since the last time Loren had looked this closely.

A few minutes later, the prime minister arrived with plenty of pomp and fanfare. He and his wife quickly formed a receiving line, and many of the guests lined up to greet him.

But the attention never wavered from Khali. If there had been any doubt about who ran this country, there was none in Loren's mind now.

"He's impressive, isn't he?" Daniel said to Loren when Khali was still one hundred feet or so from them.

"Yes, he is," Loren answered. "He commands everyone's respect."

"You know, he's been in power since before the assassination," Daniel said. "I always wondered how he's made it through the different times of trouble. Now I know. He has the backing of every officer in this room."

The former president of Algeria, Mohammed Boudiaf, had been assassinated several years earlier. Just moments after Boudiaf had called out, "We are all going to die," an assassin in uniform had killed the seventy-three-year-old president with a submachine gun.

Boudiaf had not been speaking of his own demise, but news of the timing and the brutality of the slaying had reverberated around the world. The pictures had played over and over on every national television network around the world. More than forty others were wounded by subsequent gunfire and grenades.

Boudiaf was gunned down during his first trip outside Algiers—in the Mediterranean port city of Annaba—following a military coup that had thrown out the national election triumph of the Islamic Salvation Front.

The Algerian media immediately reported that the killer was a member of the security service, who had acted out of religious conviction. The Algerian government was largely silent on the subject.

Naturally, the world immediately laid the blame for the assassination at the feet of the ousted Islamic Salvation Front, whose election had been overthrown by Boudiaf and the military.

The Islamic Salvation Front was banned, and ten thousand suspected members of the organization were subsequently arrested. Shortly after the arrests, militant Muslims killed as many as one hundred soldiers and police officers.

But despite the obvious conclusion that the Islamic Salvation Front was behind the assassination, there had been persistent rumors that perhaps factions of the army—Khali's army—were responsible.

There had been rumors for months that Boudiaf planned to investigate and punish high-level corruption in the military. Perhaps the army was nervous about such an investigation, and had Boudiaf murdered, the rumors said.

And behind it all, both before and after the assassination, stood Khali. He ran the country before Boudiaf's death, and he clearly ran it now, regardless of who the prime minister or president happened to be.

As he neared Daniel and Loren, the defense minister turned and looked in their direction. Loren's eyes locked with his. Khali gazed intently in her direction and, with his eyes still firmly locked on hers, shook a greeter's hand.

Loren suddenly felt trapped in time—trapped inside a country she knew very little about, facing a potential enemy who scared her quite badly, confronting a frightening possibility that she felt powerless to do anything about.

The reactor in the Algerian desert had certainly been built with Khali's blessing and encouragement. And if there was a nuclear missile deployed in the mountains, it, too, was done, if not by Khali's hand, then certainly by his direction. And should there ever be a decision to push the button and launch such a missile, toward Israel or perhaps somewhere else, then it would be by Khali's hand or direction as well.

Loren did not want to meet this man. She did not want to talk to him. Not now, not ever. She wanted out. She wanted to be as far away from this place as she could manage. But it was too late, much too late for that.

"Ms. Anders, how nice that you have joined us this evening," the defense minister said an instant later. Khali gave Daniel a passing glance. All of his attention—for the moment—was directed toward Loren.

And the attention was intense. Khali's eyes fairly glistened with the sharpness of his gaze. His eyes never once wavered from Loren's, not even to admire her considerable beauty, as many men did upon meeting her.

Khali's English was flawless, and he had virtually no

accent. Or, rather, his accent was distinctly neutral, as if he'd grown up in Ohio or perhaps Kansas.

"Sir . . . Mr. Defense Minister, thank you for inviting us," Loren said, trying not to stammer.

"The pleasure is all ours," Khali said with a smile. "We are honored that you have chosen to visit our country." He turned to Daniel then and extended a hand. Daniel gripped it firmly, and the two shook hands vigorously. "And you are Mr. Trabue, correct?"

Daniel nodded. "Daniel Trabue, yes. I am here representing Senator Jackson, the chairman of the Senate Intelligence Committee." Daniel knew that would mean very little to Khali, but he felt somehow that it was important to state it nevertheless.

Khali shrugged. "Oh, yes, I recall now from my days at Harvard. Your parliament, your . . . ?"

"Congress," Daniel answered for him.

"Your Congress has many leaders in it, all of them in charge of this or that in the government. Your Senator Jackson is in charge of intelligence? Is that not correct?"

"Yes, it is somewhat correct," Daniel said, trying not to laugh. Actually, Khali had it about right. Every member of the Senate wanted to be president, and virtually every member of the House wanted to run for the Senate. And they all thought they were in charge of something.

"And your president, Franklin Shreve, he sends his warmest regards as well, I am sure?" This was less a question and more a statement. Loren glanced at Daniel, who offered no encouragement either way.

"Yes, he does," she offered quickly. "I am here representing the president, and he does send his regards."

"Yes, as I suspected," Khali said, nodding. His entourage began to move on, but Khali did not budge from his spot. There was clearly more on his mind.

"Now," he said to Daniel and Loren, taking a step closer so that only they could hear his words, "you two are here in our country. Why? To see the sights? Visit the Mediterranean?"

Daniel and Loren had talked this through because the question was inevitable—if not from Khali, then from someone else.

They had disagreed on the best answer. Loren did not want to lie, but she also did not want to give away the true nature of their visit. Daniel wanted to lie. It was easier that way, he'd argued.

Daniel had eventually won the argument, and he answered Khali's question now. "There are major American corporations considering overseas investments," he answered, "and Algeria would be ideal for such investments."

Khali's eyes bore in on Daniel's. "And American corporations are so powerful they can command the time of envoys for the president of the country and the American Congress? You would come here just on their behalf?"

"American industry is very important to the health of our country, as your own industries are to yours," Daniel said hastily.

"I see," Khali said. "I cannot say that I remember such importance when I was there last, but it has been a few years." Khali looked sharply at Loren. "And is that what you say as well? Is that why you are here?"

"Mr. Defense Minister," Loren said, changing the subject, "might I ask a favor?"

"Yes, you may, of course," Khali responded, "but I cannot assure you it will be granted."

"We would like to tour the countryside. You know, drive around a bit. Would that be permitted?"

"To look for your investment sites?" Khali asked playfully. "Would that be the purpose?"

"Yes, it would," Daniel answered without hesitation.

"I see," Khali mused. "And would you object if I sent two of my officers along to make sure they are helpful to you in finding your way around the countryside? The Algerian terrain can be treacherous, you know."

"I don't think it's necessary to waste their time," Loren offered.

"It is no problem," Khali said firmly. "I insist. Please. My men are here to serve you. They will await your departure at your embassy, first thing tomorrow morning."

Just as Loren thought Khali was about to turn on his heels and continue his tour through the crowd, he took a sudden step forward and closed the remaining distance between him and Loren. He was so close, Loren could smell his expensive cologne.

"Ms. Anders, remember this," Khali whispered intently. "We are not your enemy. I am not your enemy. The world is not always as it seems. There are masks upon masks, and reasons within reasons. Look deeply before you condemn. That is all I ask."

Khali retreated a step, then bowed slightly to both Daniel and Loren, and moved on, grasping hands as he went by. It had been quite a show. Loren could see why some said he ran the country with an iron fist.

"I don't think he believed you," Loren whispered so only Daniel could hear when Khali was well out of earshot.

"Yeah, obviously not, or he wouldn't have put two of his officers on us," Daniel said. "But I couldn't just tell him the truth. That would have gotten us nowhere."

"Perhaps. But you know he won't let us get near the place," Loren said.

"I know. We'll have to think of something," Daniel said. "But with his goons around, what can we do?"

"I don't know," Loren said, grimacing. "But we'll find something. I know we will."

Chapter Eleven

TUESDAY, JUNE 16

The trawler had just two distinguishing marks—its flag, that of the country of Tunisia, and a small anchor-and-circle logo with a name that had probably once read "Medco Shipping."

But the *d* and the *c* were now gone from Medco, and Shipping had lost its first and second *p*. Which left "Meo Shiing"—the proverbial slow boat to China—to someone standing on shore watching the trawler go by.

It made no difference anyway because both the flag and the name were meaningless unless you knew to ask the right questions. The flag was mostly worthless as an identifier, and the faded "Medco Shipping" probably stood for Mediterranean Company Shipping. So there was virtually no way to tell where it had come from or what its cargo might be.

It was not unusual on these seas. Ships sailed in and out of the Mediterranean under different flags day in and day out. The flags, many times, were ones of convenience. Sometimes they reflected their true point of origin or destination. Many times they did not.

This particular trawler was even more nondescript than usual. It was almost as if the owner (whoever that might be) had searched the seas for a rusting hulk to carry cargo that no one would ever think to look at twice.

Very few sailors were up on deck, which meant that it was mostly carrying heavy cargo that required little handling or attention. Most likely, the ship's captain would crew the unloading at the other end, wherever that might be.

The ship moved quite slowly and deliberately down the coastline, attracting no attention. Tourists did not even notice it. It was much too ugly and ungainly. It was certainly not one of the famous cruise liners that often sailed the Mediterranean waters.

In fact, the shipping clerk at the port of Tripoli in Libya would not have bothered to make a notation for inclusion in his report had it not been for the fact that his CIA contact had told him to be on the lookout for such a ship. Specifically, that he should look for anything sailed by Medco Shipping.

His contact had said that they were looking for unmarked cargo—though he wouldn't say what—and that he should note anything unusual. Especially older ships that had much newer, more sophisticated navigating or electronic equipment.

The trawler, as it turned out, fit exactly the description his contact had given him. Barren of virtually all markings, the trawler nevertheless had a fairly impressive array of radio antennas and a modern small satellite dish. The electronic gear was fairly well hidden, but the clerk regularly scanned the decks of passing ships with a pair of high-powered binoculars and he spotted the gear.

The clerk had served once in Turkey, near the Soviet border, and he was almost certain that he'd seen that kind of radio and satellite equipment there. He wasn't positive. But it definitely was worth a notation.

"Tunisian trawler, Medco Shipping, expensive electronic gear aboard, possibly Soviet electronics (from the black market?), no other markings, cargo/destination unknown," the clerk scribbled in his worn notebook.

He took a second look out his finger-smudged window at the slow-moving trawler. He wished he had the ability to pick up radio frequency signals. He might get a crack at what was being beamed in and out of the ship captain's office.

But he was just a lowly clerk, who made a little money on the side each month by filing his speculative briefings and reports with his CIA contact at the local U.S. embassy.

The clerk didn't really care, of course, whether his contact was CIA or not. All he knew was that the man paid cash, in local currency, for his reports. He didn't care where the money came from or where his reports went to.

The clerk closed his observation notebook and returned his gaze to the seas. It was the middle of the month, and he'd file his two-week report with his contact soon. He was glad. He could use the money. It had been a bad year for his family.

The clerk had been doing this kind of work on the

side for nearly two years. He decided that perhaps this month, he'd ask for a raise. Not a big one. But enough to make a difference. He did good work. He deserved the raise.

It was only fair, he smiled to himself. After all, no one else wanted to work for the CIA anymore. The money was lousy, and the risks were too great. You could make more money spying for the big multinational corporations than you could for the American government these days. He knew, because he had friends who did that, too.

But as he sat there and stared at the Tunisian trawler making its unstately way along the coastline, the clerk had an even better idea. His CIA contact had been insistent about looking for just such a ship. And he had found it. That deserved a bonus, a reward. He would ask for it. If he was even the slightest bit lucky, there would be more than enough to pay the extra bills his family had racked up that month. Which would be very, very nice.

He would call his contact when he got off work and arrange to meet him and show him the notebook. He had found something valuable for the CIA. It was only fair that they reward him for it.

Chapter Twelve

8:00 A.M., WEDNESDAY, JUNE 17

Sure enough, the car was waiting for Daniel and Loren outside the embassy the next morning, across the street from the American ambassador's guest quarters. Loren had peeked out the blinds, and two of Khali's officers were waiting patiently in the front seat of the black limousine, the engine apparently running.

Over a quick breakfast of black coffee and a couple of semi-stale Danish rolls, they were briefed by the CIA's station chief, John Verdis, who was listed officially on the embassy's register as the deputy director for policy evaluation.

"We haven't turned up a thing," Verdis told them. "Nothing. Not a shred of evidence of any suspicious imports. No record of any substantial dealing with the Chinese, other than what we already knew about the reactor. The only thing in that mountain is a big hole."

Loren wondered if Verdis wasn't indulging in more

than a little bit of wishful thinking, but she kept her thoughts to herself. There was no use in making the poor man's life any more miserable than it already was.

Verdis told them confidentially that they had turned every single CIA agent and paid operative loose on the project, and they still had not turned up anything.

"Did you check corporate records?" Daniel asked.

Verdis looked at Daniel with contempt. "First thing, of course. No record of any unusual export or import activity. Nothing out of the ordinary."

"Did you check the national petroleum company records?" Daniel asked.

"Yes, of course. Their usual activity. Nothing more, nothing less."

"Would you mind showing me the file on what you found there?"

"The oil company records?"

"Yes, those."

Verdis hesitated. "Those are code word now due to the current request, so . . ."

"Mr. Verdis, I've had code word clearance for years. So has Loren, I imagine." Daniel looked over at Loren. She nodded, but said nothing. "So, in light of the fact that we are here at the direct request of the president of the United States, I don't think you'll want to deny us access to those records. Do you?"

"No," Verdis said with a scowl. He pushed his chair back hard, almost causing it to topple over. He left the room briskly and returned an instant later.

"They're being copied. You'll have them before you leave," Verdis said curtly.

"Thank you," responded Daniel.

"But I'm telling you, you're on a wild goose chase," Verdis said emphatically. "There's nothing here. Nothing. When they've finished building that reactor, that's when we'll have to press."

"Why not now?" Loren asked.

"Because the government won't engage us diplomatically." Verdis shrugged. "We've all tried. The ambassador's tried. We've had letters flown over from the States from other high-ranking officials. They won't see us."

"On what grounds?" asked Loren.

"On no grounds," Verdis said. "We don't have anything on them. We have no leverage at all. The government exports oil—which is where all its money comes from—to the Netherlands, the Czech Republic, Romania, Italy, and France. Just a little to the U.S. And it imports from France, Italy, Germany, other parts of the European Community. Just a little from the U.S."

"So even if we cut off both exports and imports, it wouldn't have a big impact?" Loren said.

"Exactly."

"What about pressuring our European Community partners to support the threat of sanctions if the Algerians don't open up the reactor site to inspections?" Daniel asked.

Verdis laughed. "You're kidding, right? France is going to support us on something like this? No chance. The French would sell their grandmothers to the Islamic fundamentalists if the price was right. And the others, like the Italians and even the Germans, are almost as bad."

Verdis was right, of course. Both Loren and Daniel knew it. They'd seen it a thousand times in many other situations. The United States and the European Community nations were partners in name only. On trade issues especially, both sides could be incredibly vicious and cutthroat. Even when regional security was at stake, the EC nations rarely joined the U.S. in the use of force. They were quick to trade and sell—not fight.

"And has there been any movement toward getting Algeria to sign the nonproliferation treaty?" Loren asked.

"None. The Algerians won't even talk to anyone about it. They're just marching ahead."

"But there *has* to be some leverage somewhere," Loren sighed. "What about China?"

"They don't care, and it wouldn't matter anyway," Verdis answered. "The materials are all here, and the reactor's almost finished. The Algerians could hire out help even if the Chinese walked, at this point."

"And loans?"

Verdis brightened at this. "They've got a couple of whoppers, from IMF and the World Bank. Got 'em both about three years ago. They were done quietly. We didn't hear about them until they were already signed, sealed, and delivered."

"What were they for?" asked Daniel.

"Remember when oil prices plunged? Well, it just about killed their national petroleum company. Algeria promised to take a whole lot of the loan money and privatize, and also look to export other things like natural gas. But a lot of it also went to the oil company to look for more places to dig."

"To dig?" Daniel asked.

"Oh, mostly in the desert. But in other places as well.

Wherever their hired geologists told them there might be oil reserves."

"And have they found any oil?" asked Daniel.

"Doesn't look that way. Their export numbers haven't gone up appreciably. So they must have hit some dry wells."

"So have we talked to IMF and the World Bank?" Loren interjected.

"Sure. But there's not much they can do as long as Algeria makes the payments. If it fails, well, that's a different story. Then there's some leverage."

"But not until?" asked Loren.

"Not until."

Verdis's secretary walked into the breakfast area, carrying two files. She handed both to her boss, who glanced through one of them and then handed it over to Daniel. "All yours," he said. "Keep it safe. Do you have a lock-and-key briefcase with you?"

"Yes, I do, to carry my other classified files with me on this one," Daniel responded. He began to leaf through the file. He'd look at it more closely later. But something jumped out at him almost immediately—the name of a shipping company the oil conglomerate had been using.

"You might want to ask the CIA to run a quick search on this transport company, Medco Shipping," Daniel said, showing the name to Verdis.

"But I'm not CIA," Verdis protested.

"Yeah, not officially," Daniel said, sighing. "But consider it anyway, okay?"

Loren pushed her chair back from the table. "We should be going."

Daniel rose as well. "Thank you for your time and for the files."

"You won't find anything in there," Verdis predicted. "Just run-of-the-mill stuff."

"If you say so." Daniel laughed. "But I always like to be thorough."

Daniel and Loren exited out the front and walked directly to the waiting car. As they drew close to the car, they noticed a quite small Algerian flag on the hood— two vertical bands of green and white with a red five-pointed star inside a red crescent; the colors and shapes were traditional symbols of the state's religion, Islam.

One of the officers stepped quickly from the car and held the rear door open for Loren. He let Daniel fend for himself with the other.

As they slid into the backseat, Loren couldn't help noticing that both officers wore guns. The driver had placed his beside him on the front seat, and the other's was still fastened inside his holster.

Neither Daniel nor Loren could tell if they were high-ranking officers, and neither wanted to ask. The driver started the car and pulled away from the curb. He did not ask them where they wanted to go.

"Uh, excuse me, but do you speak English?" Loren asked tentatively.

"Yes, quite well, thank you," answered the officer on the passenger side of the front seat.

"Oh, good," Loren said. "Well, we'd like to go west of the city, somewhere near . . ."

"You will see Algiers," the officer interrupted. "Visitors love Algiers. You will want to see Algiers."

"But . . . ," Daniel protested.

"You will want to see Algiers," the guard said force-fully. "It would be quite rude to the prime minister if representatives of your great country came to ours and did not see the sights of our most important city."

Daniel and Loren looked at each other. There was nothing to do but sit back and enjoy the ride. They were going to see Algiers, whether they liked it or not.

Chapter Thirteen

WEDNESDAY, JUNE 17

The temperature was beginning to soar. It had to be at least 110 degrees, even in the shade. There was no relief anywhere, except in the one building near the center of the refugee camp.

In all directions, wherever you looked, the horizon shimmered unevenly from the waves of heat that rolled across the barren land. Mirages floated in and out of people's views like uninvited ghosts.

People were still arriving in the camps in droves. Dozens, hundreds, of refugees were crossing the border at all hours. There seemed to be no end to the people making their way to the camp.

The Christian Medical relief worker took his hat off and wiped the sweat from his brow before it could slide down into his eyes. He sighed once and stared at a family of nine just entering the outskirts of the camp. Their sole valuable possession, an ox, pulled all of their belongings in a run-down wagon that barely bumped along the dirt path.

Garrett Sutton wondered at how the word went out to these people. For the word had, indeed, gone out. War was coming—awful, terrible, bone-crushing war—and these people knew it. They were fleeing the country as fast as they could to escape the carnage.

The war was as old as the history of the nation itself. Once, there had been two tribes in the nation of Rwanda. But one tribe had grown faster than the other and had taken over much of the government apparatus.

The other tribe had done its best to coexist peacefully with the majority tribe. But a day had come when the tribe had begun to set neighbor upon neighbor, and hundreds of thousands of innocent women and children had died in a sudden, violent surge of civil war.

The smaller tribe had fled to the mountains and the refugee camps. And it had waited for its day to come. Its people gathered themselves, formed secret war councils, and stockpiled weapons.

Then, one day, the message had come from its leaders down through the ranks. The day had arrived. They were well armed—though no one could ever seem to quite figure out where the arms came from—and they had laid their plans carefully with the help of a few mercenaries who were experts in this sort of warfare.

And they had struck, first in Kigali and then the rest of the land. They quickly captured the communications and government centers. They rounded up all the leaders they could find and publicly executed them in the central squares of the tribal villages.

Some leaders were murdered viciously while their

wives and children watched in horror. Atrocity piled atop atrocity. Then the emerging victor broadcasted that all members of the tribe that had been in power before would be killed if they did not leave the country immediately. The exodus had begun that day and had never really stopped.

But there had been an uneasy peace for several months nevertheless. At some point, the refugees into the camps surrounding Rwanda in Zaire and Tanzania had begun to slow to a trickle.

Until the day before this one. That was when the word had mysteriously gone out again that there would be a new round of killings and murder.

The reason, Garrett presumed, was that the United Nations humanitarian relief forces had begun to have some success in convincing refugees to leave the camps and return home. Planting season was only a few weeks away, and if they didn't return now, they never would.

The UN had a fairly substantial presence in Rwanda and the surrounding countries, and it worked hand in hand with the new global power in relief and humanitarian affairs, Unity. The combined economic and diplomatic might of the UN and Unity had been enough to convince the government of Rwanda to accept the refugees back in and begin reconciliation efforts.

But the military authorities in Rwanda were not the government, and they had clearly made a unilateral decision to block the efforts of the UN and Unity to bring the people back to their homes.

Garrett hardly blamed the military of Rwanda. Or to be more precise, he understood their actions. He still blamed them. They were wrong, morally wrong. God

would surely hold each and every one of them accountable for their actions.

But Garrett did understand what they were doing.
They were still the minority tribe, even if they did hold
power. If the tribe that had formerly ruled over them
returned, eventually they would grow in power again
and make an effort to form a civil rebellion movement.

The most effective way to counter such a movement
was to keep the people out of the country of Rwanda, in
the refugee camps across the border. They could not
organize in such camps, at least not into military units.
The "blue helmets" of the UN did not allow that, and
the Unity workers served almost as spies for the UN to
enforce that directive.

So the Rwanda government was planning a second
wave of terror across the countryside to make sure the
refugees either stayed in the camps or returned to them.
And there didn't seem to be much anyone could do
about it.

A Unity jeep roared by at that moment. The worker
driving the jeep glanced over but did not wave. Garrett
glanced at the insignia emblazoned on the side of the
jeep—three circles touching each other to form a triangle, with a large circle surrounding all three.

It was a curious symbol for the Unity movement—
very symmetrical, very distinct, hard to miss. The three
smaller circles seemed to spiral into each other, almost
as if someone had begun to draw a design and had never
stopped. The larger circle surrounding the three gave it a
sense of purpose, a kind of cohesion, which is what the
artist had obviously intended.

It was similar in some respects to the five interlocking circles of the Olympics. But the Unity symbol was cleaner, simpler, more elegant, Garrett thought. He had no idea what it meant, of course, but it was impressive looking.

Garrett often wondered about the Unity movement. His organization, Christian Medical, was a well-established relief charity that relied heavily on donations and support from traditional Christian denominations in the United States. It provided donated medicine to poor people and refugees in more than one hundred nations.

Unity had come from nowhere, it seemed. In just a few short months, at the height of a crisis of colossal proportions in the sub-Sahara of Africa, this organization had suddenly begun to flood the run-down airports with C-5s and C-130s, brimming with badly needed supplies, food, and medicine for people dying from malnutrition, starvation, and ill health.

What had been so incredibly unusual about the Unity movement was that the multimillion-dollar donations had been cobbled together virtually overnight, the board of directors had been assembled in a matter of weeks, the headquarters had been *purchased* in Geneva—not rented—and the staff had been hired from virtually every relief organization almost overnight.

Unity had plucked the best and the brightest from World Vision, CARE, Ameri-Cares, the International Red Cross, the Baptist World Alliance, and every other international relief group that had been helping people for decades.

Unity was well represented among all the major religions as well, not just the Christian community. Most worldwide relief groups were Christian, Garrett knew.

But Unity was more than that. The central, organizing principles of Unity were religious in nature, but not necessarily Christian. They were based on a somewhat unusual premise, that knowledge of God could be learned through scientific experience and discovered through rational exploration. There was no mention of faith in the organizing principles.

Unity's leaders explained that the world had been torn asunder by religious wars over the centuries, and they were trying a different approach. They explained that they looked for common threads running through all religions—sort of the best that everyone had to offer.

They developed a set of laws common to all religions that everyone could agree to—sort of an expanded version of the Ten Commandments. They never said anyone had to live under these laws, only that they were common unifying principles to strive for.

No one seemed to know where the money had come from. There were no obvious billionaires on the board— the board members seemed to have been picked more because they represented a faith or an ideological movement than anything else.

Within months of Unity's formation, Unity planes were in the air to every disaster around the globe. Unity was nearly always first on the scene, first to set up a refugee camp, first to dig the latrines, first to sanitize the water system, first to build reconciliation panels, first to help direct the UN multinational troops to the sources of conflict.

Garrett knew how difficult it was to buy the kind of transport planes, earth-moving equipment, and fleets of overland vehicles that Unity seemed to have more than enough of. Every relief organization struggled with the logistics and transportation of goods. Except Unity. Its workers always seemed to have more than what they needed and triple what anyone else had.

Where the International Red Cross, for instance, had scraped together its last bits of money to buy old, dilapidated Russian transport planes, Unity had found money to buy almost-new transport planes from Boeing and Lockheed, as well as newer-model Russian and Chinese transport planes.

It was almost as if some very rich council of wise men and women had said, "All right, what can we do with all our money to help feed, house, clothe, and treat poor people and sick people around the planet? Let's create an organization, give it more money than anyone's ever seen, and then let it do its good work."

Yet Garrett and everyone else could only guess at how Unity had been formed and for what purpose. Garrett knew that the Bible said you could tell the hearts and minds of people from their words and deeds—their "fruits."

Well, Unity's "fruits" certainly seemed of the highest, noblest sort. Its workers were always there, doing everything they could to help poor people.

And yet. Garrett had been in the field a long, long time. He had seen many organizations come and go, with purposes noble and grand. He stayed with his own organization, Christian Medical, because his born-again faith in Christ was shared by many others in the small, but determined, band of medical missionaries.

But he had never seen anything quite like this Unity movement. They were organized and disciplined, unlike most relief charities that operated on a prayer and a shoestring budget. Their source of funds was secret, unlike the sources for organizations such as the Red Cross that opened their books for the world to see.

Unity's board met in secret in Geneva and other parts of the world, and their directives were almost as closely guarded as the pope's decrees. Unity's "troops" carried out their marching orders without question, which was also not similar to the chaos that often surrounded other relief organizations.

And Garrett had seen at least a couple of instances—especially lately—where Unity had intervened in a highly unusual manner to block something that had seemed to be for the common good.

The most recent example was a U.S. company that had teamed up with his organization, World Vision, and the Baptist World Alliance to build a factory and distribution center in central Africa. The purpose of the facility was to make and distribute oral rehydration salt packets to other organizations operating water supply systems in drought-stricken parts of Africa like the Horn and the sub-Sahara.

It was a simple, but wonderful, idea, Garrett thought. He'd been helpful and somewhat instrumental in getting some of the logistics for the operation worked out. Dehydration was the biggest killer in Africa—far beyond anyone's imagination really—and the only way to treat it was to get these salts into the right hands. Yet no one had ever made the effort until this company had come along with the right technology and know-how to both make and distribute the oral rehydration packets cheaply.

Then Unity had entered the picture unexpectedly, just months before the operation was to begin. Unity's representatives began to meet with various governments and the UN, and urged them to block the group's efforts to distribute the packets widely. The argument was that handing out the packets might save lives in the short run, but it would discourage efforts to solve the overall problem of water supply development in each of the African nations.

The argument enraged Garrett. He couldn't imagine arguing that people should die violently of dehydration so that governments and industries would be spurred to develop water supply systems that did not exist. It was inhumane beyond belief, Garrett felt.

But Unity had won the day, and the governments had buckled under its diplomatic efforts. The oral rehydration facility had crumbled under the weight and was now a vacant warehouse for rats and other creatures that wandered in from the blazing sun.

Garrett could not understand Unity's motives. They made no sense. He understood that development needed to occur in these African nations. But saving people's lives—now—was what truly mattered, and he did not understand how doing that would hinder bigger development efforts.

The Unity jeep skidded to a halt in front of the only erected building in the camp, the UN Humanitarian Relief Headquarters. The worker jumped out and raced into the building, clearly on a mission of some sort.

Garrett wondered vaguely what that mission might be, but then decided that it was really none of his business. He had his own work that day, which would consume every last ounce of his effort. He had to get a new shipment of a popular antibiotic unloaded and distributed to the medical teams throughout the camp.

With the influx of new refugees, the teams would desperately need the antibiotic. And Garrett's organization was the only one with the product to supply, so it fell to him to make sure it got around.

Still, he would try to remember at some point during the day to ask one of the UN team members he was friendly with what was going on. Because clearly something was happening, perhaps beyond their own little corner of the world.

It would be nice if he at least knew what kind of catastrophe was headed in his direction. Not that he could actually *do* anything about it. But it would be nice to know.

Chapter Fourteen

6:00 P.M., WEDNESDAY, JUNE 17

Daniel and Loren were bone weary by the time they returned from their fun-filled day of sightseeing through Algiers. The officers had clearly been given a prearranged agenda because they drove from sight to sight without any discussion.

And when they stopped at each place, one officer would get out, open the door for Loren, and point them in the direction of whatever sight they happened to be visiting. The officers waited patiently until they returned.

Had they been tourists, the day would have been interesting, perhaps even exciting.

They visited the National Library, which Daniel discovered was founded nearly 150 years ago. It reportedly had a million books. Neither of them particularly felt like examining whether that claim was true.

They found another seven hundred thousand books sometime later at the University of Algiers library, which also had quite a collection of art and other works on African subjects.

In the afternoon, they visited the Prehistory and Ethnographic Museum as well as the National Museum of Antiquities, both founded near the turn of the century. And they finished the day at the Museum of Fine Arts.

At one point during the day, as they were resting in the middle of a walking tour of the museum of antiquities, Loren had leaned over and rested her head on Daniel's shoulder. It had been a natural thing. Loren was exhausted from the long trip over anyway, and they'd walked a lot.

Daniel had reached an arm around to hold her up. Loren didn't remove his arm, although Daniel kept expecting her to at any moment. But they stayed that way for quite a while, until Loren mumbled that they needed to keep moving.

Daniel had not dated much in college, and he had dated even less as an adult in the working world. Friends had sometimes tried to set him up on blind dates, but they'd all turned out badly and Daniel was rapidly growing weary of even thinking about asking women out on dates. It was all too painful.

But he couldn't help himself. When he looked at Loren—or especially when she looked at him in a certain way—it was all Daniel could do to think straight. Just the way Loren tilted her head sometimes made Daniel go a little crazy inside.

He'd never felt this way before. He'd never been so unable to control his emotions. It worried him and made him wonder just what in the world was going on.

In one of the museums, they stumbled across a whole

section of religious art. Loren had been quite fascinated by it. Daniel had looked at it politely, but he had managed to steer clear of any conversation about it.

Later in the day, though, he'd gotten up the courage to ask her about it. Casually, of course. You just didn't blurt out questions like that. But he was genuinely curious. And Loren had answered his indirect question quite directly.

"Am I a Christian? Yes, I have given my life to Jesus Christ. I call Him Lord," she said simply, not wavering in her intensity about this as in all other things in her life.

Daniel was more than a little surprised. "So you go to church and everything?" he asked her.

Loren smiled and answered, "Yes, I go to church and everything. I have for years, since I gave my life to Christ. It is an honor, not a duty."

Daniel let it drop at that. He wasn't sure he wanted to force the issue any further. But he *was* curious about this part of Loren's life—like he was curious about almost everything else she was involved with.

He didn't say that to her, though. He didn't dare. And perhaps he never would. Most likely, they would return from this trip, go their separate ways, and that would be that. Daniel would never get up the courage to call her, to actually ask her out on a date. He just couldn't. He didn't know how.

When the officers let Daniel and Loren off outside the embassy in the evening, they asked them whether they would need a car in the morning. Daniel asked them whether they would be able to go elsewhere, outside Algiers.

"There is much to see in Algiers," one of the officers answered.

"So does that mean we cannot go outside the city?" Daniel pressed.

"There is much to see in Algiers," the officer said simply.

"Much that we did not see today?"

"Much, much more," the officer said, smiling. "They say that you cannot properly see Algiers unless you have spent ten days, perhaps two weeks, in the city itself."

There was a stony silence. They had reached an impasse. "I will need to discuss it with my superiors," Daniel said finally. "We'll let you know."

The officer gazed intently at Daniel, his hand resting comfortably on the gun that rode high in his holster. "If you choose to go out, call. We will provide a car for you. We would not think of letting a guest of our government go without an escort. That would be rude."

"And if we secure our own driver?"

"We will provide you with one," the officer said firmly.

Daniel sighed. There was no getting around this. They were really left with no choice but to draft one of the embassy staff members to chauffeur them—and risk the wrath of the Algerian government. Most likely, they would be stopped somehow, but they would probably have to risk it.

"Fine. We'll call," Daniel said, and turned to enter the embassy. Loren joined him.

A moment later, the car roared away. Loren watched it from the stoop of the embassy and then went inside. Daniel came inside a moment later. He demanded to see Verdis, who arrived in the front foyer of the embassy almost immediately.

"How was your day?" he asked brightly.

"We saw the sights," Daniel said angrily. "They never let us get beyond the city. Nor will they."

"As expected." Verdis nodded. "They won't let you out of their sight."

"So we want a car, an embassy car," Daniel demanded. "To drive us to the mountain regions. We'll stay overnight nearby if we have to."

Verdis grimaced. "That would be . . . how should I say it? Impolitic. Not quite proper?"

"Look, I don't care!" Daniel exploded. "Didn't I tell one of your staff that I wanted you to secure permission to travel outside Algiers? Didn't I?"

"Well, yes, that was reported to me."

"And did you make the effort? Did you?" Daniel's voice rose a bit with each word.

"Yes, of course, the ambassador's staff made an inquiry."

"And the answer was?"

"The answer was that you should be quite pleased that the major general has provided you with a limousine and a driver," Verdis said dryly.

That was too much for Daniel. "And you *accepted* that answer?" he exploded again.

"Mr. Trabue," Verdis said, trying to remain calm, "please remember our conversation this morning. We do not have a great deal of leverage here. We do what we can. But there are limits."

"Well, I can tell you one thing," Daniel said, crossing his arms viciously. "We are *not*—I repeat—*not* going to spend our time running around in circles. No chance. We're not doing it. Got it? So I want a car, and I plan to go where I want to go. If they kick us out, fine. I have no plans to come back for a second visit anyway."

Verdis held up a hand. "But I'm also afraid that our embassy cars aren't exactly equipped for the kind of terrain you might encounter where you'd like to go."

"Well, then find us a car that is," Daniel said, his anger subsiding only a little. "There has to be something around. I know you can scrounge something up."

Verdis thought for a moment. "There is an old Humvee, I think, out in the garage. Came here years ago after some strange mission."

"A Humvee?" Loren asked.

"You know, like a jeep," Verdis explained. "Only a lot bigger. And it's quite open. The whole world can see who's driving it."

"We'll take it," Daniel said quickly. "And a driver?"

Verdis pursed his lips. Loren felt fairly certain he was running through the list of people at the embassy who were expendable—people who could be expelled without any discernible loss of intelligence-gathering expertise or who might create a stir when they left.

"We've got a new staff clerk, apparently knows how to drive the thing," he said finally.

"Fine. We'll go first thing in the morning," Daniel said. He turned on his heels and left Verdis standing there.

"Kind of has a temper," Loren said, apologizing for her traveling companion. "Especially when he's under stress."

"Well, aren't we all, Ms. Anders?" Verdis said. "But we can all remain civil, can't we?"

"Yes, of course," Loren said. "I wish the government here felt the same way."

Chapter Fifteen

2:00 P.M., WEDNESDAY, JUNE 17

Amy Estrada began her search as high as she dared—the assistant director for protective operations, Herbert Black, who was Amy's boss three levels up and who reported to the Secret Service director.

Black listened patiently to Amy's story, but told her he didn't have the resources to go chasing after a wild goose. She could do some work on her own if she liked, and he would pass the information on to both the FBI and the White House.

Amy argued a little, but gave up when she saw that she was getting nowhere. The Secret Service was a monolith that didn't crack easily. Had the news of the Algerian terrorists come to the Service through other channels—like *from* the White House or the FBI—then the place might have been turned upside down. As it was, Amy knew that she'd have to run this down—if there was something to it—with her own resources.

She turned first to a friend in another part of the Service, the Office of Protective Research, on the eighth floor of their building at the corner of Eighteenth and G Streets. That office handled mundane things like information management, technical security, and the law enforcement institute, but it also had an intelligence division. Her friend, M. J. Bristol, was the deputy special-agent-in-charge in that division, and she offered to help immediately.

First, they used the computer to track entries and visas during the year. All kinds of Algerians turned up, many of them promising leads. A number had entered East Coast ports in the past couple of days alone.

Next, they cross-matched situation reports with other government agencies like the FBI, just to make sure they weren't missing something. They weren't. There was no mention anywhere, in any bureau, of Algerian terrorists.

From there, they ran a quick profile of all terrorist activities in the past several years, cross-keying words like *Algeria* and *Islamic Salvation Front* with the searches.

They found nothing. Or, rather, they found several matches with the Islamic Salvation Front, but none linked to Algeria. Other countries, yes, but not Algeria.

They did find one very obscure reference to a group in Sudan with a tangential tie to the Islamic Salvation Front. It was a medical supply and educational group, with its primary funding from some other international group called Unity.

The group, Biomed, was promoting an AIDS awareness program throughout most of northern Africa, thanks to funding from Unity, and a delegation arrived in the U.S. in just the past week for some training at the American Red Cross. Its link to the Islamic Salvation Front was that the group had asked Biomed to intervene once in a medical emergency.

Amy had never heard of either the Sudanese group or the group that funded it. She'd have to check both, though she was sure it was a dead end.

"So what now, kid?" M. J. asked her when they'd run down the last of the computer searches.

"Can you come up with more on the recent Algerian visas?" Amy asked her.

M. J. nodded. "Sure. Got a friend at State, who can run the visas through if I invoke protective operations."

"I'll get you the signature," Amy said.

"So what will you do next?"

What she really wanted to do was run down the Algerians in the country, but that was better left in M. J.'s hands for the time being. She could narrow the search a lot quicker from a desk than Amy could with her feet.

"I'll close the file on the Sudan thing," she said. "That shouldn't be too hard. Then I'll be back for your Algerians."

Chapter Sixteen

9:30 A.M., THURSDAY, JUNE 18

Their driver, it turned out, was still wet behind the ears. He was easily no older than twenty-three, maybe twenty-four.

"John Robison," the young man said, extending his hand to Loren and Daniel as they emerged from the embassy.

Loren shook his hand. "You work here at the embassy?" she asked him, a little incredulous.

"My dad's a bigwig at State. He got me this job for the summer."

Loren groaned. "So you're still in college?"

John puffed his chest out. "Yale. I graduate next year."

Daniel whistled. "Well, Yalie, you got your hands full today. Anybody tell you what we have planned?"

John shook his head. "No, Mr. Verdis just told me to drive you wherever you say."

"Do you know your way around the country?" Daniel asked.

John nodded conspiratorially. "Everyone tells you to be careful around here, with the government and all. You're not supposed to go to certain places. But I've been *out* if you know what I mean."

"No, we don't," Loren said. "Tell us."

"Well, you see," John said, his voice almost a whisper, "on the weekends, when the embassy staff doesn't know it, I hitchhike all over the country. I just take off. I've seen the whole country like that."

"You hitchhike?" Loren laughed.

"Yeah. It's a great way to see places."

"So have you been to see the mountains, my young hitchhiker?" Daniel asked him.

John nodded. "I have. Parts of 'em. But the central parts are all shut off. You can't get in or out without a uniform and a pass."

Daniel took a deep breath. "Well, John, that is precisely where we want to go."

"But you can't," the young man protested. "Like I said, not without a pass. I know for a fact that they wouldn't let a foreigner near the place."

"John, we don't have time or a choice in the matter. We must get as close to the place as we possibly can," Daniel said.

A look of fear flitted across the young man's face, replaced by a look of fierce determination. "It must be important then."

Daniel nodded. "It is."

"Then I'm your man," John said eagerly. "If we can get there, I'll find a way."

The three of them walked around the embassy to the

back. John had already moved the Humvee from the garage, and they climbed aboard.

Verdis had been right. The Humvee was a strange vehicle. It felt more like a tank—and rode that way—than a car. Its tires bit into the road, and the shocks didn't absorb much. The wind whipped the interior of the car through mysterious openings.

But it sure felt solid, like it could withstand a bazooka blast. *Which maybe it was designed for*, Daniel thought ruefully. *I hope it won't be tested in such a fashion today.*

As it turned out, John really did know where he was going. He left the city of Algiers like a seasoned pro, making turns without consulting a map, and found the outskirts of the city with little trouble.

Two hours later, John found the sole highway leading into the mountains. On that road, they drove for another hour or so, and never once met an oncoming car. That, in itself, seemed strange to Daniel. But what seemed even stranger was that no one was following them. He expected at least some kind of surveillance.

As they crested the second ridge of the mountain ranges, John began to slow down, though. "We're getting close to one of the guard boxes," he explained.

Daniel looked around the landscape. "I don't see any fences guarding a perimeter."

"I've never seen fences," John said. "Only guards along the road. Though I've never been inside further. They might have fences at some point."

Daniel glanced at Loren, who hadn't said much. "This goes off road, doesn't it?" he asked. He could feel, not see, Loren move uncomfortably in the seat beside him.

"Yeah, I guess. You want to try that, get around the first set of guards?"

"You think they'll shoot?" Daniel asked.

John thought about it for a second. "I can't say as I remember if they have guns or not. I think not."

"Daniel," Loren said quietly, "we shouldn't do this."

Daniel turned to her. "Do you want to see it or not? We can't really go back without something, can we?"

"But we can't do this, either," she said, her voice trembling. "It isn't right. We're breaking laws."

"Look, I know you're scared," Daniel said soothingly. "But it'll be all right. We're just going to try and get a little closer, that's all."

"We shouldn't, Daniel. Really. It isn't right," Loren insisted. There was greater resolve in her voice now.

Daniel looked at Loren, then at John, then back at Loren. He thought about all the people back in the States who were waiting for their report. If they didn't do this, if they didn't come up with *something*, then they'd have failed.

"We're going. Drive," he said, tapping John on the shoulder. He turned to Loren. "Do you want out? Or do you want us to take you back first before we try this?"

Loren shook her head and wrapped her arms around herself. "No. But I wish you wouldn't do this."

"We have to," Daniel said, looking away from Loren's pleading eyes.

John revved the engine once, shifted the vehicle into four-wheel drive, and veered off the road to the right quickly. The vehicle almost felt better whizzing across the grass than it had on the dry pavement.

"See how easy this is?" Daniel said, almost gleefully. "This thing was made for off-road driving."

Loren didn't answer. But she did reach out and take Daniel's hand. Her hands were like ice cubes. Daniel held the hand tightly, trying to reassure her.

John was pretty good at the off-road stuff. He had a sense for where the bumps might be and avoided them like a pro. He drove up and over two hills, and then began to veer back to the left. "I think we've made it past the first guard gate, at least," he said.

Sure enough, they met the road again a short while later, and there was no guardhouse—and no perimeter fence blocking them—in sight. Everyone breathed a sigh of relief. They pulled back onto the road and sped along again toward the heart of the mountains.

They could see for miles in either direction. They kept their eyes peeled for oncoming vehicles, but never saw any. And as they got toward the top of ridges, they always slowed to make sure there wasn't a guardhouse on the other side.

They spotted another guardhouse about five miles after the first one. John adroitly pulled the same trick as before, going well to the right, up and over several smaller hills, and then making his way back to the road safely. They were starting to get the hang of this.

Daniel expected that he would be able to recognize the terrain from the NSA photo. But now that he was actually here, on the ground, everything looked the same. He had no real idea if they were anywhere close.

Only instinct told him they were headed in the right direction.

As they began to near a very high ridge, John slowed the vehicle once again. They began to work their way slowly to the top, as they had before.

There was a faint sound off in the distance, almost like the sound an eggbeater or a blender makes. The sound began to grow louder, and then louder still. Whatever it was, it was coming at them in a hurry.

"Quick!" Daniel shouted. "Go right! Fast!"

John jerked the wheel hard and floored the Humvee. There was a jerk, and the wheels spun a little. The vehicle raced off the road and over the grass.

An instant later, a huge black monstrosity came roaring up and over the ridge. Loren glanced over in a panic, expecting a tank or something to ram them.

But it was a helicopter with huge sweeping propeller blades. The thing was absolutely the largest helicopter any of them had ever seen. It flew straight at them, pulled up hard, and circled around to head them off.

"Go!" Loren shouted. "Go, John!"

But there was nowhere to go. They couldn't outrun the black monster of a helicopter. The thing was on them in a matter of seconds. It was hopeless.

Daniel thought about getting into the foothills and hiding somewhere. But that, too, was pointless. You couldn't really hide a Humvee. They'd have to give it up. There was no choice really.

"Slow it down," Daniel ordered. "We'll have to see who it is and take our lumps."

Loren gripped Daniel's hand even tighter. Daniel returned the squeeze. He wasn't exactly scared. But he wasn't feeling altogether confident, either.

The helicopter set down in front of them as John slowed the Humvee to a stop. One of the side doors opened, and a passenger emerged.

Daniel and Loren stared in total shock at the insignia on the side of the helicopter and at the uniform of the figure striding across the grass toward the vehicle. The insignia was a flag—the flag of the United States of America. And the officer was a United States Marine. He saluted as he neared the vehicle.

"Ms. Anders? Mr. Trabue?" he asked them.

"Yes, yes, that's us," Daniel answered, still stunned.

"If you would come with me, please," he said. "Orders from the White House."

"The White House?" asked Loren.

"Yes, ma'am. From the highest levels."

"The president's orders?"

"From the highest levels," the marine answered. "That's what I know."

"But how did you know where . . . ?" Daniel was still totally confused.

"We were told to keep an eye on you," the marine said grimly. "It seemed prudent to get you now, before you got in any real trouble."

"Real trouble?" Loren asked.

"Let's go. You'll see," the marine said, holding out a hand for Loren. She took it, left the Humvee, and headed for the helicopter.

A moment later, they were airborne.

Chapter Seventeen

8:00 A.M., THURSDAY, JUNE 18

The vice president tossed his coat onto the back of his high-backed chair in his West Wing office and strolled out the door, grabbed a couple of M&M's he always kept in a bowl on his secretary's desk, turned left, right, then left again, and headed down the long corridor that led to the Oval Office.

He nodded at Will Samuels, who was on the phone, and kept walking. No one ever really said much to Lucius Wright when he was in the White House. For that matter, no one even asked where he was going or where he'd been.

They kept him in the loop, of course. They had to. He was second in command. Should something happen to the president, he would have to take over at a moment's notice. He was the proverbial heartbeat away from the presidency.

And yet, Lucius Wright knew he was light-years away

from the real nexus of power. It wasn't that anyone deliberately excluded him from decision-making councils or policy-making sessions. It was just that they didn't think to include him.

It had always been the case with vice presidents. Unless their one and only supervisor, the president, chose to include them, they were, by the very nature of the job, excluded from meetings where everything happened.

Wright had never said anything, never quibbled about his lot in life. People said he was biding his time, building up chits for the day he would run for president.

People said he had ambition, but it was deep-seated, hard to read. People said he kept his own counsel, never let on what he was truly thinking.

It was certainly true that he kept one very firm rule in his dealings with the power brokers who always jockeyed for position inside—and outside—the Oval Office. Lucius Wright always advised the president privately. He never gave advice to his boss in even small, exclusive meetings. Never. It was his one inviolate rule, and every single senior aide at the White House knew it.

No one ever challenged his authority or ability to deliver news privately to the president, either. In fact, some—like Liz Barton at the State Department—often used that back channel to the president to get decisions made or, at least, moving in their direction.

On more than one occasion, senior staff orchestrated some decision, only to see it reversed mysteriously after a visit by Vice President Wright. No one would ever know for sure—and the president obviously remained silent on such matters—but everyone still *knew*.

Wright's footsteps echoed down the hallway. He glanced in the Roosevelt Room on his left before continuing his walk down the hallway that joined his office to the president's.

A number of deputy assistants to the president were engaged in some sort of briefing for industry officials, and they were delighted to see someone of stature look in on the meeting.

Wright graciously entered the room, shook hands all around, sat down for several minutes to listen to the briefing, then excused himself. Wright promptly forgot everything he'd heard in the room. The occupants he left behind would talk about the surprise visit for months to come.

Wright knew the president was in his office because he'd had his secretary check. He also knew the president didn't have another meeting scheduled for at least fifteen minutes. Just enough time to deliver the message he wanted the president to hear.

Franklin Shreve looked up as his vice president entered. He did his best to keep a look of annoyance from passing across his face. He only partially succeeded.

Wright was the only person within the confines of the White House grounds who could walk into the Oval Office like this unannounced. And it always bothered Shreve, more than a little. Even his wife usually scheduled appointments before she showed up at his office.

It wasn't that Shreve *disliked* his vice president. That wasn't it. He actually didn't mind the guy. It just annoyed him that Wright took advantage as others would not and barged in on him.

There was something else that Shreve had never quite

gotten around to thinking about. There was something about his vice president, something he couldn't put his finger on.

Some White House aides dismissed Wright as something of a lightweight, a politician who preferred the golf links or the cocktail hour with banking types to the hard, grinding work of policy making.

But Shreve knew better. He knew—perhaps more so than anyone else on the planet—that Wright was simply waiting for his chance to run someday. He was biding his time.

It was pointless for Wright to throw his weight around or to try to effect too much change in the White House. He wouldn't gain any advantage politically for the day he ran for the Oval Office. If anything, too much involvement in policy scrapes could get him in severe trouble with certain key constituencies.

And Shreve knew that his vice president was far from a lightweight. Quite the contrary. Wright's counsel to him, in private, was the best he received. By far. No one approached his grasp of foreign policy, for instance, and Wright had an uncanny knack for predicting how financial markets would react to certain policy pronouncements.

The president put his pen down—the infamous veto pen, as it turned out at that particular moment. He'd just spent the past fifteen minutes wrestling with a complicated recommendation to veto the latest crime bill sent to him by Congress.

The new Congress, more liberal than recent ones, had voted in a constitutional amendment banning the death penalty in the states as racist and inhumane. In the end, despite some contrary advice from his staff, he'd decided to veto the legislation.

"The veto pen?" Wright asked his boss as he strolled into the room toward the sofa at the other end of the room.

"Yes, as a matter of fact, it is," the president sighed. "This was a tough one."

Wright settled in comfortably at one end of the couch. "The new crime bill?"

The president nodded. "Yes. It seems crazy how far the pendulum has swung in just the past few years. But I had to veto it or risk losing the South during reelection."

"Congress is clueless," Wright said, looking out the window at the Rose Garden, which was magnificent in early summer. "They don't get it. People *like* capital punishment. They like having the death penalty around. It makes them feel safe. Even if they aren't."

The president didn't respond. Wright's analysis was probably correct, but he still hated that he had to buckle to that kind of logic. "So what's on your mind today, Mr. Vice President?"

"Just a small matter of state, Mr. President," he responded with a laugh.

Franklin Shreve eased his way out of the chair behind his desk and walked over to where the vice president sat. "Okay, try it out on me."

"It's about this Algerian situation," Wright said, watching for the president's reaction.

"Yes?"

"I wasn't at the initial briefing, you know, but I've had a chance to catch up, so to speak."

The president smiled. Wright was good at this sort of thing. He was quite capable of palace intrigue, despite his best efforts to mask that ability. "And what's your take on it?"

Wright leaned forward in his seat. He looked the president straight in the eye. "I think you need to be prepared to act forcefully. If Algeria has deployed a nuclear weapon—no matter where it's targeted—I think you have to move to take it out."

"Preemptively?"

"Yes, preemptively," the vice president insisted. "I don't think you have a choice. Algeria is not China or Russia. Or even North Korea, for that matter. The situation is so unstable in that country, almost anything could happen."

The president met Wright's even gaze. There was something to what he was saying. But the United States had never acted in such a manner before. Israel had done so, on several occasions. But Israel was in a vastly different strategic situation from that of the U.S.

"What would our NATO allies think?"

"Our NATO allies?" Wright snorted. "You must be joking. They're spooked by their own shadow these days. They can't even commit to sending a few thousand troops to routine UN peacekeeping missions anymore without a full-throated debate. If it weren't for Unity's prodding them all the time, nothing would ever happen in some of these countries."

The president nodded vaguely. He knew his vice president served on Unity's board of directors. His own White House counsel had ruled, early in the term, that Wright could remain on the board as long as he took no pay for his involvement with the nonprofit charity work.

Wright—and one or two others involved in foreign diplomacy—always sang Unity's praises, and for good reason. In the past two years alone, Unity had defused a handful of very tense situations in troubled nations and then had allowed the U.S. to appear to play an active mediating role.

"But we've always consulted them on decisions of this magnitude," the president said.

"Times change," the vice president said evenly. "And so do allies, I might add. It wasn't so long ago that both Germany and Japan were our mortal enemies."

"So you would strike first, ask questions later?" Shreve asked him. "And worry about consulting allies later?"

"If you try to mobilize world opinion against Algeria before a surgical strike, it won't work. Algeria would have too much time—perhaps to move the missiles out of there. You have to take them by surprise."

The president leaned against the wall. He was, to be sure, still quite uncertain about the proper path to follow with Algeria. Despite the intense pressure he'd placed on certain Cabinet members, he had no confirmation of any substance. The small team that had been sent over had yet to report back. The CIA station chief in Algiers had turned up nothing. The armed forces were primed and ready, but for what?

And to make matters worse, there were some sudden armed flare-ups in other parts of Africa. A number of them, in fact, that might erupt into something even larger before the day was done. And as the word of the fighting spread across the continent, more took advantage of the chaos to start their own little insurrections.

His treasury secretary had also informed him of some important international monetary decisions looming in the near future—decisions that could place a severe strain on the global financial markets. They were events that would ordinarily command his full and undivided attention. Only he didn't have that kind of time right now.

So the president knew he couldn't really afford to devote all his energies to an Algerian solution, not with so much else going on. But what choice did he have?

"And how would you explain it," the president asked, "if we were to take the site out?"

"I'd prepare my speech ahead of time for a prime-time national television address," the vice president answered. "Send in the planes, take the site out, and then go on TV. It's foolproof. The American people will understand the necessity, and they'll applaud you."

Perhaps, the president thought. *If the mission succeeds. If it does not, and there is a botched mission— like the idiotic attempt to rescue the Iranian hostages that had contributed to the ouster of a former occupant of the Oval Office—then it was not such a great idea.*

"Well, that's why they pay me the big bucks, to make these kinds of decisions," the president laughed.

"Yes, Mr. President, you're right," Wright said softly. "But on this one, the choice is easy. Take out the Algerians before it's too late."

Chapter Eighteen

3:00 P.M., THURSDAY, JUNE 18

The black helicopter, which had huge missile pods on either side and laser-guided gun turrets at both the front and the back, covered the ground quickly. It flew just a dozen feet or so above the ground, following the contour of the land.

Loren and Daniel had learned enough from particular briefings to know that the helicopter was one of the new stealth copters developed recently under one of the black programs Daniel distrusted so much.

But, right now, Daniel was grateful for this particular black program that had produced this particular piece of machinery. "It's flying under radar?" he asked the marine sitting beside him.

"Yes, sir," the marine said, shouting slightly over the interior noise. "We were offshore, and when we got our orders to come in and get you, it didn't take us long."

"And you said you spotted something?" Loren asked. "On the way in?"

"Yes, ma'am, we did," the marine said. "We had other orders, that if we came inland, we were to fly near a coordinate on the map. We did. You'll see what we found in just a second."

Loren and Daniel pressed their faces to the window to see. "By the way, why'd you come get us?" Daniel asked, his face still up against the window.

"We got an urgent request from the basement of the White House," the marine replied.

Daniel looked away from the window for a moment. "The Situation Room?"

"Yes, sir. They said to fly in and retrieve you."

Daniel looked out the window again. That was odd. He wondered how they were tracking his movements from there. But, of course, he should have known. They'd approved money for it not more than two years ago.

Yet another black program defense contractor—under the auspices of the now-defunct strategic missile defense office—had developed a satellite tracking system so sensitive it could pick up individual movements on the ground quite clearly and instantaneously. It was designed to immediately detect missile launch, but it had other missions as well—like following someone's movements in a hostile country. The system had been deployed as a test during the Persian Gulf War, and the president had almost used it to target Iraq's Saddam Hussein for assassination. At the last moment, the president's national security aides had gotten cold feet and had pulled the mission back. But the capability was there.

So Daniel felt fairly certain that they'd used it here to

track them. But he also got a very strange feeling in the pit of his stomach. If they had such an ability to see so clearly from a satellite platform, why in the world were he and Loren here, risking their lives to gain information that was more easily gained without human intervention? Why, indeed?

Just a minute or so later, Daniel had his answer. The helicopter went screaming up the side of a hill. Only when they had neared the apex did it become clear what they were flying over.

The mountain was made by people. Or, rather, the structure inside the mountain was made by people. The sod, trees, boulders, weeds, and everything else needed to make it look like just another small foothill had been planted recently.

As the helicopter slowed and began to hover over one part of the "mountain," parts of the structure beneath were visible to the naked eye. He could see it. So could Loren. But it would be almost impossible to pick up with certainty from the sky. You had to be here, within yards of the structure, to know for sure what you were seeing.

And near the very center of the apex of the mountain, Daniel could make out an unnatural straight line running north and south. He turned to the marine. "I want a look at it," he said.

"Sir, we have to . . ."

"Let me down," Daniel said firmly. "I want a look at it."

The marine hesitated only a moment and then ordered the pilot down. Daniel climbed out the bay door a second later, dropped to the ground, and ran to the unnatural line. He knelt down to examine it. Sure enough, beneath the sod were heavy metal doors on either side of the line.

This is the proof, he thought triumphantly. *This is a bunker.* He knew of only one use for such a bunker out in the middle of nowhere. And it wasn't for research. He knew, because the U.S. had bunkers such as these in remote parts of less-populated states like West Virginia, fully loaded.

Daniel knew they now had something to tell the president, something important. Then, he hoped, all of this really would be above his pay grade. Way above it.

Chapter Nineteen

10:00 A.M., THURSDAY, JUNE 18

It had been some time since all of the Joint Chiefs had met in the Tank. If anything, they'd all avoided being in one place at one time—and that meant a forced rendezvous in the place the Pentagon middle management called the Tank.

The reason was simple. All of them—the respective chiefs of the once-vaunted air force, marines, navy, and army—were now reduced to tomcats in a back alley brawling to save their own services in the middle of massive downsizing.

All four services were undergoing what nearly every major corporation had undergone since the 1980s—a huge cut in services and personnel. They were supposed to be leaner and meaner as a result. But they weren't. They were just hollow shells without much esprit de corps.

Each of the armed services chiefs had developed his own network on Capitol Hill and throughout the corridors of the White House. Each was desperate to cut the other guy's budget to save his own. And all would do nearly anything to accomplish that mission. That didn't leave a whole lot of time for policing the world.

But they had no choice now. Their commander in chief had ordered them to work together to solve the Algerian problem.

"Do whatever it takes to get to the bottom of it," he'd told them, without any of the political apparatus around. "And fix it if there's a problem. We'll worry about the consequences after the fact."

They'd seen the NSA photo, of course, and they'd all scoured the ends of the earth for information that might provide a clue to what that gaping black maw in the center of the mountain might be.

In the end, they'd all come to the same basic conclusion. It seemed incredible beyond belief, but there was really no other possibility. It looked an awful lot like the fixed exit for an intermediate-range ballistic missile.

Nobody put ballistic or GLCMs—ground-launched cruise missiles—in silos anymore. That was crazy with a satellite's ability to countertarget ground-based missiles from space. No, GLCMs were moved around constantly from flatbed truck platforms, and the ballistic missiles were now placed in what amounted to hardened silos buried inside mountains and other remote, inaccessible places that could be protected.

None of them could believe that Algeria had actually put such a facility in place without the world knowing about it. Or perhaps more important, *why* it would build such a facility.

But the Algerians had cut the deal with China to

build the nuclear research reactor in the desert, and the reactor was almost fully built and operational by the time an NSA satellite picked it up. The Chinese had built it for Algeria without anyone else knowing, and there was no reason to believe that actual deployment couldn't have happened the same way.

Still, deployment was incredible if that was what was going on in the photo. Where had the money come from? Where had the technology come from? It was one thing to dabble with fissionable material and reprocessed fuel. It was quite another to build the platform and make the missile that could fire with such technology.

Algeria wasn't even a second-rate power. It was just out of the colony stages. There seemed no earthly reason why the country would leapfrog into the twenty-first century and the nuclear arms race as North Korea, Pakistan, India, and others had.

Unless—and this was the fear that resonated within the Tank as the chiefs spoke of the situation—someone had paid big money for what was, in effect, a surrogate nation.

Every intelligence report for the past five years had indicated that Iran had moved fully into Africa, especially into Algeria and Sudan. Full-blown Islamic fundamentalist movements were agitating in both countries, thanks to Iran. But Iran had never had the money to pay for much more than uprisings. Iran was still, to this day, recovering from the effects of the devastating war with Iraq. The Iranians were strapped for cash and couldn't even finish their nuclear deals with China and Russia.

So what exactly was going on in Algeria?

Members of the military intelligence community were now wise to possible nuclear reactor shifting of plutonium from spent fuel rods to reprocessing plants in certain nations, and they had a rough idea just how far along each nation was in its nuclear program. They could almost track Iran's progress, for instance, based on the types of shipments into the country from the black market and places like Russia.

If you truly wanted to mask a buildup—for a possible launch at an enemy like Israel, for instance—then you had to build and deploy your missiles elsewhere. Like Algeria.

The mountain ranges outside Algiers were just within the range of the intermediate-range missiles Russia had spent tens of billions of dollars building. The technology for developing a ballistic missile with the right parabolic arc to get to Israel from a nation like Algeria was now almost common knowledge in the scientific community. It could be done.

But who could manage to pull the funds together for such a project? That's what had the chiefs baffled. And why? What could they possibly hope to gain by putting such a project together?

Perhaps they'd hoped that the world community would not find out until it was too late. If that was the case—and there really was something to the NSA photo—then their scheme was about to come unraveled.

Because the chiefs had come to a very swift conclusion that day in the Tank, one they all agreed to with only a small amount of discussion. The four U.S. armed services would throw their combined weight at the problem. They'd gotten their marching orders from the president and others in the chain of command at the White House, and they didn't have to ask twice.

They immediately deployed half of the American nuclear submarines carrying SLCMs—sea-launched cruise missiles—into the area. Two carriers were dispatched as well, and their air base in Saudi Arabia went into overdrive. Every other command force anywhere near the region was put on alert.

It would take a couple of days before the world's intelligence community would catch the signals, but that made no difference. No military power in the world could hope to match full, worldwide U.S. deployment. No one would dare try.

The most anyone could do—if anyone had the courage—would be to go to the media or perhaps the United Nations Security Council and then the media. But, again, it didn't matter. Diplomacy was the president's responsibility. Theirs was to solve the equation and be prepared in case the worst occurred.

If there was something in Algeria, they wanted to be in position to either take it out with cruise missiles or bomb it into oblivion with their planes. It would be just like Iraq and the Persian Gulf War all over again.

And should the need arise to go into Algeria to take out the sites, it would galvanize American public opinion. It might be just the thing—as the Gulf War had been for a short time—to get the services past this horrendous budget-cutting nightmare in Washington. They desperately needed a crisis. And Algeria just might be that crisis, the Joint Chiefs reasoned.

Curiously, they'd been prepared for this type of emergency for several months. A task force on regional conflicts at the White House—headed nominally by the vice president but really run by the national security staff—had been engaged in mock simulation of this type of crisis since the first of the year.

Everyone now prepared for regional conflicts that had the potential to escalate. A developing nation with an armed nuclear weapon was at the top of everyone's nightmare scenario. And almost by magic, one had appeared on their doorstep overnight.

So they were actually prepared for the scenario, unlike others such as Iran's hostage crisis that had taken them by complete surprise.

It was just too good to be true.

Chapter Twenty

10:00 A.M., THURSDAY, JUNE 18

In another corner of the Pentagon, nearly a half mile away through the labyrinthine corridors of the five-sided building, the defense secretary, "Big Bill" O'Donnell, was meeting with a handful of political appointees—two of his special assistants, his legislative affairs director, his public affairs chief, and his policy director.

They were people he could trust. They had all been with him in his corporate job and had come over to the Pentagon with him. The White House had saddled him with other political appointees, but his core staff—these four men and one woman, the public affairs chief—were the people he turned to in a crisis. He ignored all the rest of the bureaucracy.

And there was no doubt about it to O'Donnell. It was crunch time. He had to act, privately and, ultimately, publicly.

"Look, this Algeria thing is for real. No matter which

way it cuts," O'Donnell said, spreading his huge hands out before him on the massive desk that separated him from his staff, who were arrayed in a semicircle around the desk.

O'Donnell had fully briefed all of them. None of them would leak to the press—not unless their boss told them to.

"But what if it's a dud, there's nothing there?" asked his policy director, Samuel Addison.

"It isn't a dud," O'Donnell said quietly, remembering that NSA photo and all the satellite photos of their own ground-based missiles and those of the old Soviet systems.

"But what if it is? Won't we look stupid if we overreact?" pressed Addison.

"Does it really matter whether we look stupid or not?" asked one of the special assistants, Jonathan Hoyle. "We have to act as if it's the real thing. No one can hold us accountable for overreacting."

"Unless we *do* something," Addison said.

"Like what?" asked Hoyle.

"Like, I don't know, some sort of a strike," Addison said.

O'Donnell shook his head. "We wouldn't move in unless we had better information. Hard information."

"And how will we get that?" Hoyle asked.

"We have a team going over, a small one, to do initial reconnaissance," O'Donnell said. "And then, if we have to, we'll send in the diplomatic team. Or anyone else we have to."

"And the Joint Chiefs? What do they say?" Addison asked.

"Whatever I tell them, I would presume," O'Donnell said with just a small amount of uncertainty. Everyone in the room had been there long enough to know that no defense secretary controlled the Joint Chiefs. They answered only to the president. And even he did not have complete control over them.

Jackie Hart, the public affairs director, leaned forward in her seat. This was history in the making. She could sense it, like any good PR counselor would. And she wanted to be out in front, not catching up.

"Can I brief the networks off the record?" she asked her boss. "Just to be prepared. I want them thinking— *knowing*—that you were there first. Prepared. Ready. Taking command of the situation. Then when the cameras have to roll, they'll know how to position the story. In our favor."

Jackie Hart was a real pro, perhaps the best PR director in any of the Cabinet departments. She was very good in front of the camera, but she was also smart enough to know when to step aside and turn every single ounce of her energy toward promoting her boss in the spotlight. This was one of those times.

O'Donnell hesitated for only a moment. "Do what you have to," he said, looking at her and then away, off into space. "Whatever makes sense. I don't need to know the details."

Jackie nodded. She'd done this countless times before. If it worked—if she briefed the networks, and they held the story, didn't break the confidence, and go off half-cocked—then she'd be in control. She could direct the story line from the start.

But if it didn't work—and that had never really happened to her, to be honest about it—then she'd take the fall. It was understood between the two of them. O'Donnell wouldn't think twice about shifting every bit of the blame to her if something like this should ever blow up in her face.

"What about our allies?" asked Addison. "Shouldn't we let NATO's high command know?"

"Why?" O'Donnell asked. "They have no role here."

"But don't they have ships in the Mediterranean?" Addison said somewhat plaintively. He hated it when people didn't do things at least a little by the book.

"I suppose so," O'Donnell sighed. "But they have no strategic mission in Africa. And defense of Israel or the Middle East is stretching their responsibilities an awful lot."

Addison grinned widely. "Then why are *we* there? What's our mission in the region?"

"We don't need a reason." O'Donnell laughed. "We're the United States. We can do anything we want."

"All right," Addison said, ignoring the laughter around him at their boss's remark, "then what are we going to do? We aren't going to notify any of our allies . . ."

"Which would be the State Department's job anyway," Hoyle interrupted.

"And we really can't do much with our troops until we have better information," Addison continued. "So what do we do? Sit here and twiddle our thumbs?"

"Well, for one thing," O'Donnell said, "we need to reassemble the tactical and strategic teams we had in place during the Persian Gulf War. Just in case we need them. Because if we go into a nation like Algeria, we'll risk setting off unrest in that part of the world again. No way around it."

"And what do we call the teams?" Addison asked. "What name do we give them? Why are they being created. Or re-created?"

"We'll just war game it for a little while. That should keep everyone in place for at least a few days," O'Donnell said. "And by then, I hope we'll have enough information to make some other decisions."

"So we're really gonna do this?" Addison asked, shaking his head in disbelief. "This is real? It's not just made up out of whole cloth to test military readiness or something crazy like that?"

"It's real—as real as anything gets these days," O'Donnell said. "We don't want to overreact. But if that NSA photo was for real, then something very ugly and sinister has taken place in that corner of the world, and we need to act immediately to deal with the threat."

Chapter Twenty-One

10:30 A.M., THURSDAY, JUNE 18

Veronica Gray wasn't doing anything particularly helpful or useful at the moment, but something would turn up. It always did. It was just about that time of day—midmorning—when things had a habit of turning up.

Veronica wasn't her real name. Only a few hundred people knew her real name. About fifty million others knew her as Veronica Gray, which was just the way she'd planned it.

She was now one of the best-paid news correspondents at the television networks. She'd had her choice of plum jobs during the last round of contract negotiations, and to the surprise of her colleagues, she'd chosen the Pentagon. Not the higher-profile White House or more glamorous State Department.

But Veronica knew what she was doing. She had her eyes on a greater prize. She didn't want a cushy beat job at State or the daily grind of the White House. She wanted to sit in the anchor's chair in New York. And you got there, she figured, by proving yourself in other, unexpected arenas.

If she, a woman, could master the arcane world of the Defense Department, that would do it, she figured. She'd have a shot. And she would make the most of it. Plus if you didn't mind sitting with generals all the time, the Pentagon wasn't a half-bad place to do stories from.

There was a soft knock on her door. Veronica looked up and almost broke into a smile. Something, indeed, had turned up in the form of Jackie Hart, the defense secretary's "flack." She never showed up without something in hand.

"Got something?" Veronica asked her.

Jackie looked up and down the hall, and then stepped in quickly and closed the door to the cubicle office behind her. Even though Veronica was a big network correspondent, she was stuck with a small office in the place.

"This is confidential, and hold for now," Jackie started the conversation.

"But not necessarily off the record?"

"Let's say it's off the record for now. Use this as guidance. You can revisit some of this for attribution later, when the time is right."

Veronica nodded. They'd established the ground rules. She'd honor them for as long as she could. "Okay, what gives?" She pulled her notepad over to take a few notes.

"We have . . . a situation," Jackie said, trying to phrase her words carefully.

"A situation?"

"Yes. Possibly a very tricky one, involving missile deployment in an unusual place."

Veronica frowned. "Where, like Cuba again?"

"No, no, not Cuba. Not even anywhere that threatens the United States. But in a place where it shouldn't be, maybe aimed at a country it shouldn't be."

Veronica had been around long enough to know that there was only one other part of the world the U.S. even considered nearly as strategic as its own—the Middle East, around its longtime ally, Israel.

"Okay, it must be an Arab country then. Iraq? Iran? Syria? Egypt maybe?"

Jackie shook her head at all those guesses. "No, it's on the African continent."

Veronica wasn't exactly a whiz at geography. Arab, on the African continent? The only country she could remember, at the moment, was Libya. "Gadhafi again?" she asked.

"No, not Libya. West of Libya."

Veronica didn't give Jackie a hard time for the runaround. It was the time-honored way of doing business. Jackie could later say that she'd simply confirmed information for Veronica, not given it voluntarily, if the network correspondent guessed right and asked the right question. Albeit with a little help.

So what was west of Libya? She glanced over at the world map tacked up above her desk. She scanned the map quickly. It had to be Tunisia, Algeria, or Morocco. Tunisia was too small, and Humphrey Bogart told her Morocco was out.

"Algeria?" Veronica asked. "You've found something in Algeria?"

Jackie nodded. "Jackpot!"

Veronica scrunched up her face slightly—not enough to create any lines—and considered this information. "Wasn't there something in Algeria a couple of years ago, a nuclear reactor?"

"You got it," Jackie said. "A nuclear reactor four times the size it was supposed to be. They've been making fuel. Now, they seem to have a use for the fuel."

Veronica's eyes popped wide open at that one. "You mean, they've deployed a nuclear weapon? Algeria? A real nuclear bomb?"

"And with the Islamic Salvation Front so active in the country, guess where it's gonna be aimed?" Jackie said, hoping she hadn't gone too far. Only time would tell.

Veronica whistled softly. This was a hot one. No question about it. It had all the elements of one whale of a story. Just the kind of story to get her up and out of this hole for good, right into the anchor's chair.

"Okay, I'll start getting pictures together," she said.

"But hold for now," Jackie warned her. "I'll give you the high sign when it's time."

As soon as Jackie closed the door, Veronica was on the phone to her producer. Within minutes, they had satellite time booked for that afternoon, and a crew hired in Algiers. They'd have pictures ready for the newscast that evening.

Her second call was to a longtime trusted source at a very senior level in the White House. They chatted for a few moments. Her source confirmed everything she'd just heard, and then some.

In fact, the White House was in full pursuit of the situation, her high-level source informed her. They had a small team in Algiers, which had finished its mission and was on the way back home. They could probably take pictures of the team at the airport if they hurried and used a long-lens camera.

The missile site had been positively identified. Algeria had deployed, the source said. There was a likely shipment of new missiles on its way to Algeria right now aboard a nondescript trawler. What's more, there were unconfirmed reports of Algerian terrorists just arrived in the United States.

The Pentagon and the Joint Chiefs had ordered U.S. forces into the region, and bases in Saudi Arabia and Kuwait were on the highest alert.

When Veronica got off the phone, she was trembling more than a little. Not with fright, but with anticipation.

It was a huge story, and she had it exclusively. The United States was on the verge of war with Algeria over the deployment of nuclear weapons—possibly aimed at Israel—and the story was hers. All hers.

She made her decision at that moment. Off the record or not, she was going with it. She couldn't afford to wait. Tomorrow, everyone else would have this. She had to move it tonight. Why else would her source in the White House have confirmed all the essential elements of the story if they didn't want it known?

She grabbed a makeup kit from her purse to fix her face up. Tonight's broadcast would make her career, and she wanted it to look exactly right.

Chapter Twenty-Two

7:00 P.M., THURSDAY, JUNE 18

Loren rested her head on Daniel's shoulder on the ride out to the Algiers airport. They accomplished their mission. They could report to the president. And others could decide a course of action.

There were just a few unanswered questions nagging at the back of Daniel's mind. And when he mentioned them to Loren, she said she had some of the very same thoughts.

Like who had given the orders to retrieve them? And why? They never *had* seen any Algerian troops near the site, just the guards. It wasn't as if their lives were in jeopardy.

Granted, they weren't moving straight at the target— they were easily five miles too far to the east and likely would have missed the built-up mountain bunker entirely—but that couldn't have been the reason for the timely rescue, could it?

And why had they been allowed to get so close to the missile site if it was such a state secret? Where were Khali's forces? Why wasn't the place guarded more closely? A perimeter fence would have been a dead give-away obviously, but they could have set up electronic sensors or *something*.

Finally, why hadn't they been informed that their movements were being shadowed offshore by a stealth mission? They were entitled to that sort of information—both of them were, even if they were staff.

Something wasn't quite right. They could sense it. They just couldn't trace it back to the source. The whole thing had become a series of jumbled events, reaching to the one inescapable conclusion they would report to the president.

Algeria had deployed. There could be no question of it. That's what they would report and feel confident about it. They'd seen the site with their own eyes.

As they pulled into the Algiers airport, Daniel helped Loren with her bags. She accepted gratefully. In their short time together, she'd come to trust him more at every turn. She wasn't entirely convinced, but he could at least carry her bags.

Neither of them noticed the camera mounted on a tripod some one hundred yards or so away, filming them as they emerged from the embassy limousine and climbed directly aboard the aircraft. The camera was too far away.

As the plane lifted off for a direct flight to Dulles International in the U.S., the cameraman packed his bags and sent the tape on its way to the satellite trans-mission studio through a courier who was standing by.

Not more than twenty minutes later, the pictures had reached the network studio in Washington, D.C. And just a half hour after that, selected parts of those pictures were already B-roll for the piece Veronica Gray would air that evening to lead the newscast.

Chapter Twenty-Three

1:00 P.M., THURSDAY, JUNE 18

Watch out," one of the CIA director's three secretaries whispered across the foyer outside their boss's office, "the chief's on a rampage."

The second secretary, who had been at the doctor that morning, nodded and didn't even bother to hang up her jacket. She tucked it behind the chair, quickly turned her computer on, and retrieved the first file she came across. The last thing she wanted was to be caught in idle chatter or with nothing to do should Branigan come storming through the double doors to his office.

Sure enough, Branigan's bellicose voice boomed a moment later. "Sharon, where in the devil is that shipping and transport file I asked for this morning?" the CIA chief yelled through the closed doors.

The other two secretaries gave Sharon—the CIA director's executive secretary and their office manager—a knowing, sympathetic smile. Branigan had been storming around Langley like a Nazi general for the past three days, nonstop. Sharon had traced the "rampage," as they referred to it, to an early morning meeting on Monday with the president and a subset of the national security team.

It had something to do with Africa. They could tell from the briefing teams that had been scheduled incessantly from that meeting onward. Virtually every African research specialist had been in to see the director. Every African file had been dredged up from both the archives and the active files. Every incoming report from anywhere near that part of the world had been analyzed to death and sent in to the director.

But today had been especially brutal, and the day was only half over. Sharon sighed quietly and steeled herself for the near-certain inquisition she would face when she peeked into the room.

Like so many other support staff in and around the power centers of Washington, Sharon was a career professional. She had seen CIA directors come and go. She'd been the executive secretary for the last three directors.

Branigan was by far the worst of the lot. Like the others, he was self-important, brusque to support staff, officious at times, and he worked the front office staff to the bone. But he was also mean-spirited on occasion, and he fired or reassigned people for even minor errors or omissions. People lived in constant terror of the summons, "The director wants to see you in his office."

Branigan justified such actions to himself, at least, on the grounds that the national security of the United States demanded his full attention and discipline. He expected the very best from those around him, and those who did not—or could not—deliver in a timely fashion had to be swept out of the way. There was no other choice.

Branigan had made a pact with himself, in a way, that he would be nice to others when he left the job he was in. Until then, he would do whatever it took to get the job done.

But the job was not getting done right now. Not by any means. No one had been able to come up with a plausible rationale or scenario for what was in the NSA photo.

It was driving him insane. He knew his job was on the line. No one had said anything to him, but every professional instinct screamed to him that he had to be first to the cause, if not the solution.

He'd held four separate meetings the previous day alone. The first had been on the humanitarian relief effort under way in the Horn of Africa. A massive drought had swept across six countries. There was civil unrest in five of them, and at least three major wars were on the verge of breaking out. But not in Algeria. They had water there, thanks to the Mediterranean.

The second briefing had been on the quite severe economic situation confronting the socialist government in Algiers. The projection for oil production in Algeria was dismal at best, and the global outlook for the price of oil was equally dismal. There seemed no relief in sight for the government of Algeria. But this was nothing new. Every specialist in Africa knew all of this. It was common knowledge—not to the people of Algeria, of course, but to anyone who paid even a minimal amount of attention to the affairs of African nations.

The third briefing had been on the most recent report from the CIA station chief in Algiers. The report had been worthless. Completely worthless. The station chief, desperate for any scrap of information, had thrown everything but the kitchen sink into the report. None of it made a small amount of sense, even his speculation about a sea transport company that "confidential sources" indicated may be connected somehow.

There were reports of imports and exports at the ports, everything from pots and pans to bushels of corn flour. But no high-tech imports. They'd scoured earlier reports for some mention or hint of an import company operating in the Algiers district, attempting to bring in even modestly sophisticated equipment for a basic industry. There had been nothing, not a hint of an unusual import operation. The lack of findings was maddening.

The fourth briefing was from the arms control group that shadowed the efforts of the U.S. Arms Control and Disarmament Agency, the State Department, and the White House national security team on nuclear disarmament and test ban treaties. Branigan wanted to know where things stood in the dismantling of the Russian and Ukrainian nuclear arsenals. The group had been tracking the progress of the destruction of the intermediate-range missiles under the INF Treaty, and they briefed the director on the never-ending discussions over the fate of the long-range missile talks that had been called SALT I, SALT II, START, and other names over the years.

The arms control team gave their usual ridiculous picture of the arms control talks. Even in collapse, Russia would never voluntarily give up its intercontinental ballistic missile capability. Never. Branigan knew that. He wondered why the dolts at ACDA, State, and the White House didn't realize it as well. Perhaps because the American people demanded at least a show of effort by their politicians toward global disarmament, Branigan reasoned.

According to his team, all of the INF missiles in the United States and the former Soviet Union states had been either destroyed or dismantled. At least, that was what the reports said. But there had been other reports of parts and pieces of these dismantled INF missiles shipped out of both Russia and the Ukraine into the black market. Some of those parts had allegedly begun to show up in North Korea, Iran, Iraq, Pakistan, India, China, and even Israel.

Branigan did not doubt that Russia was turning the dismantling of old, outdated INF weapons into hard currency. He did not doubt it in the slightest. Russia felt no moral obligation toward anyone to destroy those weapons.

Under the absurd terms of the agreement, Branigan knew, the U.S. had not demanded that the core of the missiles themselves be destroyed—only what was, in effect, the outer casing for them. The actual components that made up the missile could be used piecemeal in other things—or sold to the highest bidder among the second-tier nations frantically assembling their own nuclear arsenals.

Four briefings, four presentations that amounted to nothing, a day wasted in a fruitless search for a piece of the puzzle that made any sense. Branigan felt like he was losing his mind.

Sharon poked her head around the door. "The shipping and transport file I asked for! Where is it?" he barked.

"That was five minutes ago, sir," Sharon responded mildly. "I told the African section you needed it ASAP."

"Check on it personally, will you?" he growled. "Go down there yourself if you have to. I want it on my desk in five minutes, or someone will be in one whale of a lot of trouble. Oh, and have someone with at least half a brain walk it up who can explain it to me."

"Anyone in particular?"

"Yeah, not a section chief. I want an analyst, someone who understands the data."

Sharon nodded. She closed the door quietly behind her and went back to her desk. By now, she knew every five-digit number by heart in the entire Langley complex, and she dialed the number to the sea transport office without thinking.

"Hi. Sharon in the chief's office," she said in a hushed tone when someone answered on the other end of the line. "You have the shipping and transport file ready for him? He's screaming about it already." Sharon nodded at the response, satisfied that it would arrive momentarily. "And you might send Frank Donley with it if he's up to taking a beating today."

Sharon knew Frank Donley was the best that section had to offer, and he was young enough to weather a berating. Sharon had a deft eye for talent. In the past, she'd regularly guided directors to good, solid talent two and three levels down in the vast bureaucracy. Others had appreciated that ability. Branigan did not. He was oblivious to it.

But this job would require the best the CIA had to offer. She knew it instinctively. She could sense that something big had happened or was about to happen. The whole agency had a sense that some earthquake was opening up under its feet.

Donley arrived out of breath two minutes later, carrying the file with him under one arm. "The director . . . ?" he began to ask. Sharon waved him right into the director's office. Donley knocked timidly, and then entered when Branigan grunted for him to enter.

Donley placed the file on the desk and remained standing while Branigan glanced over the hurriedly prepared executive summary—for the CIA director's EYES ONLY—and then leafed through the rest of the document.

Donley knew what was in there. He regularly kept up with reports from the field. It was a trick he'd learned on his very first assignment as a special assistant to the director of intelligence in the office of the Pentagon's Joint Chiefs of Staff. Read everything—and that meant everything—and then sort it out later. Boil it down to its essence and give even minor scraps of possibly useful information to your superiors. You never got in trouble that way. And you earned promotions.

He'd done that here as well. That's why he knew there was not anything of any consequence in the report. He'd seen the actual field reports that had been the basis of the report, and he didn't need to read the analysis of them.

Except for one item that had been brought to his

attention by someone else in another section—someone in the intelligence-gathering part of the agency who had a parallel responsibility to track field reports from each of the CIA stations in Africa—nothing stood out.

And the one item that had been flagged for him wasn't much, either, just a report of a foreign-flagged trawler off the coast of Libya with what appeared to be quite sophisticated Russian electronic surveillance and tracking gear on board.

An unusual sighting, but perhaps a mistake as well. The people the CIA paid to report such events often fabricated things to make a little more money.

Branigan looked up. "All right. What's your name?"

"Frank Donley, sir."

"All right, Donley, tell me what's in here. Anything useful?"

"Can you tell me perhaps whether you're looking for anything in particular, sir?" Donley asked, trying to keep the fear out of his voice.

Branigan clenched his jaw. "Useful. Important. Out of the ordinary. Those words mean anything to you, Donley?"

Donley swallowed hard. "Yes, sir. They do. And no, sir, there isn't anything in that report that fits the description of what you're looking for."

"Nothing?"

"Well . . . um . . . ," Donley said hesitantly.

"Yes?" Branigan asked sharply.

"There . . . um . . . there is this report that was brought to our attention about a foreign flag on a trawler near Libya," Donley said, thankful that he'd been literally given the information before he'd come up here. It might save his job, he thought.

"What flag?" Branigan demanded.

"Tunisian, I think."

"You think?"

"No, well, I know, sir. It was a Tunisian flag on an ugly trawler. Name was Medco Shipping."

"Medco Shipping?" Branigan sat bolt upright at his desk, a cold, delicious shiver sweeping through his body. "You're sure of that name?"

"Yes, sir."

Branigan almost smiled. Almost. Medco Shipping was the name of the sea transport company given to him by his station chief in Algiers not too long ago.

"And the significance of this is what, do you think?" Branigan asked sharply. "There are a hundred foreign flag ships there every day. So what's new about this one?"

"This particular trawler had sophisticated, expensive Russian electronic gear on board, according to the report."

Branigan sat forward in his chair. His eyes bored straight ahead. Donley could see the wheels and cogs spinning at thermonuclear rates inside the CIA director's head. Donley knew he'd hit pay dirt. He almost felt like leaping for joy.

"And it was headed for where? Was it going west along the coast of Libya or east?" Branigan asked, holding his breath.

Donley panicked. He blanked on the answer. But then, yes, he remembered something his contact in the intelligence-gathering section had pointed out to him.

The ship had been heading toward Algeria, he'd said. That was west of Libya.

"It was moving west, sir, west of Libya," he said quickly.

"Toward Algeria then?" Branigan asked.

"Yes, sir, toward Algeria."

"You're sure of this? It's in the report?"

"Yes, sir, it's in the document. It's based on a field report from one of our regular paid contacts—a shipping clerk in the port of Tripoli if I'm not mistaken—who spots unusual activity in his corner of the world."

"He's reliable?"

"Yes, sir, he's been filing reports for years."

Branigan sat back in his chair, the first smile in three days breaking across his face. At last. The first piece of the puzzle had fallen. He had something. His gut told him that this was the real thing, that it fit into the picture. He knew. And he was first. The CIA was first on the scene for a change.

Without any hesitation, he picked up the secure line and dialed into the White House for the president. Franklin Shreve was on the phone a minute later. Branigan explained the find for him and asked him to authorize a rescue mission immediately.

The president hesitated only a moment and then concurred with the finding. Such a mission was worth the risk. The stakes were already high. No point in worrying if this made them just a little higher.

Chapter Twenty-Four

9:00 P.M., THURSDAY, JUNE 18

They waited until the ship was almost to port, but still far enough away from Algiers that they could legitimately claim afterward that the incident had occurred in international waters of the Mediterranean.

Not that it really mattered. It wasn't like there was a World Court or a superpower left in the world that could challenge the U.S. military.

Still, the orders had been handed down from the highest levels. Seize the ship near Algiers, so its destination was obvious. Get the job done quickly, efficiently, with as little loss of life as they could manage, and then get the goods to the U.S. air base in Germany immediately so they would be on display for the public, should the need arise.

The two navy cruisers sped silently toward their mark, careful to steer clear of other ships. A larger, bulkier navy freighter pulled up the rear to carry whatever cargo they retrieved.

The cruisers were not challenged as they neared the trawler. With all the fancy electronic gear on board, the trawler's crew surely must have known of the approach. But they did nothing, though there wasn't much such a slow-moving trawler could do anyway.

The captains of both cruisers nevertheless maintained soundings for submarines right up until the moment they flanked the trawler on either side. It all seemed a little too easy. They still expected some sort of challenge.

But there was none. The crew of the trawler emerged on deck when challenged and lined up alongside the rail as the navy cruisers prepared to board. As the security detail boarded the trawler, it met no resistance whatsoever.

The crew was international and rough. Only the captain seemed remotely competent. The others looked as if they'd spent too many days at sea.

A captain of one cruiser joined his crew on board the trawler. He wanted a firsthand glimpse of the cargo so that he could give the report to Washington himself.

As they entered the cargo bay area, they saw debris strewn everywhere. Much of the area at the bottom of the trawler was empty. Some boxes of oil-rig machinery were spread around the circumference to give the appearance of being somewhat full to a casual observer.

But in the middle was the real, precious cargo of the ship, quite secure. Stacked neatly in several rows, packed and repacked, with large instructions printed on storage and handling, were twenty-four gleaming missiles, minus their nose cones.

The navy captain recognized them immediately, even

if they were representative of another branch of the military. They were Russian intermediate-range missiles banned under the INF Treaty signed between the former Soviet Union and the United States. They should have been destroyed years ago as part of the treaty.

But they obviously had not been destroyed. They were right here before the captain's eyes. And they were on their way to Algiers. There could be no question of that. None at all.

It was not his job to question how they had come to be here, who had paid for them, why Algeria would be purchasing two dozen intermediate-range missiles, or where the Algerians intended to aim the weapons of mass destruction.

His mission was to seize the missiles and deliver them to an air base in Germany. An hour later, the missiles were aboard the navy freighter, and a videotape of the operation was on its way to Washington via secure satellite.

The banned INF missiles would be in Germany by the end of the day. The crew and the ship's captain were detained under ship arrest aboard their own vessel.

Chapter Twenty-Five

6:00 P.M., THURSDAY, JUNE 18

It had all worked like clockwork. Everyone at the network was jubilant. This evening's broadcast would send their ratings through the roof, maybe for months to come. And breaking such a story on Thursday was simply too good to be true. It would carry like wildfire right through the weekend.

First, they'd gotten the shots of the two U.S. envoys in Algiers. They had turned out to be a senior aide to the chairman of the Senate Intelligence Committee—which meant the Hill was already up to its eyeballs in this deal—and a senior aide to the president's national security advisor.

Then almost out of nowhere, they'd picked up the scrambled satellite transmission of footage from a nighttime Mediterranean sea mission. It took a little doing, but the technicians managed to unscramble enough of the footage to give Veronica at least three stills of the capture of the Soviet INF missiles aboard the trawler.

175

To make sure she wasn't out on a limb, she confirmed it with her high-level source at the White House.

Last, but by no means least, her source at the White House had also provided the means by which she could obtain a highly classified satellite photo, which could only have come from the NSA's picture files.

Veronica and her source had done this kind of thing before, so the routine was in place. But the stakes had never been this high before. Once, the source had provided NSA pictures of a Soviet nuclear installation in a location they had maintained was not covered by the START talks, which the network had obligingly aired. But that was nothing compared to this particular photo.

It was clear to Veronica that the NSA photo showed the actual deployment site within Algeria. No distinguishing landmarks surrounded it, but she knew her White House source was not steering her wrong.

Veronica was surprised there had been no action at the White House, according to the three correspondents they had there. Nothing out of the ordinary. She assumed that her White House source would tell the president that something was about to break, and that the staff would soon start to get in gear. But maybe not. Stranger things had happened. And anyway, they'd know soon enough.

They also had confirmed reports of fleet movements toward Algiers off the coast of Morocco, in the Atlantic Ocean. And she'd been able to have someone confirm the base alerts in both Saudi Arabia and Kuwait.

Veronica had this one dead to rights. It was airtight in every direction, and she knew it.

The network was giving her the first ten minutes of

the broadcast to lay it out—an extraordinary amount of time for network news. But the executives had felt, rightly, that it was big, and that the coverage time was warranted.

At precisely 5:45 P.M., eastern daylight time, Veronica had called the White House press secretary and the public affairs chief at the State Department to ask for official reaction to her story. She did not give them any time or leeway to talk her out of the story. She simply asked for comment.

The White House aide said he had no comment. The State Department aide, when pressed, said State would look into the matter and discuss it with their Russian counterparts—if, in fact, banned Russian missiles had been seized.

At precisely 6:00 P.M., Veronica Gray went on the air, live, with a report from the grounds of the Pentagon.

The United States was on the verge of war with Algeria, she reported, over the deployment of banned Soviet INF nuclear missiles that may be targeted at Israel.

A shipment of the missiles had been seized just outside Algiers, and they were identified as "Russian INF missiles" in the pictures the network broadcast as she read a voice-over.

The U.S. had obtained pictures of the deployment site, also shown on the air, and the U.S. military had moved into position to strike at Algeria if they did not agree to immediately open up the area for inspection, she said.

The U.S. had sent two envoys to Algeria on a secret fact-finding mission, and they were now on their way back to the White House. The network flashed pictures of Daniel and Loren, complete with their names and titles, boarding the plane in Algiers.

At 6:10 P.M., Veronica finished her broadcast. She'd been flawless. She clearly enunciated every word. The word had gone out. The story had been launched. More important, her career had been shot into the stratosphere.

At 6:12 P.M., the president of the United States slumped back wearily in his Oval Office chair and then called an emergency meeting of the National Security Council.

Later, he would attempt to sort through how, and why, all of this was now on very public display.

Chapter Twenty-Six

7:00 P.M., THURSDAY, JUNE 18

Loren was asleep when the first pictures showed up on CNN. But she wasn't asleep for the second half hour of news, nor would she be for the remaining hour of their trip across the Atlantic.

By the second hour of CNN, every passenger on board the aircraft had seen the broadcast and knew that the two White House and congressional aides identified in the report as the U.S. envoys to Algeria were sitting toward the front of the plane and had been sitting there the entire flight.

Veronica Gray's network had refused to give out any of its own footage, so the other networks were scrambling for new pictures to match the breaking story.

CNN had somehow found two old stills of Daniel and Loren. Daniel recognized his as an old Senate ID photo, and Loren's was from her bio file at the White House. Neither of them was especially flattering.

They were both aghast at what they were hearing and

seeing on CNN. About the only thing missing from the news reports was what Loren and Daniel had found. But that wasn't on full display as well because they hadn't had time to tell anyone yet over a secure line. They'd decided to wait and brief the president personally. State was sending a summary via secure cable.

As the plane came in to land at Dulles, Loren had that awful, sinking feeling again in the pit of her stomach. It kept getting worse the closer they got to the gate.

Their plane taxied by one of the lobby windows. They counted at least twenty cameras with their lenses pressed up against the windowpane, shooting the arrival of the plane.

As they began to get off, one of the flight attendants stopped them and asked them to step off to the side.

"You might want to wait," she cautioned them.

"Why?" Loren asked.

The flight attendant shook her head. "Because there's a crowd of about one hundred reporters waiting for you at the end of the ramp. I'm not sure how you'll get through."

Loren instinctively grabbed Daniel's hand and gripped it hard. She was scared of what was happening. It had gotten very big, very fast, and they were right at the center of the storm.

"It'll be all right," he said quietly. "No one says you have to answer those jackals. Just push your way through them, and hold your head high."

"But what if they keep shouting questions?" Loren asked plaintively.

"Just shake your head and say, 'No comment.' This is

a free country. You don't have to answer their questions."

They waited until all the passengers were off the plane and then made their way up the ramp slowly. As they turned the corner, dozens of reporters spotted them and surged forward en masse.

"Ms. Anders!" they all seemed to shout at once. She served the president, so it was logical to attack her first. The questions were all a blur. Why did they go over on a secret mission? Had they found evidence of the deployment site? Was the U.S. declaring war on Algeria? Had the U.S. entered diplomatic negotiations? Would there be a backlash from the Arab world?

Loren had no answers to any of the questions. It wasn't her job to answer any of them. They began to push their way through the crowd of reporters. Several cameras smashed into Loren's head as she tried to fight her way past.

About halfway through, a young man grabbed Loren by the hand and started to pull her through the crowd. Loren started to resist, but the man flashed a White House ID badge at her. He was an assistant White House press secretary. "They sent me here to get you," he explained, "in case something like this happened."

"Well, it's happened," Daniel growled. "Now, get us out of here."

"Yes, sir," the aide said, and then like a lead blocker for a running back, he began to plow straight ahead, clearing a path for the two of them.

Minutes later, they were clear of the madness and on

their way through an underground tunnel that security had pointed out to the White House press aide. They would be back at the White House safely within the hour

Chapter Twenty-Seven

7:00 P.M., THURSDAY, JUNE 18

Malcolm Hopewell usually checked his computer E-mail messages first thing every morning. Just for fun. He was an unusual journalist in more ways than one.

He didn't mind, for instance, when weird people called him about stories he'd written for *Time* magazine. That was just fine with him. He almost preferred hearing from people like that. It kind of connected him to the world he wrote to and about.

And he loved to get E-mail from people all around the United States. He had widely circulated his E-mail address on the Internet, CompuServe, America Online, and every other service he could subscribe to. He had invited people to send him stuff through E-mail—any old kind of junk. It didn't much matter to him. Almost all of it was worthless, of course. But every so often, well, something popped up that he could use.

Malcolm's job for the magazine, ostensibly, was to

cover the United Nations in New York. But that didn't take much of his time. The UN, despite its massive budget and membership, was worthless. It never did anything. Except talk. It was very good at talking. He often wondered why anyone even bothered to keep the place going, especially when private groups were cropping up that seemed to know how to get the job done much more efficiently.

Like this new Unity movement. They were everywhere the UN was, only they got jobs done. They didn't talk much. Unity just moved the troops in and made things happen.

On the side, Malcolm had learned to surf through the various on-line services. It was like trolling for fish in the ocean. You never knew what you might catch. That, and what he got in his E-mail, allowed him to provide useful tidbits to other parts of the magazine and keep from being totally bored.

Malcolm had really been treading water lately. He'd risen like a rocket through the ranks of reporters and writers at *Time*, landing the job at the UN when he was only twenty-seven years old.

Malcolm was very, very talented. He had to be in the career he'd chosen. For Malcolm was a Christian—he'd learned his faith in the Presbyterian church his mother had grown up in—in a field that was openly hostile to people with deep religious beliefs such as his own.

Journalists, by and large, were loners who lived by one simple creed. Whatever it takes. Get the story, no matter what. If you have to lie or cheat or steal to get it, don't get caught.

There was a kind of honor code among journalists,

which included things like not burning or giving up sources and not cribbing too blatantly from the work of other journalists. But those were more for self-preservation than anything else. People would never speak off the record to a reporter if they thought they might get hung in the public square for their comments, and plagiarism could get you drummed out of the journalists' corps.

Malcolm, though, was unlike his peers. He didn't have to cut corners to get information or skulk around in back alleys with "Deep Throats." He just worked very hard from a multiplicity of sources to get honest information that no one else seemed to pay much attention to. He'd actually landed a number of sensational stories that way. If you took yourself out of the herd that usually stampeded after the same stories, you had a chance to find some real gems of stories.

When he'd turned on his computer that Thursday morning in his cubbyhole office at the UN's headquarters, his E-mail box contained twenty-three messages. He began to flip through each one of them quickly to see if any was worth studying more carefully.

He stopped at number fourteen, a message from a usually reliable source in Anaheim, California, who seemed to have nothing better to do with his life than remain logged on to the Internet. The guy—Malcolm presumed it was a guy, though you could never quite be sure in these cyberworld discussions with people at the other end of a keyboard—was more excited than at any other time he'd dropped a message into Malcolm's E-mail address.

"Urgent, flash, urgent. Hope. Gotta pay attention to

the request for info I stumbled across on the Net this AM," the message to Malcolm read. "Too way out to believe. But doesn't sound crazy. Sounds like some chick in real trouble. Doesn't know how to handle the info. She left word in the coffeehouse on Main Street. Asked if anyone could confirm or deny. Something about Japan's parliament, Diet, IMF bridges, Chile, London falling down and the World Bank, marks and dollars, and a loan to Russia. Stuff like that. Figured you're the MAN on this one. Got your sticky fingers in so many pots . . ."

Malcolm sat back in his chair and gazed at the screen. He'd known about two of the items mentioned in the E-mail. There was an IMF meeting in Geneva sometime soon, maybe the next day or so, to go over the status of some bridge loans to three or four nations. He couldn't remember which ones.

And he'd heard recently from a couple of financial sources at the UN that people were worried about Chile defaulting on its World Bank note. Some weird things had happened there recently. Some sort of an ecological disaster had all but wiped out a couple of its export crops.

Chile had struggled, in fact, ever since the U.S. Food and Drug Administration had found some cyanide in a few grapes and had blocked entry into the U.S. of their second-largest export. The ordeal had cost the Chileans billions and almost destroyed their export capabilities. They were only now recovering.

Then, during the past growing season, something had contaminated groundwater in large portions of the country, spoiling water supplies and ruining whole crops. People were desperate for water, and the crops had been essentially wiped out.

So it wouldn't surprise him if there were rumblings of a Chilean default on loan obligations. Without export money, Chile would be in deep, deep trouble. But a default? That seemed unlikely.

Still, Malcolm decided to check it out. The other items intrigued him anyway. Perhaps there was something to them.

He quickly tapped into the Internet. The "coffeehouse" on "Main Street" was a usual hangout for Internet junkies. It was a little like a real coffeehouse you might find in a small town where people could wander in, sit down, gossip with friends or acquaintances, and shoot the breeze.

The only difference, of course, was that the "town" was all of America, and the people who wandered into the place on "Main Street" did so over a telephone line and through the use of a keyboard.

You had to be fast to strike up conversations in the coffeehouse. Most people just typed in notes and waited for others to respond. Malcolm assumed that's what the "chick" his California E-mail buddy had referred to had likely done.

Malcolm logged in and went "back in time" to early in the morning. He trolled through each of the notes posted on the electronic bulletin board and hit pay dirt at about 9:10 A.M. New York time.

"Coffeehouse patrons," the note read, "I need some help confirming or denying information I've run across. Is anyone out there who might know about any of the following events over the course of the next three to four days?

"A Diet vote in Tokyo on a previously undisclosed budget deficit, scheduled for two days from now, that would drive the Nikkei stock index price down and trigger a massive derivative scare.

"An IMF meeting in Geneva in two days on bridge loans to Algeria, Sudan, Brazil, and Panama, and an offer from an organization to step in and consolidate all those loans.

"Rumors of Chile's impending default on a World Bank note, and an offer by a private group to help pick up the note and take the World Bank off the hook.

"A Treasury Department directive to convert marks into dollars, with a group in Geneva serving as the broker.

"A State Department cable about the latest move by Russia to break off talks with the U.S. over an emergency loan, which might be picked up by a Geneva-led consortium.

"Big London bank about to collapse because of bad bet on Japanese stock market, and talk of a private consortium coming in with the Bank of England's blessing to keep it out of bankruptcy.

"I need help. Leave a message if you can help. I'll get back to you. Yours, Sarah in New York."

Malcolm was surprised that the woman had signed the note with her name. If that was, in fact, her real name. No one used a real name in these cyberspace talk shops. Everyone was role-playing as someone else.

But this had the feel of the real thing. So Malcolm quickly typed in a response, indicating that he had information on at least two of the items she'd listed, left his E-mail address, and waited for the mysterious "Sarah" to get back to him.

Having delivered his message, Malcolm then forgot about it. The day went by. He paid close attention to the breaking evening story about Algeria and nuclear weapons coming out of Washington. It sounded like the kind of thing he'd get dragged into fairly soon.

About an hour after Veronica Gray's broadcast, Malcolm was still at his office, tinkering with a story on his laptop. His desktop computer beeped twice, which meant someone was trying to get through to him directly via on-line. The person was using the Internet direct-to-direct on-line service, and Malcolm logged in and answered.

"Knock, knock," Malcolm typed into his computer. He watched the answer appear on his screen an instant later as it was typed in, a process that always fascinated him to no end.

"Who's there?" came the reply.

Malcolm thought about it for a moment. "The big bad wolf," he typed in finally.

"My house is built of brick and stone," the reply came back. "Are you really a wolf?"

Malcolm didn't like the direction this was heading, so he switched gears. He decided to guess that the caller was the elusive Sarah from the coffeehouse. "No. I saw your message in the coffeehouse. I know about an IMF meeting, and I know about the Chilean loan situation. Are you Sarah? What's your angle?"

"No angle. It's strictly business. And, yes, I'm Sarah. What's your angle?"

Malcolm considered masking his identity. But he didn't operate that way. He wasn't into playing games. "I'm a reporter for *Time* magazine. I'm at the United Nations."

"Really?"

"Yes, really. I trade information for a living. You?"

There was a pause at the other end of the line as Sarah (or whoever she was) decided how far to commit. "I trade. And share information. It's what I do for a living," she said obliquely.

Malcolm racked his brain. Trade. Shared information for a living. Worked in New York. He laughed out loud and then typed in his response. "Okay, Sarah. You work on Wall Street, right? One of the big brokerage houses?"

"Lucky guess. But you'll never figure out which one."

"Probably not. Doesn't matter. Is Sarah your real name?"

"What's yours?"

He didn't hesitate. "Malcolm Hopewell, intrepid reporter."

"Yes, Malcolm Hopewell, intrepid reporter, Sarah is my real, given name. But that's all you get. Not a smidgeon more."

"Fair enough. Now, why are you so interested in those items you posted in the coffeehouse?"

"For my business. It helps with my trading."

"That's the only reason?"

Sarah didn't answer right away. Malcolm waited patiently on the other end. "I'm worried," she typed in slowly. "I wanted to tell someone."

"Why? Why are you worried?"

"Because I've never seen events like this lining up.

I've never seen governments and international financial institutions hanging like a thread—and so willing to turn their affairs over to a private group."

"But how do you know each of these things will happen?"

But Malcolm already knew the answer. He didn't need to see it appear on the screen before him. He knew because he could see them as well. He heard the same still, small voice that had been speaking to men and women of God down through the ages.

"I know," she typed. "I just know. Leave it at that."

Malcolm decided to take a risk. It was almost as if someone else was typing the words for him. Which, in a way, was true.

"Do you believe in God?" he typed slowly. "Are you a Christian? Is that why you are so certain of what you're feeling? Of what you're seeing?"

Sarah could scarcely believe what she, too, was seeing and typing. "Yes, I am a Christian. And, yes, it is my faith that makes me so certain. Every part of me is screaming to do something. I feel like I'm a very, very small part of something that is much, much larger than me."

Malcolm took a deep breath. "We'll do something about it. I promise. You tell me what you see, and I'll do something about it. I give you my word."

There was no answer on the other end of the line. Malcolm waited. A minute passed, then another. Still no words appeared on the screen before him. Malcolm wondered if perhaps one of the computers had disconnected.

But then the words appeared on the screen, words that, he knew, would change his life forever.

"Can I see you? Now?" Sarah asked.

"Yes," Malcolm answered as speedily as his fingers could manage. "Tell me where."

Sarah typed in the address to her home. It was less than five minutes from his office in Manhattan. Malcolm said good-bye, signed off, and flipped the computer off.

He was out the door an instant later. He didn't bother to lock the door or turn the lights off as he left. He knew he'd be back anyway after his meeting.

Several long—but exceedingly interesting—hours later, Malcolm was onto one whale of a story, provided he could run down some of the essential elements of it. But there was clearly a common thread, one that Malcolm could follow.

Thanks to Sarah's ability to keep track of seemingly unconnected events around the world, he knew where to look. It was now a matter of tracing them and explaining them to a world that didn't seem to care about such things.

The following day was Friday. With events breaking so sharply on Algeria—and with Sarah's information linked to that situation, it seemed—Malcolm knew he'd have just one day to tie the loose threads together.

But he was confident he could manage it. It would require a little effort, a little cooperation with bureaus around the world—and a little luck—but he could pull it off.

Chapter Twenty-Eight

8:00 P.M., THURSDAY, JUNE 18

They were whipped, exhausted, and furious that they'd just had to fight their way through a savage media pack. But the worst was yet to come. Both Daniel and Loren knew it.

The president had convened an emergency meeting of the National Security Council for that night. Attendance was mandatory.

And the guests of honor? Daniel Trabue and Loren Anders, in person. Bedraggled and absolutely dead tired, but in person.

Daniel volunteered in the ride over to the White House to do most of the speaking if that was what Loren wanted. She gratefully accepted the offer, though she knew they'd both end up doing a lot of talking.

The meeting was still being convened, so they waited in the press secretary's office. It was up on the second floor, down the hall from the Oval Office. Usually, reporters streamed in and out. But tonight, for them, they sealed off the hall.

The president's chief spokesman had one of the nicer offices in the place, a big room dominated by a weird-looking desk shaped in a semicircle.

The press office staff left them alone in the room, which was just as well. They were too tired to talk. They were saving their energy for the security council.

Twenty minutes later, a secretary came in to retrieve them. The president was waiting. She led them down the hall to the Cabinet room.

Daniel was surprised at that. He would have assumed they'd be meeting downstairs in more secure facilities. The Cabinet room was for show, not so much for privacy.

As they entered the room, both Daniel and Loren immediately realized—too late—why they were there. Photographers immediately started snapping pictures, and a couple of the less polite reporters shouted questions. They'd walked dead into a photo op.

"No questions, please," the president said, holding up a hand. "We'll get to those."

The reporters grumbled, but asked no further questions. Two press aides ushered them out of the room a moment later.

President Shreve turned to Loren first, and then Daniel. "Sorry about that," he said, smiling broadly. "But we have to show our best face—you know, doing something positive—in the midst of a thing like this."

"I understand, sir," Loren said. She wanted to tell him that she resented being used as a prop for his larger public relations efforts, but she said nothing.

The room was quite full. All members of the security council and their key staff were in attendance. There was not an empty seat in the room. Which meant, of course, that Daniel and Loren would have to stand throughout the meeting.

Once, the National Security Council had been a small, select group. Only the president, the vice president, the defense secretary, and the secretary of state were members. The CIA director, the chairman of the Joint Chiefs, and the Arms Control and Disarmament Agency (ACDA) chief were statutory advisors.

But the previous occupant of the Oval Office, Bill Clinton, had expanded the council to include the secretary of the treasury, the head of the White House economic policy committee, and the U.S. representative to the United Nations. National security, it seemed, was purely in the eye of the beholder.

As a result, these meetings had turned into a zoo. And today, all the animals had been turned loose from their cages.

Once the doors were closed and the media were forced to cool their heels not more than one hundred yards from where they were meeting, the president jumped right into it.

"All right, let me first tell you—both of you—what a fine job you did," the president said. "We've all read the written report sent us by State. I have just one question, for starters. How was it you were able to get so close to the missile site without being detected?"

Daniel stepped forward. It had been his plan, and he would suffer whatever consequences resulted. "We chose to drive past the guards, sir. We drove around them in a Humvee. We asked our driver to swing wide around the guardhouses and then get close to the site."

"And no one challenged you?" the president asked.

"No, sir. No one challenged us." Daniel glanced around the room. Every Cabinet secretary, every staff aide, was sitting forward, riveted on his words. "But we would have missed it if we hadn't been picked up by the marine helicopter."

There were surprised murmurings from around the room. There had been no mention of a marine helicopter in the written report. The president looked genuinely stunned by the news.

"A helicopter? One of ours?" the president asked after a short silence in the room.

"Yes, sir," Daniel said. "I planned to put it all in our report, but State said they'd take care of it. I guess they left that part out."

Vice President Wright leaned forward in his seat, rested one elbow on the table, and then gestured casually to the president. Shreve acknowledged him.

"Mr. President, if I might explain," he said. "I was in charge of the Situation Room, as you know, when this incident occurred. That marine helicopter picked them up under my orders."

"Your orders?" the president asked.

"Yes, they were in imminent danger," Wright explained, "and I had to act immediately. I ordered the chopper in to get them, and they obviously made good use of the ride."

The president nodded. There was no need to explain their satellite monitoring capability to this group. They knew the capability. They would have had plenty of information at their fingertips, more than enough to make such a decision. And it had proven to be the correct one.

"Good call, Lucius," the president said, nodding. "Very glad you went in and got them."

"Thank you, sir," Wright said, settling back in his chair.

Daniel almost blurted out a question—about why the vice president thought they were in "imminent danger"—but did not. They hadn't seen any troops, but perhaps they were just around the corner nevertheless.

The president turned to Loren then. "And your report of seeing the actual missile site? It *is* correct, I presume? No other details?"

Loren nodded, gripping her pen hard to keep from getting too panicky. "It was Daniel who actually walked across the site, but yes, it was there. I saw it with my own eyes."

"And I walked the length of the doors, lifted the sod," Daniel added. "It was man-made. And the doors opened up and out, like the ones we have in our own sites. Same size. Same kind of man-made hill."

The rest of the briefing went easily. Daniel and Loren described their brief encounter with Khali, the obvious loyalty he commanded from the military, and then described the open countryside where they'd found the missile site. They fielded a few questions, and the briefing was over. They'd survived.

The president thanked them again for coming at such a late hour and then excused them. They closed the doors behind them, and the National Security Council continued their discussion about what to do with the Algerian situation.

As they walked back down the hall, Daniel noticed quite a few uniformed officers cooling their heels in the private waiting room next to the Roosevelt Room. *So,* Daniel thought, *they were going to the military. Not State. That meant a strike.*

A secretary walked them down the corridor, past the Oval Office, down some stairs, out a side door, and then over to the Old Executive Office Building. From there, they would be able to leave unobserved from an exit on Seventeenth Street.

Loren took Daniel's hand as they left and hailed a taxi. Daniel accepted it gladly and gave it a little squeeze.

"We survived," he whispered to her.

"Barely," she answered wearily. "But I feel responsible, somehow. Like we started a war or something. I mean, our faces are everywhere."

"Just remember," Daniel said, trying to reassure her, "we didn't leak all this stuff to the press. We were just doing our jobs. And we sure didn't start any of this. They did."

Loren turned and faced Daniel as a cab finally pulled over to pick them up. "Who are *they*? The Algerians?"

"Yes, of course," he said, confused.

Loren's usual steel resolve wavered briefly. "Are you so sure of that, Daniel? Are you? Is war that simple?"

Daniel held Loren's hand tightly. "No, I'm not sure," he said softly. "And, no, war is never that simple."

Chapter Twenty-Nine

6:00 A.M., FRIDAY, JUNE 19

Amy was probably the only one not cursing in the vice president's security detail. The guy *never* ran. He golfed. He didn't run.

But here Wright was, at 6:00 A.M. Friday, jogging with the president. And the detail jogged, too. All of them, including Amy.

Amy knew why Wright was up and jogging with the president. The Algerian bombshell the evening before had really lit the place up. Wright probably knew this would be the only time of day he would get alone with the president.

The Friday newspapers had the story in huge World War II-era headlines. The United States was going to war with Algeria over a nuclear weapon, it seemed. They'd discovered a cache of banned nuclear missiles in the port of Algiers, and an eyewitness had seen the site where other missiles were deployed.

Amy didn't mind their detail this morning. She kind

of liked the change of pace. She was in great shape. So jogging with the veep and the president was a piece of cake. They were eight-minute milers, at best. Amy could tick miles off at under six minutes each, and still not breathe too hard.

The president ran every morning, had since he'd been in office. At first, it had been a curiosity. Large crowds used to line the streets of Washington, shortly after inauguration, to catch a glimpse of him as he and his entourage went by.

But as the weeks and months wore on—and as traffic continued to get snarled whenever the president was out running around the capital—the crowds thinned. But the president continued running.

The Secret Service had tried—and failed—to get the president to vary his route. He wouldn't, not under any circumstances. He loved the views the run offered, and he refused to give them up. It was the one and only shining, clear moment of the day for him.

He always warmed up on the south lawn, just beyond the Rose Garden. Then he, and those who were power jogging with him, left the White House grounds out the southwest gate and ran due south across the grounds of the Ellipse and then across Constitution Avenue.

From there, it was a straight shot to a jogger's heaven. The president always made the same loop: south past the Washington Monument, across Independence, around the eastern side of the Tidal Basin, past the Thomas Jefferson Memorial, along the softball fields in West Potomac Park, past the Lincoln Memorial and then the Vietnam Veterans Memorial, along the Reflecting Pool, through the Constitution Gardens, and then north onto Seventeenth Street, east onto E Street, and then north again into the White House grounds.

It was a truly breathtaking run, especially in the early morning light. You could catch nearly every memorial in Washington during the course of the run.

After a while, the Secret Service began to breathe easier as well. It was easy to manage the detail for nearly the entire run. Almost all of it was in wide, open spaces where they could see someone coming for one hundred yards. Plus, it was early, before many people were up.

They were especially nervous this particular morning, though, what with all the Algerian hype. War talk brought out the crazies, the Secret Service knew.

Amy noticed all of this as they left to follow the president and his vice president. Only the special-agents-in-charge jogged with the two men. Everyone else ran either ahead or behind, on the perimeter. And, of course, there were those "other" agents stationed at points along the route, the agents who were never officially counted in the detail, but who were there nevertheless.

As they made their way into the run, Amy grew less anxious about their protection. There was nothing to it. Only when they left the grounds of the Washington Monument and turned north onto Seventeenth Street to head home did she and the other agents look around a little more than at other points of the run.

But even this was harmless. The president ran by only one fairly tall building before entering the White House grounds, and it was completely benign—the American Red Cross building at the corner of E and Seventeenth Streets.

As they ran up Seventeenth, the Red Cross on their left, Amy realized that she'd not followed up on a loose end of her search for the mysterious Algerian terrorists. Her friend, M. J., was narrowing the search for Algerians who'd entered more recently, and she had a couple of live names for Amy to track down. But Amy had vowed to find the Sudanese delegation from Biomed first to close that loop. They had been scheduled to meet for training sessions at the Red Cross. Jogging by the building triggered the thought.

The last time she'd spoken to someone at the Red Cross, the delegation had not yet checked in. Then a couple of days had gone by, and she'd almost forgotten to follow up. She had a little time that morning, after her charge had gone into the White House, so she'd use her time wisely and close the loop.

"Be back in thirty," she told her special-agent-in-charge as the president and vice president went to shower down and dress for the first meeting of the day, their usual CIA briefing. The day had been uneventful, as always. The two leaders had talked up a blue streak during the run, but nothing much else happened.

"You headed somewhere?" her supervisor asked her.

"Business. At the Red Cross. Be right back," Amy said. It was almost seven. Perhaps someone would be at the front desk.

Her supervisor nodded, and Amy headed out the door, flashed her ID badge at the gate, and walked briskly the block and a half to the Red Cross building.

She entered the main entrance on E Street and asked the receptionist to ring the training office. Several very long minutes later, an older woman came ambling out of the ramshackle elevator that served all, great and small, who walked the corridors of the venerable Red Cross.

"Can I help you with something?" she asked Amy.

Amy glanced down at the woman's nameplate on the front of her white smock. "Yes, Ms. Bates, you can . . ."

"Mrs. Bates, please," she smiled. "Eight grandchildren."

"Yes, of course, Mrs. Bates," Amy said. "I was here before." She held out her Secret Service badge and let the woman inspect it.

Mrs. Bates frowned. "Is there a problem?"

"No, no problem," Amy said quickly. "I just need to close the loop on something, make sure there's nothing to a rumor we picked up."

"And how can I help?"

"Well, I'm looking for a delegation from a group called Biomed. From the Sudan. They're supposed to get training here, I believe."

The woman thought for a moment. "Yes, I believe they arrived yesterday morning. They were delayed for some reason. Can't recall why."

"And are they here?" Amy asked. "Can I speak to them?"

"Why, I don't see why not. No state secrets here. Just helpin' folks." The woman turned, and Amy followed.

"Don't I need a visitor's badge or anything?" Amy asked as they walked to the elevator.

"Not when you're with me, dearie," she said and punched the button to the top floor.

They turned left off the elevator on the top floor of the building, then right down the hall. They came to the last room on the hall, a big conference room at the corner of the building, facing Seventeenth Street.

The room was jammed full of people—perhaps a dozen Red Cross personnel and the members of Biomed—which was surprising at this time of day. Equipment was strewn everywhere. People were poking and prodding and talking, all at once. It reminded Amy of a triage unit in some distant war.

Biomed appeared to be a scraggly scientific lot. Most were men in their fifties, Amy guessed, who'd done medical work in hospitals and clinics all their lives. There were only a couple of younger men, who appeared to be lower-level staff along for the ride, for neither of them seemed to be doing much at the moment except staring at the younger Red Cross women in the room.

Amy walked into the room. Mrs. Bates pointed out the Red Cross official in charge, who at the moment was explaining something to a small group at the opposite corner of the room.

Amy picked her way carefully through the people and equipment and walked up to the Red Cross official. She waited patiently for him to finish his briefing, looking out the window as she waited.

They had a lovely view from the conference room at the corner of the top floor of the three-story building. A magnificent view, in fact. *You can see the Washington Monument past the Ellipse from this view*, she thought.

A sudden jangling thought struck her. Perhaps it was because she had just jogged on detail this morning, past this building, on this street, but there was something else quite interesting about this room.

It offered a clear, unobstructed view of Seventeenth

Street, the only such unobstructed view along the entire route of the president's run each morning. There was no other vantage point in all of Washington, D.C., from which a sniper could secretly take aim at the president.

A cold chill settled on Amy. She took a second look around the room. It was quite chaotic and stuffy right now. But snipers didn't need much for success—just an open window and a direct shot at the target. You got both in this room.

A still, small voice was telling her to pay attention. Be alert. Listen and understand. She always heeded that voice.

"May I help you?" the Red Cross training official asked her, startling Amy.

"Yes, you can," she said, stepping off to one side so the others in the room could not overhear their conversation. "I had a couple of questions for you about this training session."

"And you are . . ?" he asked, frowning.

Amy didn't want to flash her badge here, so she leaned close and said softly, "I'm with the Secret Service. Please hold that information in confidence if you would. I just need some answers."

The official hesitated. Amy thought for a moment that he might ask to see some identification, but then thought better of it. "Okay, how can I help, then?"

"This delegation from Biomed," she said. "How well known are they to the Red Cross? How did they come to be here, using your training facilities?"

The official thought for a moment. "I don't think the Red Cross knows a thing about them, other than what we've learned here today."

"Is that usual, to entertain groups like this?"

"Oh, they came highly recommended, from a group we've partnered with in dozens of countries in Africa and Latin America. If I recall, the group made a direct request to our president to let Biomed come here this week for training."

"A group did? Which group is that?" Amy asked.

"Why, Unity, of course," he said. "They do so much for people, and they've helped out so many of our Red Cross chapters in other countries, that it was a small thing to lend our training personnel for a group they wanted to send us. If Unity says they're okay, then that's more than good enough for us."

Amy looked around the room and saw everyone in it with new eyes. "And how long will they be here?" she asked.

"Oh, a week, including even tomorrow and Sunday."

"Is this building secure?"

"Yes, of course," the official bristled. "No one gets in without a pass or an escort."

"But once you're in here, you can wander on your own?"

"I suppose," the official said. "But what is all this about if I may ask? The Red Cross has never . . ."

Amy held up a hand. "No one is questioning the Red Cross. Believe me, that is not my motive here. I just have one more question at any rate. What time will your training sessions begin each day?"

The official smiled wearily. "Alas, Biomed asked to start early, with breakfast in the mess on the ground floor, so that their delegation could see the sights in the afternoon during their stay here."

"And what time is that?" Amy held her breath.

"A time that only birds should be up and about—six o'clock in the morning. It's dark when I leave home to get here by then."

But not dark when the breakfast starts. Or when the president jogs beside the birds hunting for worms, Amy thought grimly.

Chapter Thirty

8:00 A.M., FRIDAY, JUNE 19

There had to be at least twenty-five people crammed into the conference room on the sixth floor of the State Department by eight o'clock in the morning that Friday, all of them poring over every cable that had ever been sent in or logged from Algeria.

They'd all been there since ten o'clock the previous night. All twenty-five of them. They'd worked through the night, at the secretary's order. Now, ten hours later, they were all ready to drop in their tracks.

Liz Barton had sent them scrambling immediately after the close of the emergency National Security Council on the Algerian situation. A phone chain had roused them in the night Thursday, and gotten them to come in for a massive manhunt. No one was very happy about it.

There were hundreds and hundreds of cables to sift through, on subjects ranging from speculation about Algeria's position in OPEC talks to the fallout from the assassination of Algeria's president and the national election results where the Islamic Salvation Front had almost taken over the reins of the country.

They had their marching orders from the secretary: find something, anything, that would help her weather the political storm over the Algerian problem. They had to have proof, now that this thing had blown sky high.

Liz Barton had been in the Game—the unspoken one that everyone in Washington played but never actually described in any detail—long enough to know that the stakes on this one were now very, very high.

The revelation a number of years ago that China had almost completed a sixty-megawatt nuclear reactor in the Algerian desert had sent shock waves rippling through the diplomatic community.

This second revelation that Algeria had deployed some form of a nuclear weapon, or was about to, had come as an earthquake to the diplomatic world.

CNN had been live on this thing since the moment Veronica Gray broke her exclusive. They were fourteen hours in and counting. And they wouldn't shut down until it had reached its conclusion.

Liz Barton knew she had to be out in front of the pack—now, at this moment in time—or she would be swallowed up in the crush of world opinion that was about to weigh in.

Cabinet secretaries with any kind of a stake in the Game were turning their places upside down for anything that might help their position and standing with the White House.

The Pentagon, for instance, had immediately gone to

its highest alert—the lights from the building lit up the sky and its gargantuan parking lot was half full at midnight—and had put a massive command post in place. It almost duplicated the Persian Gulf War effort.

The CIA had never gone to sleep the previous night, either. The lights at Langley had burned throughout half the building all night long.

And every operational NSA satellite anywhere near the African continent was now in high gear, snapping a million pictures.

Liz Barton knew she had to produce. She just didn't know what to tell her people to look for, so she gave this vague instruction: "I want to see anything that might help."

During the first few hours, staffers came trooping into her office with some piece of paper or news. None of it was worth anything. There wasn't a shred of evidence anywhere that might lead anyone to guess that something unusual was going on in the mountains south of Algiers. Nothing. It was maddening.

"Eleanor!" Barton yelled from behind her desk. Her longtime executive secretary, Eleanor Holmes, who'd been with her from one professional incarnation to the next, entered the secretary's office quickly, a notebook in hand.

"Yes, Ms. Barton?" asked Eleanor.

"Take a note to the president, please," she said curtly. "Dear Sir—or whatever it is I call him—please be advised that the State Department has reviewed all cables and correspondence with Algeria over the past two years. We have turned up nothing of note. There is no communication, of any sort, to confirm or deny the existence of the situation."

Eleanor jotted the words down quickly in shorthand, and then looked up at her boss. "Ms. Barton, are you sure you want to send this note over to the president?"

"And why shouldn't I?" she exploded. "We haven't found anything. It seems like we're on a big wild goose chase. Why not tell him so?"

"Have you checked with the other Cabinet secretaries to see what they've uncovered?"

"No. Why should I?"

Eleanor didn't answer right away. It usually took a planted suggestion to get her boss thinking. Especially when she was furious like this.

"Why don't you check in with the vice president, see what he's heard?" Eleanor suggested.

The vice president and the secretary of state were on unusually good terms. They often traded valuable information. "I could, I suppose," she mused. "But he can't possibly be over at the White House this early, and I don't want to call the residence."

"Ma'am, I do believe he *is* in. I believe I remember hearing on CNN that he was out jogging with the president this morning," Eleanor said. "Shall I get him on the line for you?"

Liz Barton frowned. She hated it when her own secretary prodded her along like this, even when she was right. "Oh, all right," she sighed, accepting the inevitable.

"And shall I hold off on this note just yet?"

Liz Barton glared at her secretary. Every so often, she

half wondered who worked for whom. "Just get him on the line."

"Yes, ma'am." Eleanor left the office and quickly punched in the number of the direct line into the vice president's West Wing office. Lucius Wright had two offices, a quite ornate one in the Old Executive Office Building, and a second in the West Wing just down the hall from the Oval Office.

Like previous occupants of the office, he was never in his OEOB office. You could almost always find him— when he was in town—at his West Wing office. That's where he was now.

"The vice president is on line one," Eleanor called out a moment later.

Liz picked it up. "Lucius, how are you?" she asked in her sweetest voice. "Long time no see."

"At least eight hours. An eternity," Wright said easily in his smooth baritone voice. "And I'm fine, all things considered."

Liz Barton knew exactly what he meant. It was Friday morning, and it still seemed like Thursday. "Say, Mr. Vice President, I was just curious . . ."

"You're going in circles on this Algerian thing, too?" he asked sympathetically. "Don't worry. Everyone else is as well. The whole place is burning to the ground. Crazy. Frantic. Everyone stumbling across everyone else."

"Well . . ." She paused, then jumped right to her request. "What've you heard? Anything?"

"You know, as a matter of fact, ol' Wilkinson over at FBI did mention something to me in passing the other day," Wright offered casually. "Perhaps it's useful. Perhaps not."

She held her breath. Wright had never been one to pass on gossip lightly. There was usually something to what he passed on. "And?" she asked finally.

"Well, he mentioned something about Algerian terrorists. In the United States. You might want to check on visas. That is the State Department's area, isn't it?"

Liz Barton's mind was already racing frantically. They were looking in the wrong direction. There wouldn't be anything in the cables. That was a dead end.

If there *were* Algerians in the States—and the department had let that fact slip through without flagging it—then she was in deep trouble. And she knew it.

"You're sure?"

Wright sighed on the other end of the line. "That's what he said. Told me he'd stumbled across something, and he was pretty sure of it."

"Thanks. That's helpful. I'll let you know what I find."

Within five minutes of her conversation with the vice president, Barton had ordered three of her staff—one of them an expert in computer searches and the other from State's counterterrorism unit—to the part of the State Department where visas were granted.

Less than an hour later—after searching through records of entries at ports like Baltimore and New York, and airports like LaGuardia—they had found what they were looking for.

Seven men with Algerian passports—several with clear ties to the Islamic Salvation Front—had entered the U.S. within the past week. All seven had entered by different routes, at different points of entry. Two had entered through the West Coast, four had come in on the East Coast, and the seventh had entered through a Gulf Coast port.

There was no record of where any of the seven had gone. Their entry visas indicated New York, but all people said they were going to New York when they came to the U.S.

It made no difference to Liz Barton. She had succeeded. She had something to deliver to the president's desk, something real, something tangible.

She drafted the memo herself, with Eleanor's help, and had a courier hand carry it over immediately. It arrived at the White House by 9:30.

The secretary then put herself on the president's schedule later that day to brief him more fully on the findings. She'd have to remember to stop by Wright's office first, though, to personally thank him. His tip had bailed her out in a huge way, perhaps more than he could know.

At 11:00 A.M., live from the White House lawn, CNN began reporting on the investigation of Algerian terrorists in the U.S.

Chapter Thirty-One

11:00 A.M., FRIDAY, JUNE 19

Wilkinson had been just about sixty minutes too late with his own confirmation, and he wouldn't have made that if he hadn't gotten a chance call from his golfing buddy, the veep, on Friday morning about their next outing to Burning Tree Country Club.

Wright sure is a golfing fool, Wilkinson thought. *He has golf on the brain, like so many senior executives with time to kill and not a whole lot of responsibility. One day it will catch up with him.*

In the course of picking a golf date, Wright had also mentioned in passing that the radar screen was heating up on the Algerian terrorist thing, and that Wilkinson might want to goose his boys a little.

Wilkinson did. He lit into his two deputies to nail down their findings on the Algerians they'd been tracking, and he got the report over to the White House by midmorning—an hour after State had already confirmed it and just thirty minutes before CNN began reporting it.

Fortunately, for Wilkinson's sake, the State people only confirmed the entry of the Algerians at different ports—nothing beyond that. The FBI, on the other hand, had tracked two of the seven, and both were in Washington.

One had checked in a Crystal City, Virginia, Marriott hotel. The other had signed it at the Willard, in the District.

Pretty fancy hotels for the likes of them, Wilkinson thought. *That means money.*

It surprised him that they were using their own names, but he'd seen stranger things. Still, when the FBI followed up that Friday, after the reports, both were long gone. Maybe they weren't so dumb after all.

But they'd run them down before long. The FBI always did with these cases. So far, they had acted more like two-bit hoodlums than professional terrorists, which should make it relatively easy to zero in on them.

And when they did, he'd be a hero to the press. His office would make sure of that.

Chapter Thirty-Two

11:30 A.M., FRIDAY, JUNE 19

Daniel was still asleep when the phone started to ring and ring and ring. His one effort to maintain some control over his life was his refusal to keep an answering machine hooked to the phone in his small efficiency apartment two blocks northeast of the Senate office buildings.

But this particular Friday morning, he wished he'd given that up. This particular caller was awfully insistent, ringing every minute or so. Daniel was still so tired and groggy from the flight over and the White House briefing that all he wanted was for the world to go away. At least for one day.

After the sixth time the phone had begun to ring insistently, he cursed loudly, rolled out of bed, and picked up the phone next to his bed.

"What *is* it?" he growled, glancing at the clock. It was 11:30. He'd been hoping to make it at least until lunchtime.

"The president is calling," the polite voice said on the other end of the line.

"The president of the United States?" Daniel sputtered.

"Yes, sir. Please hold."

There was a brief silence, and then a voice he immediately recognized came on. "Daniel, my boy, how are you? Recovered yet?"

"Well, no, sir, not exactly," he replied.

"To be expected," Shreve said. "Hard duty, getting back in the saddle after a trip across the Atlantic. Don't like it much myself."

Daniel almost said he wasn't *quite* back in the saddle yet, but held his tongue. "I'll live, I guess," he mumbled.

There was a brief pause on the other end of the line. For a moment, Daniel wondered if perhaps they'd been cut off. "Have you seen the news reports this morning?" Shreve asked finally. "About the Algerian terrorists here in the States?"

Daniel glanced over at the TV, which was black. "Uh, no, sir, I was just about to."

"Well, I just got the blasted report on them from State. The FBI confirmed it had been looking into the situation, too. And an hour later it was all over CNN and the other networks," the president said somberly.

Daniel was surprised at how calm the president was. But he was probably used to it by now. The White House was crawling with aides eager to leak information—even highly sensitive information—to curry favor with the national press. But Daniel also wondered why the president was telling *him* all of this.

"I'm sorry, sir," Daniel offered. "We have the same problems with leaks on the Hill, as you know."

"Yes, I know. I most certainly do," Shreve said, and then paused again. This was clearly hard for him. Something was on his mind. "Look. I've been talking to Loren Anders this morning. I've asked her to look into something. She asked specifically that you be involved as well. She said she trusted you. Which means I will have to as well."

Even if I do belong to the other party, Daniel thought ruefully. "Thank you. You can," he told the president. "And I think I would probably trust Loren with my life. If that means anything."

Daniel could almost feel the president smile on the other end of the line. "It does. Funny. She said the same thing about you. Anyway," he said, coughing gruffly, "about this Algerian situation. As you can imagine, we're under enormous pressure, both here and overseas, to do something about it quickly. Every last one of Israel's friends has weighed in. They say if we don't take Algeria out, then Israel will."

"That would be unfortunate, sir," Daniel said. "Israel going after Algeria, I mean."

"Most unfortunate, yes. And not an option in my mind. No, the U.S. will have to take this one on, especially in light of the fact that war seems to have broken out across half of the African continent almost overnight. The international community will have to respond."

Daniel had heard reports of some of that fighting on the flight over. It seemed isolated, though almost certain to spread up to Algeria's borders. "What do you want Loren and me to do?" he asked.

"I want you to look at something for me," the president said quietly as if he was afraid someone might overhear him. "I've given a file to Loren on it. On a group called Unity. You might have heard of them."

Daniel remembered the Unity captain that Algeria's Khali had been so enthralled with. "A little."

"Take a look at the file. Check it out. Get me an answer on it as soon as possible. Can you and Loren do that?"

"Mr. President, why me if I may ask?" Daniel was genuinely curious. He'd really never met this man before, and now he was being asked to undertake a new mission on his behalf.

"Three reasons," the president answered crisply. "One, Loren trusts you, and I have decided that I have to trust her. Two, you are not part of this snake pit here at the White House. And three, time has run out. I need answers right now before certain decisions—irrevocable decisions—are made. And I believe you can deliver those answers."

Chapter Thirty-Three

FRIDAY, JUNE 19

They left before dawn four days after they'd begun their ascent. Colonel Asher wanted to make it up and over the last ridge before the sun was up. He wanted a chance to get close to the missile placements under the cover of darkness if at all possible.

The night had been cold, but his men were used to that, especially on this kind of mission. None of them complained. They just did their job—quietly, efficiently, in a workmanlike fashion.

They had packed and loaded their gear in less than fifteen minutes. They fell into a single line without question, following Asher up the ridge.

Asher checked his compass and map one last time as they crested the ridge. They had less than half a mile from this point. Every step would be critical from here on out.

Asher had no way of knowing what he might find at

the top. He wasn't exactly sure what kind of troops would await them. They could be Lebanese, Syrian, Palestinian, even Russian, for all he knew.

It didn't matter to him or his men really. They were quite confident in their abilities, no matter who the foe. They'd seen combat against all manner of enemy. No one was better trained, or better equipped, at this kind of action.

Asher called a halt about seven hundred yards up and over the ridge, which looked out over the whole of northern Israel, parts of the Golan Heights, Syria and, further into the mountaintop, southern Lebanon. This was the highest point in the entire region.

They waited for a few minutes and then pressed on again. Several hundred yards later, Asher spotted the shadowy outlines of several soldiers moving up on the summit. All of the men in Asher's outfit stopped at once. They'd all seen the movements.

Now came the hard part. Asher separated his men, sending half to the east around the position. The other half went with him to the west.

They had their orders. Shoot to kill if they must, but attempt to take the position with stealth and no shots fired if at all possible. There was no way of knowing, just yet, what other positions were established on the summit.

As they drew near the position, Asher knew instinctively that something was wrong. The whole setup was strange, unlike anything he'd seen before.

He was expecting a short-range mobile system of some kind, something that could lob shells into the land north of the Sea of Galilee. What loomed before them was nothing of the sort.

Though it was difficult to see in the murky darkness, Colonel Asher couldn't believe what he was staring at—a tactical short-range nuclear-tipped missile. There was no mistaking it, even from here. It was a weapon he'd never seen in this part of the world, a tactical nuke that could travel up to two hundred miles.

These weapons had once been deployed all across Central and eastern Europe, aimed at places like Berlin and Prague and major cities in Russia.

At one point in time, there were so many short-range nuclear-tipped missile positions throughout both West and East Germany that an exchange by both countries would have obliterated both instantly. It didn't take much to get from one country to the next in Central Europe.

But those positions had been dismantled, by and large, with the reunification of Germany. The breakup of the Soviet empire had also prompted many of the former Warsaw Pact countries to remove their arsenal of short-range nuclear missiles.

Israel had invested heavily in maintaining nuclear control over the Middle East region. Though Iraq, Iran, and other Arab nations had tried to achieve nuclear parity with Israel, thanks to intelligence and covert military efforts, none had come close to achieving that goal.

And yet, here was proof that the world had somehow changed, almost overnight. A short-range nuclear missile now overlooked Israel. It was but a relative stone's throw from all of Israel's major cities.

Colonel Asher and his men moved in for a closer

look. There seemed to be just a handful of men surrounding the missile site, and they weren't being especially vigilant.

At a predetermined time, Asher took out his small digital handheld two-way radio and turned the power on. It was already preset to a little-used frequency. There was some risk that others might pick up their conversation, but not much.

"Are you in position?" Asher asked quietly.

"In position. Will wait for your go," came the reply.

Asher waited a few moments longer to make sure there was nothing else in the area he might be missing. But only a handful of soldiers were on the ridge, surrounding the position.

He beckoned to the men by his side to get prepared for a silent charge, and then held the two-way to his lips. "GO!" he commanded.

Both parties charged up the hill to the missile site in unison. They did so without yells or screams. The only sounds marking their passage up the hill were the soft "thuds" of boots meeting hard earth.

An instant later, they stormed the position. They took the soldiers completely by surprise. Only one of the defenders managed to get a shot off, vaguely in their direction, and he was quickly felled with a blow to the head.

The remaining soldiers gave up immediately. They held their hands up, clasped behind their heads. Colonel Asher's men surrounded them and ordered them to the ground, their hands still behind their heads.

Only then, with the soldiers on the ground, did he recognize the uniforms worn by the men they'd captured. The shock of recognition almost caused Colonel Asher to have second thoughts about their mission.

Although each wore the uniform of his country of origin, there was no mistaking who these soldiers were. Their blue helmets told Asher everything he needed to know about who their commanders were.

These soldiers were members of the UN multinational peacekeeping force that had been almost permanently stationed in the West Bank to quell Palestinian uprisings there. He was certain of it.

And one of them, also in a blue helmet, wore the distinctive blue-and-white uniform of another organization, closely allied with the UN but not part of the military operations.

What in the world was a Unity captain doing up here on the ridge with these elite troops? What were any of them doing up here, guarding a short-range nuclear missile site? It made no sense at all to him. None.

And what's more, the short-range missile they were guarding was not pointed at Israel. No, it was aimed to the east, toward Syria.

Chapter Thirty-Four

FRIDAY, JUNE 19

By late morning, Garrett was so exhausted he could hardly move. He and two workers with Baptist World Alliance and World Vision had distributed at least a truckload of badly needed antibiotics throughout the refugee camp in Goma.

It was strange to Garrett. Just a year ago, Goma had been a small village, an outpost at the eastern edge of Zaire. Now, it had a population of some three hundred thousand and was still growing.

At last, he could rest. He took a few minutes to type his "sit rep" into his laptop. He'd send it back to headquarters the next morning.

He'd just rested his head on his pillow in his bungalow to take a short nap before catching a late supper when a large explosion rocked the camp. The explosion was quickly followed by a second and then a third and a fourth.

Garrett bolted from his cabin, searching the horizon

for some sign of what was happening. People were running around madly, in all directions, screaming and carrying on.

He tried to grab someone running past. The person shrugged his hand off and kept running. He grabbed a second person. "What's happened?" he yelled.

The person didn't answer, but pointed to the sky instead. Then Garrett noticed the thin plumes of smoke rising to the heavens. He recognized them, from other places.

Someone was shelling the camp with mortar fire and artillery. But from where? There weren't any military positions within one hundred miles of here that he knew of.

That was the whole purpose of establishing a refugee position at Goma. It was well away from where the heavy fighting and killing had occurred in Rwanda.

Garrett ducked back in his cabin. There was a succession of explosions, perhaps a dozen in all, from all directions. Someone was shelling the village pretty hard by the sound of it.

Garrett grabbed his hat, hitched up his pants, and raced through the camp toward the UN headquarters building. Three Unity jeeps were parked outside the building.

He expected to see chaos inside, but instead found the place relatively empty. A UN officer walked past, apparently not in a great hurry.

Garrett approached a UN clerk he knew, who was French but spoke some English. "Jean, where is everyone?" he asked the clerk.

Jean gestured toward the one and only conference

room in the place. The door to the conference room was closed. "In there," he said.

"So what's up? What's going on?" he asked.

"The shelling, you mean?"

"Yes, the shelling. Why are we under attack?"

The clerk shrugged. "Do not know." He glanced back toward the door to the conference room. "They say it was from the Rwanda forces. They attack our position."

"But there aren't any Rwanda military forces within a hundred miles," Garrett said.

"Do not ask me. They say there are troops. They fire on us. I cannot say."

Garrett decided not to press the clerk any further. He clearly had no idea what was happening. He was only repeating what he'd heard.

There was another loud explosion toward the edge of camp, probably several hundred yards away. Garrett stuck his head out the door and looked around. He thought it strange that he could see no damage anywhere near the UN headquarters.

Shelling was going on all around them. Garrett could see close to half a dozen columns of smoke rising at different points in and around the camp. But none here, near the UN headquarters where the officers and the Unity people operated.

And how could that be? he wondered. Above all places in the Goma camp, this was the first place to hit. This was where the UN officers and high command for the military forces of the multinational peacekeeping force were stationed.

If you wanted to hurt your opponents, you bombed their headquarters where their leaders were stationed.

Yet whoever it was hadn't. Mortar fire hit everywhere but here.

The conference room door burst open. Several UN officers, with troubled looks on their faces, emerged. They were followed closely by a virtual phalanx of Unity officials, dressed in their usual white-and-blue uniforms, the triple-circle insignia on their breast pockets.

Garrett crossed the room, careful not to get in the way of the deadly earnest group emerging from the conference room. He waited until the Unity officials left, and then he cornered one of the UN officers who'd been in the meeting, a U.S. colonel who'd been stationed in the refugee camp for nearly six months.

"The meeting. What was it about?" he asked the colonel.

The colonel grimaced. "It's not good news. There are reports of shelling, killing, mortar fire, all through Zaire, Tanzania, and Rwanda. Perhaps other countries."

"Like here?"

"Yes, like here."

"And what will happen? Who will respond?"

The colonel laughed. It was a harsh, bitter laugh, born of months of frustration of dealing with a situation beyond his control, where there was no hope. "You know the answer to that. No one will respond. No one cares."

The colonel was right, of course. This part of the world had been forgotten. There had been so much death, from starvation, drought, famine, disease, or civil war, that the world had grown weary of the ever-present specter of death shrouding all these lands.

"But someone should do something, shouldn't they?" Garrett pressed.

The colonel looked over his shoulder toward the door where people had just vacated the building. "Only Unity will. They are our only hope."

"Unity?" Garrett asked, confused. "What do you mean? How can they help?"

"A Unity reconciliation team is leaving, this very moment, for Kigali. It will intervene. I hope it can stop the shelling," the colonel said.

"Unity, negotiating with the Rwanda government?" That was unlike anything Unity had ever done. Reconciliation panels and local outreach efforts to village groups, yes. But direct negotiation with sovereign governments? That was new.

"Yes. That was what the meeting was about."

"Who gave them the authority to negotiate with the Rwandans?" Garrett asked. "Under whose flag will they negotiate?"

"They need no flag," the colonel said. "And the UN has granted them negotiating authority."

"The UN has done *what*?" Garrett was incredulous. He'd never heard of such a thing, the UN granting a nongovernmental organization that kind of authority and power.

The colonel threw up his hands. "We have no choice. There is fighting everywhere."

"Everywhere? Who?"

"The Rwandans apparently. They're striking at camps outside their border. Here. In Zaire, Tanzania. Elsewhere perhaps. And others are taking advantage of the wars to launch their own offensives. You know what it's like, once the looting starts. It spreads like crazy. Like a fire."

The colonel was right. Things could get out of hand quickly through the entire part of the continent if someone didn't intervene in a hurry.

"Do you have reports from other parts of Africa?" Garrett asked the colonel.

"At least five other countries, and rumors of more about to happen. Only Unity is on the ground in each of those places."

Only Unity. The thought made Garrett shudder. He wasn't a big fan of the "blue helmets" of the UN, but the thought of the well-heeled Unity forces negotiating peace accords around the continent made him wonder if the world hadn't suddenly gone mad.

There were several more explosions in the camp. But, again, none near the headquarters. Something clicked inside Garrett's head. Something wasn't right. None of this made any sense.

"Thanks," he said to the colonel, and he headed back out the door toward his cabin.

As he moved through the camp, he heard the sudden "whop, whop, whop" of rotor blades. He looked up. A blue-and-white Unity helicopter lifted off the ground and raced off to the southeast, toward Kigali and the seat of the Rwandan government.

Garrett felt like he had to do something. But what? It was hopeless to think he could figure out what was happening from where he was at this moment.

Ignoring his fears, he decided he had to see firsthand what was happening outside the camp—in the countryside and, if need be, inside Rwanda's capital, Kigali. He had this sudden, deep yearning to *know*.

There was a jeep on the outskirts of camp that he and some of the Christian relief workers used occasionally. It was old, but probably reliable enough to get him all the way to Kigali. He had friends in Kigali, from other relief groups and the government there, and they would help him then.

He had no idea why he was doing this. He just had this sense that he had to, that Unity was involved in something larger than Rwanda, and that events were moving very rapidly. He knew he had to move quickly. Later, he'd take time to sort through his feelings.

For now, he gathered a few belongings, raced to the edge of town, started the jeep, and roared off toward a future that was unknown.

Chapter Thirty-Five

NOON, FRIDAY, JUNE 19

Amy Estrada wasn't one to pound tables in anger, but she felt like it now. She was furious, steaming, almost beside herself.

They wouldn't let her in to see the director—not now, not in the middle of the most serious terrorist threat confronting Washington since the Cuban missile crisis.

"But I've *got* to see him," she fumed to the assistant director of protective operations.

"No chance," Black said. "None. Don't try to go around me on this. We've got the whole place looking for those Algerians."

"But . . . but they may not be the problem," Amy insisted. She *knew*. She was certain she had found the right trail among many complicated trails. But she did not have any tangible proof.

"And you think Sudan is?" Black said scornfully. "We find a nuclear weapon deployed in Algeria. We seize banned INF missiles aboard a ship in the port of Algiers. State confirms that Algerians with known ties to the Islamic Salvation Front have entered the U.S. in recent days. We're about to go to war with Algeria. And you want us to go chasing after *Sudan*?"

"Not chasing, sir," Amy said. "If you'd just listen . . ."

"Look, Estrada," Black said, cutting her off. "You can do me a big favor right now, and it isn't chasing after some crackpot Sudan theory. Keep the veep off the streets and out of sight for a couple of days. We've got our hands full with the president. He refuses to alter his schedule. No one can budge him."

Amy caught her breath. The president wouldn't alter his schedule, even with these reports? "He *has* to alter his schedule," Amy said. "He has to. He can't conduct his business as usual, not right now."

"Tell me about it," Black snorted. "Better yet, tell the president himself if you got any sway there. The director sure doesn't. The president won't budge on keeping to his schedule."

Amy shook her head. This wasn't right. She had to do something. She had to, even if she did it herself. "We'll keep the veep under wraps, don't worry," she promised.

"No golf, okay?" Black said, not smiling.

"No golf," Amy nodded. "At least until this Algerian thing blows over."

"Good," Black said brusquely. "Now get out of here. And do your job. Drop this Sudan theory. It's a loser. We need everyone's attention on the Algerians."

For the first time in her career, Amy realized as she left Black's office, she was about to disobey a direct order from her superior. But she served a higher Master, and He called right now. So her choice was simple.

Chapter Thirty-Six

NOON, FRIDAY, JUNE 19

Dr. Sullivan leaned back in his chair. He dreaded going downstairs to the Situation Room. But he really had no choice. This Algerian thing was killing him. He wished Loren were here by his side. He could really use her counsel just about now.

But Loren had been pulled off, on special assignment for the president. No one knew anything about it. Not even him. The president had asked Loren to keep it confidential, even from him, her boss.

Sullivan groaned as he watched yet another CNN report. In the past hour, his job had gotten a whole lot more complicated. Civil wars had erupted in not one, but five African nations. There were bombs and shells flying in all directions on that continent.

None of them were anywhere near Algeria. At least, not yet. That's all they needed at that point in time—a civil war near Algeria, which might get their military involved. That would really complicate matters.

Sullivan had gotten no sleep since the National Security Council meeting the evening before. He hadn't slept much at all since the NSA photo had surfaced. And the ordeal was beginning to take its toll.

This always happened to him in a crisis. He took everything so seriously, so personally, that he lived and breathed the crisis until it was resolved.

This one was especially nasty, though, because there was no clear end or objective in sight. Israel was agitating *quite* forcefully for a preemptive action. The Joint Chiefs and the Pentagon's senior brass had already weighed in. They wanted a strike. Now. Immediately. Before Algeria could prepare, or move the bunker site.

In, over, and down, the air force had said. The deployment site would be gone, vaporized, in a puff of smoke. The mission was simple, they'd argued. *Yes, and the diplomacy in its wake more difficult than anyone would know,* Sullivan thought.

Why did the stealth helicopter that had picked up Loren and that Hill aide not do the job while they were there? But, he supposed, *you had to have orders for that sort of thing. And theirs had been to pick the two up, not take the site out.*

Sullivan closed his eyes. There was yet another meeting—the sixth that day—in the Situation Room in fifteen minutes. Everyone wanted a decision that day, that hour, about what to do. Sullivan just wanted a little rest.

The phone on his desk rang. "Yes?" he said wearily.

"The president wants to start the meeting," his secretary said.

"Okay, thanks. Be down shortly," he sighed, placing

the phone back in its cradle gently. He wished Loren was here. She'd help with the decision. She had a sense of balance about her, which he missed desperately right now.

Oh, well, he thought. *Time to go decide. Bet it's a strike. This afternoon, before the Algerians can get ready. And then? Well, then, we'll have to suffer the wrath and fury of the entire fundamentalist Islamic world.*

Sullivan secretly hoped that there might be another path, that another solution might be found. What that might be he could not say.

But he felt as if the United States—and the rest of the world, for that matter—was shuffling into the onrushing hooves of the proverbial four horsemen of the apocalypse.

But who could stop it? Certainly not him. And perhaps not even the president.

The powers and principalities that ruled nations were moving much more quickly than individual men and women at the moment. It seemed unlikely—perhaps impossible—that the forces being unleashed could be held in check much longer.

Chapter Thirty-Seven

12:30 P.M., FRIDAY, JUNE 19

Daniel managed to meet Loren outside the White House gate, at the north entrance that overlooked Lafayette Square, by 12:30. It was the gate he was most familiar with because visitors came and went through that gate.

Loren looked like she hadn't slept at all. She had deep circles under both eyes, though her makeup hid them a little. But her eyes were clear. Whatever task the president had given her, she was ready for it.

"Let's go somewhere and talk," she said. "We don't have much time to sort through this."

"How much time do we have?"

"A day, I think. Today. This afternoon," Loren said somberly. "Not any more than that."

There was a cafeteria a half block down Pennsylvania Avenue where they could sit in a booth and talk, undisturbed. Daniel grabbed a cup of coffee and a Danish. Loren bought some iced tea.

As they sat down in the booth, Loren slid the file the president had given her across the table. Daniel took it and opened it. Loren sipped her tea and let him read it in silence. It had no file or code word name.

Daniel had perused classified documents for years, but he'd never seen anything like this before. Part of it was clearly drawn from intelligence work at the National Security Organization, another black program the public had never heard about. NSO's budget matched the CIA's and the NSA's combined. The results of its work were never circulated widely on Capitol Hill or the Pentagon.

Part of the file was compiled from the elite counterterrorism unit housed in the basement of the White House. Congress had once tried to defund counterterrorist activities at both the FBI and the State Department. The White House had simply transferred all the personnel and files from both offices, and put everyone on permanent detail there. As a result, they never showed up as a line item budget request for the White House.

Part of the file was the result of personal requests for surveillance from the president to the directors of both the CIA and the NSA. Both directors had delegated the surveillance to four others, who were not identified and, most likely, did not know for whom they'd been working.

In short, the work outlined in the file was done just for one person, and the file had been written and circulated to just that one person—the president. There was no explanation for the genesis of the file or for what ends it had been compiled.

Daniel read each section of the file carefully. It was quite complete. He wasn't sure what else they could add to it. Much of it could never be confirmed—not publicly, at least. It made him wonder why in the world they'd both been called in by the president.

In the first section of the report were six case studies. The second section dealt with a U.S. export-import operation that had sold advanced nuclear technology to Arab nations and whose owners were directly funded by one of the parties negotiating in Algeria at the moment. A third section dealt with the spate of civil wars that had erupted across Africa, and the group at the center of the conflicts. An appendix summarized dates, times, meetings, and personalities.

The six case studies in the first section of the report dealt with different financial catastrophes looming on the very immediate horizon. Each of them, if isolated, would bring havoc to a corner of the globe. Taken together, coming in a span of several days, they would likely send the entire planet into a massive monetary meltdown.

And waiting to pull the planet back from this financial abyss was an international organization that Daniel had long wondered about—Unity. With its military-style efficiency, its corporate-like structure and goals, its track record of government-like intervention and diplomacy, and its wealth that rivaled that of the Rockefellers and Solomon together, Unity was the savior no one knew existed. Until now.

The first case involved a long-simmering problem in Tokyo that was only now coming to light—a huge budget deficit that Japanese leaders had masked for years. U.S. intelligence had known about it for some time, but the issue was being forced in the Diet, their parliament. A vote was scheduled for Monday, and the disclosure would almost certainly send the Nikkei-225 plummeting.

The problem, outlined in the report, was that the NSO had come across a number of major banks—including three of the largest ones in the U.S.—that had tied up tens of billions in derivative trading to the overall price index of the Nikkei. Those all came due in less than two weeks.

In other words, when the Nikkei index plunged as a result of the budget deficit disclosure, all those institutions would lose billions of dollars. Several would almost certainly go under immediately.

Incredibly, though, Unity's board of directors had already intervened directly with Japan's prime minister. Daniel knew, because the file contained a copy of correspondence between Geneva and Tokyo on the subject.

Unity—with its vast resources, only some of which were on display to the world in the form of humanitarian aid—was prepared to buy blue chip Japanese stocks at whatever cost and prop up the Nikkei index. Whatever it took, Unity had pledged to keep the Nikkei above a certain level.

In return for what? Daniel wondered. *In return for what?* There was no mention or speculation about this in the report, though.

The second case in the file revolved around an International Monetary Fund vote on Sunday. The IMF planned to vote on continuing bridge loans to four countries. Algeria was first on the list, followed by Sudan, Brazil, and Panama.

Daniel was shocked at the amount of money involved. He'd had no idea Algeria was in such trouble. The country's centralized economy, it seemed, had collapsed. Only through the grace of the Western world were the Algerians providing food to their citizens.

But the IMF planned to call in Algeria's multibillion-dollar bridge loan. This Sunday. The report outlined how the IMF's board would vote, based on wiretaps of two of the board members. Several of them had direct or indirect ties to Unity.

The IMF also planned to call in the bridge loans to the other three countries on the list. Without IMF funding, their economies were finished as well.

But Unity was there again, ready to offer private financing. And the IMF was prepared to hand over the reins and the loan portfolios to Unity.

The third case might just as easily have fallen in the IMF's lap. But instead of going to that particular international lending institution, Chile had gone to the World Bank for its loan. The World Bank would vote Monday to call in Chile's note. And, again, Unity was there, willing to take the note from the World Bank.

Fourth on the list was a pure U.S. monetary initiative, which surprised Daniel a little. A Treasury working group—headed by Vice President Wright and which included an IMF executive vice president, a World Bank senior vice president, two of the Federal Reserve governors, three presidents of major American banks, and the president of one of the three worldwide credit card companies based in America—had convinced the president to issue an executive order.

That order was signed two days ago. Boiled down to its essence, the order—which was now locked in a vault inside the White House—essentially gave the Treasury and the Fed whatever authority they needed to buy marks, yen, and pounds until they had substantially affected the balance between the dollar and those currencies. The buying would begin quietly early next week.

It would be a huge, bold stroke, one that none of the other three economies would be prepared for. It would take them some time to recover. And the currency firm the U.S. would use to convert the dollars? One of the central underwriters of Unity, the Solomon Fund.

The Solomon Fund was easily one of the most successful bond and mutual funds ever established. It made billions for its investors, and it had pools of money to invest beyond any ordinary human being's imagination. It was not surprising to Daniel that the fund was linked to Unity, or that the U.S. had tapped it to handle the dollar conversion.

Fifth on the list was a very private communiqué between the Russian president and Franklin Shreve, informing the United States that Russia intended to break off talks with the U.S. over repayment of a massive, congressionally ordered bailout. Russia was going to default on what amounted to a $50 billion, American taxpayer-funded loan.

Only one organization had the muscle, negotiating skills, and talent to negotiate between the two countries now—Unity. Franklin Shreve, knowing he had no choice in the matter, had authorized the Unity talks, which were to begin tomorrow.

And last on the list was a relatively minor case, but one that illustrated just how precarious and interconnected the world was. A London bank, the largest and most venerable in England, would be closed on Monday, the report predicted. Several of its Hong Kong traders had bet unwisely in the global commodity futures market. Drought and other assorted natural disasters had wiped out the commodities, and the bank owed double its capital reserves to fulfill the futures contracts.

But Unity was already on hand. The Bank of England had privately negotiated a deal to turn the London bank over to Unity. That transaction would be announced the same day the bank was closed.

Already overwhelmed, Daniel turned to the second section of the report. It detailed a series of transactions over the past few years—some of them quite recent—between an American export-import firm called Peramco and foreign nations.

Basically, it appeared, Peramco had sold nuclear technology to several Arab nations in the past few years. There was no mistaking the trails. Someone had clearly wanted his hands on the capability to launch intermediate-range missiles, and he'd paid plenty of money for it.

Most of the transactions were to Algeria: reprocessed fuel guidelines, ballistic missile arc technology, missile cone manufacturing technology, and other assorted information that would give someone the ability to build and fire an intermediate-range nuclear weapon.

And nearly all of it had been funneled to Algeria, through this Peramco. And the source of Peramco's start-up funding just five short years ago? Unity's bond and mutual fund partners in the U.S., Switzerland, and Italy.

The third section of the report dealt briefly with Unity's mediating role in a number of African nations over the course of several months. Actually, *mediating* was the wrong word. Unity had not so much mediated as managed to make sure both sides of each budding civil war walked away from the table.

The final section—a raw appendix really—listed dates and times of meetings involving Unity officials or affiliates and their points of contact around the world. At many of the meetings, listed as a participant or occasionally as honorary chair, was the vice president of the United States, Lucius Wright. There was no analysis of any of this, however. It was simply stated as fact.

Daniel closed the file. He didn't say anything for several minutes. Loren continued to sip her tea and waited for him to speak. She'd had the same reaction to the file.

"I had no idea such organizations existed in the world," Daniel said finally, his voice almost a whisper. "No idea at all."

"Me neither," Loren said.

He put his fingers to his lips, a funny little habit that Loren had noticed about him some time ago. "It's scary, isn't it, to think that people and groups with all that money and resources have joined together to back just one organization?"

"Yes," Loren answered softly, "it is."

"And with no controls over it, none at all," Daniel mused. "I can't think of a single group that even remotely comes close to a mandate to keep track of it. And the places that might keep tabs—like the UN or the World Bank—are cutting deals right and left to keep the world from going over the edge."

Loren smiled wanly. "Now you see why I needed help with this."

"And you thought of me." Daniel laughed.

"I think of you a lot these days," she said, blinking furiously. "But, actually, you know, it was more the president's suggestion to bring you in than mine."

"But he said that *you* asked for permission to bring me in," Daniel said, confused.

"I did," she explained. "But only after he hinted quite strongly that you might be helpful."

Daniel nodded. It was all beginning to make a little sense. "So what do you think he wants us to do? Investigate all this? Confirm it somehow, like he said?"

Loren shook her head. "I think you can guess what he wants you to do as well as I can."

Daniel closed his eyes, imagining what his boss, Senator Cedric Jackson, chairman of the Senate Intelligence Committee, was going to do when he read this file. The separation of powers in America's government had never seemed so important as it did to Daniel—and Loren—at that moment.

"And what about the reference to the vice president at the end?" Daniel asked.

"No conclusion that I could see."

"No, there isn't. So what happens there?"

"Nothing, would be my guess," Loren said. "He'll run for president in a few years."

Daniel thought about poor Khali in Algeria, how

Unity and the others had him over a barrel. No wonder he'd struck a deal with the devil, so to speak. He had no choice. His country would go under without the outside help.

Daniel looked at Loren, who still looked quite troubled by all of this. "And will you come with me to see Senator Jackson?"

"No, Daniel, I can't," she said, her voice quiet. "The company mentioned in there, Peramco, that sold nuclear technology to Algeria? That's my brother's company. I will have to see him. That's the part the president gave to me."

"But he's your brother," Daniel said, clearly seeing— and understanding—the pain Loren must be feeling right now.

"I know," she said, the tears forming at the corners of her eyes, "but I have no choice. I think Michael's crossed the line, maybe even breached national security. And I have to go get him."

Chapter Thirty-Eight

FRIDAY, JUNE 19

The drive to Kigali was much, much harder than Garrett would ever have imagined. Troops from both tribes were firing at will in every village he drove through. Village after village was burning. It seemed much worse than the last time.

How had this carnage begun, and why? Had someone set a match to the fuse that always existed in places like this?

Kigali, though, was relatively peaceful by comparison. There was some mortar shelling at the perimeter, but nothing like what he'd just driven through.

As Garrett drove along the main road in downtown Kigali, he was surprised to see that—directly across the street from the seat of the central government of Rwanda—was a large blue-and-white sign proclaiming ownership of the building. It was a Unity sign with its three-circle insignia.

Garrett stopped his jeep and stared at the symbol for

quite a while. There was something almost mesmerizing about it, but he couldn't quite place why. He followed the curving lines—three smaller circles in a triangle with a larger circle surrounding all three—over and over.

And then it hit him. He could see it now. If you started at one point, near the top of one of the smaller circles, and traced from there, the symbol was really three sixes, all interlaced and overlapped to form one symbol. Each six ended and then began another six in an endless, fascinating loop. He wondered if someone had planned that, or if it was just the way he was looking at it.

A great deal of traffic flowed between Unity's headquarters and the Rwanda government complex. Couriers and officials hustled back and forth. It almost looked like a Western city, everyone was moving so quickly.

Garrett ducked into one of the Rwanda government buildings at the end of the complex. He was there to see a friend, a Christian doctor who worked for the national health service. Garrett wanted to see him because, one, he would have some idea of the scope of the civil war, and two, he had a ham radio.

Garrett had been a licensed ham radio operator for years and years. And he and many of his Christian Medical missionary friends across Africa had developed quite a network. Whenever he could get his hands on a ham radio, he and his friends would talk well into the night.

His friend, Jonas Sarumba, ushered him quickly into his office and closed the door. "I wondered if you might show up," he said to Garrett with his thick British accent common to many bilingual Africans.

"You did, huh?"

"Yes. We live in strange times, friend. Strange times indeed."

"How so?" Garrett asked.

Dr. Sarumba looked around to make sure no one else could hear him. But they were in his private office. Garrett wondered what he was so worried about.

"This war? You know its beginning?" Dr. Sarumba asked him.

"No, I don't. That's why I'm here." Garrett took a seat.

By the time Dr. Sarumba had finished, Garrett felt a surge of rage unlike anything he'd ever experienced. These people had been manipulated quite badly and for no apparent reason. Their own peacemaker and broker, Unity, had apparently backed both sides into a corner. War had been inevitable as a result.

"I wonder," Garrett said.

"What is that?" his friend asked. "What is it that you wonder?"

Garrett looked over at the ham radio on Dr. Sarumba's desk. "That thing still work?"

His friend nodded vigorously. "Never been better."

Garrett scooted his chair over next to it and put the headphones on. He moved the mike close and flipped the power on. It crackled to life.

Many, many conversations later, Garrett had lost his voice. But he'd found his answers. Actually, just the one answer.

All his Christian Medical missionary friends in Sudan, Ethiopia, Somalia, Zaire, Chad, and Niger—where some form of tribal war had broken out in the past few days—told the same story. None knew it had been replicated elsewhere.

In each and every case, the peacemaking, humanitarian agency attempting to broker peace accords among warring factions had, instead, triggered conflict. All at roughly the same time, for different reasons.

Those events combined with the nuclear missile crisis in Algeria had suddenly made northern Africa a very, very unstable place.

And the group at the heart of each and every breakdown in peace talks, which had, in turn, triggered violence across the various countrysides? Unity. At every turn, Unity the peacemaker and broker was there.

All that remained now was a simple question. Now that he had it, who could Garrett tell anyway? Who would believe such a story? In the end, Garrett knew he had very little choice.

Deep in the heart of Africa—literally in the eye of the continent—Garrett's only hope was to tell his story on the global computer network, the Internet.

He typed his observations, such as they were, into the network from Dr. Sarumba's computer. He launched them into the great computer beyond, like a note in a bottle, soon thereafter.

Those with ears, he hoped, would hear. And those with eyes would see.

Chapter Thirty-Nine

FRIDAY, JUNE 19

There was just a small story on the Associated Press wire about the offensive. The Associated Press's Jerusalem bureau chief put it out over the international wire.

The story, the AP reported, revolved around a new Israeli military offensive in the mountains between Israel and Lebanon, overlooking the plains of Israel, Lebanon, and Syria. The purpose of the mission was to root out suspected terrorists in the mountainous region, the kind of thing Israel had done time and time again in the past. That was why the report merited only three paragraphs. It presented no attention-grabbing news.

The prisoners taken by Colonel Asher and his squad would be returned, after interrogation, to their respective countries. Israel had no desire to provoke an international incident by holding prisoners from countries and allies such as France, Germany, and Italy.

Israel's military held the tactical nukes, though. Engineers quickly determined that the missiles were aimed not at Israel's sovereign territory but at Syria.

Israel's elite military special operations teams also found three more such units hidden in the mountains in roughly the same region. All had tactical nukes. All were aimed at the capitals or major cities in Lebanon, Jordan, and Egypt.

Asher and the others in the Israeli military could only guess at what purpose those tactical nukes served. To protect Israel in the event of a massive regional conflict with all of Israel's neighbors? Not likely.

To provoke mass hysteria and anger toward the nation of Israel the day after the tactical nukes fired on those four Arab countries? Perhaps.

Israel's prime minister did not complain to the United Nations, though. That was not Israel's way. He did, however, speak directly to the heads of each of the countries represented in the multinational peacekeeping force—including the president of the United States, Franklin Shreve—to lodge a formal, private complaint.

But the good news, Israel's prime minister informed them, was that thanks to the timely intervention— again—of Israel's military, a very awkward and clearly destabilizing situation had been defused.

There would be private repercussions, but not public ones. This sort of diplomacy was done very quietly, from head of state to head of state, not through foreign ministry cables.

Within hours, the supreme commander of the UN peacekeeping forces stationed in Gaza and the West Bank—a man with seven peacekeeping missions under his belt—had been reassigned to a small depot in southern Italy.

The president of the United States ordered his ambassador to the UN to fly over to Israel immediately to personally apologize for the U.S. role in the aborted mission.

And the Unity captains assigned to help the UN forces were also reassigned to different parts of the world. By the next day, all of them would be working in refugee camps in Africa or on development work in the Pacific Rim.

There was no other indication or trace of what had happened in the mountains north of Israel. But Israel's generals knew, and so did Colonel Asher. But they required no public recognition or even acknowledgment. Not while Israel was safe.

Chapter Forty

Malcolm had never read so many articles so fast, in so short a time, in his entire journalistic career. Unity stories were everywhere, all around the globe, all at once.

Sarah Jons had been absolutely, positively dead on the mark. She'd unearthed situations he would never have dreamed of connecting. And all roads led back to Unity.

There were at least six major financial earthquakes waiting to open up under the feet of those responsible for keeping the monetary world intact in the major developed countries of the East and West. In each case, as Sarah had discovered, Unity would play a role, either in saving an institution or in making sure a country had adequate financing to keep its economy going.

Malcolm had no idea whether Unity was good or bad, saint or sinner. He didn't care. Or to put it more accurately, it was not his job to report on Unity's motives. He would leave that to others.

The story that he wanted out there in *Time* magazine—and that had a pretty decent chance of making the cover—was how this incredibly well-endowed organization that had helped countless millions in refugee situations was now going to essentially save the Western financial world.

And as luck would have it, a final, critical piece to his Unity jigsaw puzzle literally fell into his lap as he was putting the piece together—a report from a Christian Medical missionary in central Africa (brought to his attention by his friends on the Internet) on Unity's extensive diplomacy efforts in the midst of a number of major civil wars across Africa. Malcolm liberally used parts of the missionary's raw, but precise, reports. His editors were ecstatic.

For better or worse, Unity would no longer be operating in secret after tomorrow, Malcolm considered. If his Unity piece made the cover, the group would operate in the full light of day. And that—regardless of the organization's principles or motives—was always a good thing.

Malcolm finished his piece shortly before dinnertime Friday evening and filed his report via phone. A half hour later, his two line editors called him back with the good news.

His story had made the cover. Nothing had remotely challenged it, they said. Unity would be a household name after *Time* hit the newsstands.

Chapter Forty-One

1:00 P.M., FRIDAY, JUNE 19

The plain unmarked envelope arrived at Veronica Gray's desk around lunchtime Friday. The courier had no return address—just orders to make sure it was delivered to her personally.

Veronica opened it carefully at her desk, careful not to spill crumbs from the unbuttered bagel she'd been munching on for the better part of an hour.

Since she'd broken the Algerian story, Veronica's life had changed dramatically. As she'd hoped, her star was shooting so high, so fast, that there was no telling where it would go.

She was anchoring one of the two nightly news broadcasts this weekend. She was flying up to New York the next morning to get ready for the stint.

And there were hints and rumors that she would be asked to anchor at least one of the weekend shows regularly, and perhaps even get a crack at some sort of regular feature on the weekends as well.

She stared at the contents of the package and smiled very, very broadly. And this, for tonight's broadcast, would be the coup de grace, the final touch on the most successful run of stories she'd ever had in her career.

The package contained exact, definite proof—complete with documents that would be rather easy to confirm and names of people to call to confirm them—of a nuclear technology trail that led directly from the U.S. to Algeria.

In other words, Veronica grasped quickly, a company with a U.S. connection had bought and then sold classified nuclear technology to Algeria. It was all right there in front of her.

Combined with the missile site and the confiscated missiles now secured in Germany, this final piece of the puzzle would seal Algeria's fate.

And she would get to report it first. Veronica loved getting stuff over the transom like this. It sent chills up and down her spine.

She had the story confirmed, cold, by two that afternoon. Producers in New York spent the remainder of the day trying to track down the elusive officials of the company in New York, but came up empty. They'd all somehow managed to vanish without a trace. Veronica's producers tried one last effort to track one of the company's partners in the Washington, D.C., area.

But it made no difference. Veronica had her proof, in black and white, on paper. The trail was self-evident and recent. She had no qualms at all about using it. None whatsoever.

Chapter Forty-Two

4:00 P.M., FRIDAY, JUNE 19

The president's National Security Council met Friday afternoon to review the bidding. There seemed no choice. They would need to respond forcefully to the Algerian threat.

The argument did not hinge so much on a direct threat to the sovereignty of the United States or the American people. The argument presented by the Joint Chiefs, the Pentagon, the Arms Control and Disarmament Agency director, and even the State Department was that this was the first instance the world had seen where a developing nation had armed itself with a nuclear weapon.

The United States had to act, they argued. The world was watching. If the United States—the world's only remaining superpower—did not act now in the face of such a flagrant violation of the global nonproliferation treaty, other nations like North Korea, Iraq, and Iran would be emboldened to move to deployment quickly.

Never mind that Algeria had not signed the nonproliferation treaty, or that it had refused to allow international inspectors inside its borders. There was no time
for diplomacy. Only a show of force would do.

The discovery of both the deployment site—which
even CNN had been able to spot and photograph from a
satellite—and the banned INF missiles aboard the ship
in the port of Algiers had worked people into a frenzy.

The United States *had* to take Algeria out. The Algerian problem could be solved with just one bold stroke.

The air force chief said her planes were already armed
and equipped with nonnuclear cruise missiles to take
out the sites as well as the nuclear reactor in the Algerian desert. The glide path to the missile and reactor
sites was already encrypted in the cruise missiles' nose
cones. All it required was a direct order from the commander in chief, and the missiles would be delivered to
their targets.

The navy, likewise, had armed its nonnuclear SLCMs
with the necessary data to take out the reactor and the
missile sites. All it required was a National Security
Council decision and a presidential order to launch.

"What if Algeria fires off its missiles first?" someone
asked. "Like at Israel? What then?"

"Then Israel's citizens had better head for the hills
fast," someone else said and laughed grimly. "Because
there is no defense to a ballistic missile attack."

Nearly every effort to develop a defense against even a
limited ballistic missile launch had been abandoned after the cold war had ended. People in Washington had
laughed the ambitious Star Wars defense program right
out of the budget.

Basically, there was no defense against a ballistic missile. If one was launched, it made it to its destination and killed tens of thousands of people. Period. End of discussion.

Not even Israel—with its seemingly endless capacity to produce a miraculous defense of its territory—had produced a ballistic-missile defense. For years, it had tried to develop at least a modest defense program with the help of two American firms working under a black DOD grant. But with the demise of the Star Wars program, Israel's effort had collapsed as well.

Of course, there was no certainty that Algeria had targeted Israel. But where else? The INF-type missiles couldn't carry beyond the theater, and Israel was the only enemy of the Arab state anywhere in the region. So if missiles were launched from the other side of the Mediterranean Sea, they would almost certainly fly to Israel.

In the National Security Council meeting, the vice president was more forceful than usual, several White House aides noted. Wright argued strenuously for immediate action in an effort to protect and shield Israel, their ally.

The president did not take part in the discussions. He listened dutifully as each member of the council laid out his or her position. In the end, it was his decision. He could choose to ignore or accept their recommendations. The decision, in the end, fell to him as commander in chief.

It was clear from the presentations, though, that the unofficial tally was nearly unanimous. Only two of the council's members expressed some caution about moving too quickly before diplomacy had been tried. But the sudden emergence of hawks at every corner of the table drowned out their voices.

The president, surrounded on all sides, knew he had little choice. He made his decision—an air force strike, to be followed up quickly by a navy launch if the air force was unsuccessful. But the air force would be successful. There was no question of that in anyone's mind.

The president gave the military twenty-four hours to prepare, though. They would strike at roughly 4:00 P.M. eastern daylight time, Saturday, fully two hours before the national network news in the U.S.

Should something else intervene between now and then, he would order the air force to stand down.

But no one expected that. Not now. The U.S. had gone to the brink and beyond. There seemed no turning back.

Chapter Forty-Three

4:30 P.M., FRIDAY, JUNE 19

Loren parked next to her brother's bright red Ferrari at his new home overlooking the Potomac River in McLean, Virginia. There was some irony to that, Loren thought.

All his life, her older brother had worked on a government salary and had been forced to live in a small suburban house and commute to the Pentagon or the CIA to do his job. Now, in his retirement, he was literally five minutes from Langley, and he never had to go there. He seemingly never had to go anywhere if he didn't want to.

Loren had not seen her brother in a year or so, even though they lived in the same city. They talked on the phone occasionally, but their lives were actually quite separate. That wasn't surprising. Michael and she had taken different paths in life a very long time ago. Michael had diligently pursued his narrow career in government, while Loren had taken the riskier path.

Now, it was obvious to both whose strategy had paid off. Loren was a senior White House aide and met regularly with the president of the United States. Michael had been forced into early retirement, having never achieved a Senior Executive Service (SES) salary level in government.

But Loren stopped in her tracks and looked around the grounds of her brother's new home. But was it that simple? Had her path been the more successful one? It hardly seemed so, not in these surroundings.

Her brother had a magnificent, breathtaking view of the crags along the Potomac River from here. Loren looked around. There was no other house within view on either side. It was quite a place.

She'd called ahead to make sure her brother was home. He met Loren at the door, a drink in hand to celebrate the end of the work week.

"Loren, how nice," her brother said, offering a hand and then a quick, almost passionless hug.

"It's been a while," Loren said, her voice muffled by her brother's jacket.

"Yes, it has. Too long."

Loren noticed immediately that her brother had gained a considerable amount of weight in the past year, perhaps as much as twenty pounds. But he still looked haggard and slightly under the weather, despite his obvious success in retirement.

"Long week?" Loren asked as she stepped inside the large foyer. Several obviously expensive vases sat precariously atop marble stands at the edge of the foyer.

"Yes, I suppose," Michael sighed. "A great deal of

pressure to deliver a new contract. But we got it done. Just today, in fact."

Loren walked into the living room and admired the two rather large original oil paintings that hung on opposite sides of the wall. She'd never seen these paintings before. She hadn't known her brother was even interested in such things.

"Pressure?" she asked. "From your new partners?"

"Yeah, them," Michael said, taking a large swig of the straight Scotch in his glass. He didn't bother to offer Loren a drink. He'd known her far too long. She didn't drink. Hadn't in years. Which, to be honest, made the Scotch taste all that much better to Michael.

"What's their name again? I always forget it," Loren said casually.

"Peramco," Michael said with a snort. "A dumb name if you ask me."

"What's it stand for anyway?"

Michael took another long gulp of his Scotch, and then walked over to the liquor cabinet for a quick refill. "I think they just smushed names together to come up with it. They stuck Persian, American, and company together. Presto, Peramco. Cute, huh?"

"So, this Peramco, it's an Arab company? Its owners are Arabic?"

Michael shook his head and took another drink. "Not really. One of them is. The others are from all over— Germany, Italy, Switzerland, even Japan. They're all over the map."

"So why the name?"

Michael shrugged. "They deal with Arab countries a lot. They say that's where all the really big money is."

"And these guys deal in big money?" Loren asked.

"Yeah, they do. It's real big-time stuff. Big time, big time." The Scotch was starting to have an effect. Michael's words were starting to slur ever so slightly as he spoke. He suddenly grinned wide. "And I get pieces of the pie. Nice pieces, too."

Loren looked around. "I can see that, Michael. You've done well for yourself. Real well."

"I have, haven't I?" Michael said with a chuckle. "Got it made. The good life."

"You always wanted that, didn't you?" Loren asked him.

"You bet." Michael raised his glass to toast himself. He took another drink. "Now I have it. And, you know, it hasn't been all that hard. A little information here and there and, hey, whaddya know, I'm rollin' in dough!"

Michael laughed loudly at his play on words. He thought it was immensely funny. Loren said nothing and waited for her brother to stop laughing. "So, Michael," she said finally, "what kind of information are you talking about anyway?"

Michael suddenly stopped chuckling. His eyes narrowed, and he looked hard at his little sister. "Say, what's the deal with all the third-degree stuff? And why'd you wanna stop by here?"

Loren took a deep breath. There was just no way around it. She'd have to give it to him with both barrels. "Michael, you'd better sit down," she said. "You won't like this."

Before they could move, though, the phone rang. It

rang three times, and then the answering machine picked it up.

Michael and Loren both listened as the person identified herself as a producer working with television network correspondent Veronica Gray on a story for that evening. Would he please give her a call?

The story that evening concerned the company he worked for, Peramco, and allegations that it had sold nuclear technology to Algeria. She left her office number at the network's studio.

Michael looked as if he were going to collapse into a puddle right there in the middle of his living room. Loren moved over to her older brother, took his arm, and led him gently to the couch.

"I've been set up," Michael mumbled, almost incoherently. "Set up. They've given me over to the wolves."

"Who has, Michael?" Loren asked him. "Tell me now before it's too late. I can help."

But Michael knew it was too late. Much, much too late. He'd taken a risk—the only one he'd ever taken his whole life—and it was about to destroy him. The hole opening up beneath his feet seemed bottomless, dark, and very lonely.

Loren reached out to keep her older brother from falling further. She felt God's presence with her, around her, guiding her. She could feel her brother's pain almost as much as he could. "Michael, tell me. Let me help. I can, you know," she repeated, a still, small voice echoing in her words.

Michael's eyes were wild with fear. He trembled and shook like a cornered beast. He wanted to run, hide, vanish from the face of the earth. But he could not. Not now, when the whole world was his enemy.

"I can help, Michael," Loren said a third time.

Michael seemed to hear her this time. "No, you can't," he said, his voice hoarse. "No one can."

"Is it true, Michael? Did you sell to the Algerians?" Loren took a step closer to her brother, trying to cross the terrible chasm that separated them.

"Yes," he said almost inaudibly.

"And did you sell them something you should not have? From your own files at the Pentagon?"

Michael started to cry. Loren had never seen her older brother cry, not even when they were kids. Michael had always schemed and plotted and connived. He hadn't felt remorse. It was foreign to him.

"I took files . . . from my office," he managed through the tears that streamed down the side of his face.

"When you left? Classified files?"

"Yes. Classified files."

"Code word? Nuclear technology? Hardware and delivery systems?"

"All of them."

Loren closed her eyes briefly. Her brother was in a great deal of trouble, more than perhaps he knew at this moment. "And it went to the Algerians?" she asked, afraid of the answer.

"No, not all."

"Not all? What's that mean?"

"Some of my files went to Algeria," Michael said. "The file reports on the destruction of the Russian INFs. Our assessments of their capabilities, what their technology looked like." Michael looked up. "You know, our missiles were much better than theirs. The Russian INFs were really awful."

"Michael, they still work," Loren said softly. "They still fly and hit targets."

"I know," he said, looking down at his shoes. Two big tears dripped off his chin, landing on his shoes. "But I didn't think . . . I didn't think anyone could actually use what I sent."

"Why not?"

"Because there wasn't *anything* about how to build the missile platforms or wire the nose cones or set off the chain reactions, or any of that stuff. It wasn't in my files."

"And that was all you sent to the Algerians, just the reports? Just those reports?" Loren saw something, an opening. She saw it clearly for perhaps the first time in the whole ordeal. The Algerian link wasn't what everyone assumed.

"Yeah. That was all I sent."

"But you said it didn't all go to the Algerians?"

Michael wiped the tears from his face. It left a smudge across his nose. "A couple of my files, just after I joined up with Peramco, went somewhere else. Algeria was only in the past couple of months. Early on, they went somewhere else."

"And what were your first two files about?"

"It was really boring stuff—who had charge of INF weapons in Russia, who was supposed to destroy them, logistics reports on where they were warehoused, profiles of the army officials who were physically in charge of the missiles. Really boring things like that. Nothing useful."

Except to an organization trying to determine who to go to, to get Russian INF missiles on the black market, Loren thought. *To them, those files were worth their weight in gold.*

"Where did the files go, Michael?" Loren asked. "Where?"

Michael hesitated, wondering perhaps if telling his sister would help—or hurt—his predicament. He decided that nothing could be worse than where he was at that moment. "You won't believe it."

"Try me."

Michael took a deep breath. "Geneva. They went to Geneva. I never could figure out why."

But Loren knew why. A light flickered and then burst into the murky darkness. She knew that she now had something to tell the president—and something to bargain with perhaps to save her brother from a charge of treason.

Algeria was not the problem. Algeria was the target—a carefully established one—but only as a decoy in a very elaborate, deadly game. The real problem was elsewhere.

"We must go to the White House, you and I. Now, before it's too late," Loren said forcefully.

Michael blanched. The fear returned, but it was less intense this time. The hole beneath his feet did not seem as bottomless.

"Okay," he mumbled. "But promise you'll stay with me the whole time."

"I promise," Loren said. "But, first, you need some coffee. And we need to talk some more about Geneva."

Chapter Forty-Four

5:00 P.M., FRIDAY, JUNE 19

Daniel and Senator Jackson met, just the two of them, in the Russell Building late in the afternoon after the morning's closed Algeria briefing had finished and a luncheon speech. Daniel asked the senator's executive secretary to hold his calls for at least an hour and to keep people from walking in unannounced.

The senator cleared his schedule at Daniel's request. He didn't ask why. Daniel said it was important, and that was enough for the senator. He knew, of course, that the National Security Council was convening, and he expected it had something to do with that.

The senator was standing at his desk, going through his box of correspondence, when Daniel walked in. Even though he'd been around for a very long time and had not been challenged for reelection his last two terms, Senator Jackson was diligent about at least looking at everything addressed to him.

He was one of the few senators who had a standing desk, with a slight incline. Occasionally, he would stand at this desk for an hour or two, tackling his paperwork, one foot propped up behind the other.

Daniel walked through the double doors and closed them behind him. He walked over and handed the unmarked file on Unity to the senator.

It was essentially the same file Loren had delivered to him, with a new executive summary from Daniel—for the senator's EYES ONLY—explaining his role and involvement with Algeria and its defense minister, Ahmed Khali.

Daniel's report also briefly mentioned what Loren had just discovered from her brother, describing how classified files on Russian INF missiles—the very same missiles seized aboard the trawler in the port of Algiers—had almost certainly been delivered to Unity in Geneva some time ago.

"Read this first," Daniel said. No ceremony was necessary. Not between the two of them.

Senator Jackson accepted the file, opened it, and began to read carefully. Daniel walked out the double doors to the balcony that adjoined the senator's personal office.

It was a gorgeous late afternoon by Washington's standards. Not too hot, a slight breeze. Senator Jackson's office was on the western side of the Russell Building, along Delaware Avenue.

To his right, Daniel could see Union Station; to his left, the Capitol building and the immaculate grounds due west of the building. Just beyond the Capitol was the start of the Mall.

At this time of day, dozens of joggers and bikers were in sight. On this kind of day, people left their jobs early and went outside to play.

Sometimes, on a day like this in Washington in the summer, you could ring an office in the city and not get an answer.

Not here, though, Daniel thought. *And not tomorrow or the next day, either.*

He stood there on the senator's balcony for close to twenty minutes while the senator finished reading the file. The senator joined Daniel on the balcony when he'd finished.

"Quite a day, isn't it?" Senator Jackson asked him.

Daniel took a deep breath, savoring the smell of the flowers planted two levels down around the edge of the Russell Building. It was nice. He wished he had more time and inclination to enjoy them. "Sure is."

The senator leaned on the balcony railing. "Quite a report. I assume it's from the president, prepared for him?"

"Yes, it is."

"And that it has not been sent here in any kind of official capacity?"

"Not even close to official."

The senator clasped his hands, thinking. "And the other members of the Cabinet? How many know of this file?"

"None that I know of," Daniel answered. "My guess is that they're in the dark."

"Except one of them, of course."

"Yes, except one of them."

"This has a direct bearing on their decision on Algeria, doesn't it?" the senator asked rhetorically.

"Yes, it does," Daniel said. "But he's boxed in, both by U.S. advisors and by the international community. There isn't a whole lot of running room. Or time."

The senator nodded once, his chiseled jaw barely moving as he did so. "Then we'll have to give him some."

"How?"

"I've been meaning to get out of the office lately. Now seems like a good time."

"To where?" Daniel asked.

"Oh, I don't know," the senator said with a twinkle in his eyes. "I was thinking the Mediterranean this time of year, just off the coast of north Africa. I'd like to meet your friend, Khali, while I'm there. Perhaps aboard one of our carriers."

"I'll arrange for the military transport jet," Daniel said promptly, unable to contain a smile.

"Make it a fast one, son," the senator said. "Very, very fast."

Chapter Forty-Five

6:00 A.M., SATURDAY, JUNE 20

On Saturday morning, the denizens of war were gathered in a corner of the world that had seen more wars than all the other parts of the globe combined.

Carriers sitting off the coast of Africa, both to the north and to the west. Planes took off from air bases in Saudi Arabia every hour on the hour. AWACS circled continuously, tracking developments.

The Pentagon's parking lot was more than half full, even at such an early hour on a weekend. Every other government bureaucracy attached to the military complex was fully awake and prepared, as well.

Despite all this activity, President Shreve categorically refused to change his schedule. He was keeping to his daily schedule, no matter what. And that included his knowledge of the FBI's conclusive proof that at least four of the Algerians were in the city somewhere. He would start his day with his customary jog through and around the monuments of the nation's capital.

No one—not the CIA director, not the Secret Service director, not his national security advisor—could dissuade him. He wanted to think, he told them. And he couldn't do that locked up inside the White House walls.

Thankfully, mercifully, there had been no mention of the decision reached by the National Security Council in the *Washington Post* or any of the other national papers that morning. For perhaps the first time, in a long time, a decision within the confines of the White House had somehow been contained, at least for the critical hours leading up to the Algerian strike.

No, the only reports in the papers that morning were details from yet another exclusive by Veronica Gray about a global company called Peramco that had bought and sold nuclear technology to Algeria. Further proof of Algeria's guilt, nearly every one of the intelligence analysts speculated publicly. Algeria had sought nuclear secrets and obtained them.

At least one unnamed American civilian—a former CIA and Pentagon official—had been taken into custody during the night for questioning about his role in providing the classified technology to Algeria. The suspect was cooperating fully with the authorities, White House aides confirmed, and no decision had been made yet whether he would be charged with treason.

That morning, while much of Washington slept, unaware of events transpiring in and around the 1600 block of Pennsylvania, at least one person had decided to take the biggest risk of her career.

Amy Estrada, countermanding a direct order from her supervisor, left the vice president's detail stationed on the grounds of the Naval Observatory. She left at about 5:00 A.M., to give herself plenty of time.

Even though it was quite early, and there would be no rush hour traffic, she did not want to risk being late. She drove her hunter green Jeep Cherokee carefully, but deliberately, down Massachusetts Avenue, past Dupont Circle, and then turned right onto Sixteenth Street.

At 5:30, two turns later, she pulled up into a side street that adjoined the Old Executive Office Building, parked her car, and went to get a cup of coffee and several newspapers to read while she waited. She had forty-five minutes to kill.

At 6:15, Amy made sure her gun was fully loaded, locked her car, and then walked down the street one block, to the front entrance of the American Red Cross building at E and Seventeenth, directly across from the White House and the last leg of the president's morning run.

She was not surprised, at this hour on a Saturday, that no administrative people were at the Red Cross. But she knew, from her conversation on Friday, that Sudan's delegation was inside somewhere meeting with the organization's training staff.

Amy started to walk around the perimeter of the building. She was determined to get inside. She hoped she wouldn't have to kick a door down in the process.

On the far side of the building, on F Street, she entered an open bay area where the maintenance and delivery trucks came in and out. She peered through the window. A guard was sitting, reading, less than fifty feet away.

Amy banged on the window loudly with both fists. The guard was inside a glass office, but he heard the banging. He shook his head, made a slashing gesture across his throat, and went back to whatever he was reading.

Amy banged even louder. She wasn't about to go away. The guard looked up, clearly put out. He stomped over to the door and opened it up with a furious yank.

"Look, man, we all closed here," the guard growled.

Amy pulled her badge and flashed it in front of the guy's nose. When that didn't immediately register, she pulled her vest back and gave him a glimpse of her holstered gun.

The guard's eyes got big and round in a hurry. "Yeah, yeah, all right, so what's the big deal already?" the guard said, taking one giant step backward.

"I need to inspect the grounds, like right now," Amy said forcefully.

The guard stepped back even further, letting Amy enter. "Okay, I gotcha. You don't, like, need my help or anythin', do ya?"

Amy shook her head. "No, just tell me how to find the mess."

"The cafeteria?"

"Yeah, that. Where they eat breakfast here." Amy glanced at her watch. It was 6:22. The president would be coming by in less than ten minutes.

The guard showed her the way, up one flight of stairs and then right down the corridor. She thanked him and left in a hurry.

The cafeteria was harder to find than she'd expected. The guard's directions had been only half right. The cafeteria was on this floor, but it had been left, not right.

It was 6:25 by the time she found the entrance.

As she'd expected, the Red Cross training team was inside, along with the members of the Sudan delegation. Amy walked over to the official she'd spoken to earlier and pulled him aside.

The man, startled, looked at Amy for a moment before recognizing her. "Oh, you . . . ," he started to say.

"Is everyone here right now?" Amy interrupted him. "Everyone from the Sudan group, are they all here?"

They both looked at the people gathered for breakfast up and down the long table toward the side of the cafeteria. Amy saw immediately that the two younger men who'd been eyeing the Red Cross women the other day were not at the table.

"Those men, the younger ones. Were they here this morning when the delegation arrived?" Amy asked, trying to keep the fear and panic from creeping into her voice. She'd been trained not to panic, but it was hard. It took every fiber of willpower she possessed.

"Well, yes, as a matter of fact, they were," the man answered. "I guess they had to go to the bathroom or something."

But Amy didn't hear the answer. She was already racing for the door.

She took the nearest set of stairs and ran up them, three at a time. Only when she was nearing the top did she slow down and glance at her watch: 6:30. The president would be coming by any minute now, depending on how fast he'd run this morning.

Please be slow, please be slow, Amy thought frantically as she pulled the gun free from her holster and released the safety. She also said a quick, silent prayer to God for safety and guidance, and then pushed the door to the hallway open slowly.

The soles of her shoes were built to give, so there were no sounds as she walked along the outside of the hallway toward the corner of the building that faced Seventeenth Street.

No light came from the conference room at the corner of the building. But the door was cracked slightly. And as she got closer, she could hear movement from within.

Amy moved along the wall quickly and took a position just outside the door. If these people were innocently checking out something inside, she was about to give them the biggest scare of their lives. But if they were not . . .

Amy burst into the room a moment after she heard the distinct "click" of a rifle. She came in low and fast, gun raised. Two men were in the room, both of them facing out toward the street. The window facing Seventeenth Street was open slightly.

One of the two men—the one who did not hold a sniper's rifle—turned at the sound of Amy's entrance. He reacted immediately and tried to pull a handgun up to get a shot off.

Amy never gave him the chance. She fired her own gun point-blank into the man's chest, opposite his heart. He jerked back once, hit the wall hard, and then slumped to the floor.

The other man—holding a sniper's rifle that was aimed out the window, toward the president's running route—looked down at his fallen comrade, back out toward the street, and then back at Amy.

"DOWN!" Amy shouted at the top of her lungs, gesturing for the man to pull the rifle down and go to the floor. She had no idea if the man understood her. But he saw what had happened to the man beside him, and he knew he faced a similar fate if he did not put his weapon down.

His face contorted in anger, the sniper pulled the gun back in. Amy moved forward quickly, jerked the rifle from his hands, and tossed it to the other side of the room.

The man struggled for a brief moment, but then submitted as Amy pushed his head down. She had him cuffed, hands behind his head, within seconds.

Her hands didn't start trembling uncontrollably until after she had the second man—who was laboring to breathe, but would almost certainly survive the chest wound—cuffed.

The president and his entourage came running up Seventeenth a minute or so later. Amy pushed the window open slightly and stuck her head out. She spotted one of the president's detail and called out to him.

Seven guns were pulled free, and they almost opened fire on her. Several other agents surrounded the president immediately.

Then they saw Amy's face, and the guns went down.

But the agents did not leave the president's side and hustled him off to the White House grounds quickly.

"I need your help!" Amy yelled. "Now! Third floor, corner room!"

Three agents broke from the detail and began to sprint through the parking lot adjacent to Seventeenth Street. They smashed the windows of the nearest door and rushed to the top floor.

Amy returned her attention to the two would-be assailants. Both of them were carrying passports in their vest pockets. Both were from Sudan, not Algeria.

Had they succeeded, though, and gotten clear of the building, Algeria would have been blamed for the assassination. And even if one, or both, of the men had been caught, Algeria would still likely be blamed because of the hysteria surrounding the news of the Algerian terrorists in the United States.

But not now, Amy hoped. Not now. Whatever link these two men held to Algeria would be sorted out—but *not* in the aftermath of the assassination of the president.

Chapter Forty-Six

SATURDAY, JUNE 20

J ust one thing rested on the coffee table of the captain's stateroom aboard *Constellation II*, a navy carrier stationed a few miles north of the port of Algiers.

It was an advance copy of the new *Time* magazine cover story about a group called Unity and its connections to current events breaking around the globe. The White House had secured it.

Senator Jackson—waiting for Ahmed Khali, Algeria's defense minister, to arrive at the not-so-neutral location—had read the story from front to back. For a journalist, this Malcolm Hopewell had quite a gift. Except for certain highly classified pieces of information, his story tracked quite closely with the contents of the Unity file the senator had brought with him.

Hopewell has incredibly well-positioned sources in high places, the senator thought ruefully, *or he guesses awfully well. Either way, Unity will have no choice now*

*but to go underground in the face of such publicity. For
a time.*

Khali arrived by helicopter a short while later. He was
disappointed. He hoped—even assumed—that the beau-
tiful American woman sent to his country a few days
ago would accompany Senator Jackson.

But Loren was not there. She was back at the White
House, detained with other matters, the senator explained.

"What matters?" Khali asked.

"Important matters of state," Senator Jackson said.

"More important than what we are about to discuss?"
Khali asked, a little surprised.

Senator Jackson thought about what Daniel had told
him as they arrived, that it was Loren's brother who had
been at the White House for hours describing the details
of the technology transfers his company had handled.
He couldn't imagine such a moment if it were his own
family involved.

"Some things come first," the senator said, imagining
Loren as he said this. "Now, please, we have much to
discuss. Some of it may surprise you, I think."

An hour later, the two men concluded their business.
Each gave something and received something in return.

Senator Jackson described in great detail the efforts by
Unity to pull Algeria into the center of a maelstrom that
would affect the entire planet. He shared other information about Unity that surprised Khali.

The Algerian defense minister, for his part, confirmed
Unity's involvement in his nation's economic affairs.
Unity had been centrally involved in the nuclear reactor

development and in an elaborate, well-financed effort to overhaul Algeria's national oil industry.

That had included the transport of oil-drilling equipment to and from the site in the mountains south of Algiers that the NSA photo had spotted. Only now, Khali claimed, had he discovered the true nature of what was being established there.

There would be repercussions, he vowed. For starters, Unity would be banned from Algerian soil, as would any of the financial partners brought to the deal.

But much more important—because time was running out, and both of them knew it—Khali also offered to personally escort an American military team to the missile site. Whatever was there would be destroyed or handed over, he pledged. Immediately, on full display for the world.

"Live on CNN," he said, his dark eyes shining mischievously.

And Khali delivered one more piece of important news, for the senator's ears only. As it turned out, he said, Algeria may not have been the only site of concern for the U.S.

There were other sites—several, in fact—around the region where the banned INF missiles may, or may not, have gone.

Where should they look? the senator asked.

If it were up to him, he would start with Iran and Sudan, Khali answered. It might be profitable to look there, Khali said. If it were up to him.

Chapter Forty-Seven

2:30 P.M., SATURDAY, JUNE 20

At 2:30 Saturday afternoon, President Shreve hung up the secure phone on his desk. In an hour, Senator Jackson promised him, the world would see an extraordinary event.

Shreve picked up the secure line again and punched in the number of the Pentagon. He spoke to his defense secretary first, and then the chairman of the Joint Chiefs. "Stand down," he ordered both.

An hour later, in the dead of night, CNN and the other American television networks—using a heavily lighted pool camera along for the inspection of the Algerian missile site—broadcast the pictures back to the Oval Office and the rest of a stunned world.

American military forces—clearly with the full blessing of Khali and his armed forces—confiscated missiles, technology, and hardware stored in a bunker in the Algerian mountains.

And it was all covered and reported live on CNN.

What was curious, though, was that the missiles were not armed. Nor were they in position to fire. They were piled into the rough-hewn bunker, almost in a haphazard fashion.

What's more, unlike the INF missiles seized aboard the Medco Shipping trawler in the port of Algiers— which were Russian—these missiles appeared to be much cruder Chinese intermediate-range missiles, which were notoriously inaccurate.

In fact, the commentators were reporting within minutes of the extraordinary inspection and seizure, Algeria would have been hard-pressed to get such missiles off the ground and delivered even reasonably close to a target across the Mediterranean Sea.

What seemed likely, they said, was that the same Chinese who had helped Algeria build the nuclear reactor in the desert had also pawned off their lousy missiles to the Algerians.

Which meant that the Algerian "threat" had never really been much of a threat at all, the news commentators further speculated. At least not for now.

Had the Algerian bunker been hit by cruise missiles or surface-to-air missiles from air force jets, none of this would have mattered—or been discovered. The cruise missiles would have vaporized the site, removing all traces of the nuclear missiles' origin or whether they had been in a position to launch. It was most curious, they said.

Yes, thought President Shreve as he watched the pictures flicker across his TV set in a corner of the Oval Office, *it is all most curious. Very, very curious.*

Once the Algerian missiles were safely in American

hands, the president convened another National Security Council meeting with a different purpose in mind. Based on Senator Jackson's suggestion, they had a new mission. It was different, harder, a great deal more complex. But at least now they had time.

Miraculously, like a bolt out of the blue, the world had been pardoned. And the president wasn't entirely sure who he had to thank for it.

Chapter Forty-Eight

SATURDAY AFTERNOON, JUNE 20

Shortly after the Algerian missiles had been seized, the leader of another organization also issued marching orders to his troops around the world. They, too, would stand down. For a time. Just for a time.

Their window of opportunity had been missed, their leader told them. Their efforts to establish a massive decoy and a blizzard of deception had been blunted, almost at the last possible moment in time.

It was merely a temporary setback, though. Another time would present itself. It always did. Until then, they would go underground and wait.

New plans would be formulated, and new orders issued. A new, complex effort to bring events into line would be organized.

They knew their theory was sound—that regional conflicts, orchestrated together, would present a worldwide opportunity to usher in a new era. Chaos, if managed properly, could lead to new organization. It would work someday.

But for now, warlike tensions would be eased across the continent of Africa. Financial triggers in several nations would be released gradually. The global efforts to make the nation of Algeria a target would come to a grinding halt.

Handpicked terrorists, with Algerian passports, would quietly return to their own countries from the United States.

All traces of how short-range tactical nuclear missiles had been transported to the mountains near Israel would be blurred or destroyed as soon as possible.

Assets to several trusted subsidiaries such as Peramco would be transferred first to a numbered account in Geneva, and later to new accounts and new organizations. Personnel involved with those subsidiaries would take leaves, and then new jobs.

And in two nations—neither of them Algeria—elite troops awaiting orders to launch intermediate-range nuclear missiles aimed at Tel Aviv, western Jerusalem, and several smaller Israeli cities would also be told to stand down.

The missiles would be used, their commanders told them. The holy war would be waged. But not at this time.

Epilogue

The ducks scattered on the reflecting pool at the edge of the Lincoln Memorial but returned a short while later after the ripples had gone away.

Daniel picked up another stone and skipped it across the water, scattering the ducks a second time. The stone skipped past them harmlessly, settling to the bottom of the pool. A few tourists glanced their way.

"Don't, Daniel. Please," Loren said. "You might hurt one of them. They're harmless."

Daniel let the remaining pebbles fall from his hand. He looked over at Loren, who was only now beginning to feel the weight of the world lift from her shoulders.

Yet Daniel knew Loren would never truly be free of her own special burden entirely.

Her brother would not be charged with treason, thanks to Loren's intervention and help, but he would go to federal prison for a long time. There was no escaping that punishment.

"You are not your brother's keeper, you know,"

Daniel called over to her softly as the ducks returned to the pond yet again and settled onto the muddy water noisily.

"Yes, I am," Loren answered, the tears coming slowly. "He is my charge now, my special responsibility. I will look after him all the days of my life."

Daniel left the side of the reflecting pool and walked over to where Loren was sitting. He took her hands.

And I will look after you all the rest of my days, too, he vowed silently. *I know I will. If you will let me.*

But Daniel said nothing. They had both been through too much, in too short a time, to utter such a vow out loud. There would be other times for that, both of them hoped.

For now, they were simply happy to be alive and well and not at work. They were just happy to be together.

They looked up. A marine helicopter, with a presidential seal on the side, sped across the sky and banked hard, around the Washington Monument, heading toward Andrews Air Force base. From their vantage point, they couldn't tell who was aboard.

"*Marine One*—or *Two*—do you think?" Daniel asked.

"I can't tell," Loren said, laughing. It was good to laugh. She felt like she hadn't done that in days and days and days. "They do look awfully alike, don't they?"